Praise for Persecuting Abi from Goodreads

'A true page turner. An easy read which kept me turning the pages.'

'How could anyone not cheer for Abi? She is a sweetheart who survived the worst and came out of it hopeful enough to fall in love. All of the characters are amazing. Some you love; some you love to hate (to me, that is a sign of great writing).'

'This is a great read! The story is brilliant, it holds suspense and has detailed characters. The story has many twists and doesn't feel drawn out, it is gripping.'

'I thought that Persecuting Abi had a great amount of romance and suspense. I felt like at times that I was watching one of the better Lifetime movies.'

'What a thrilling exciting story. What a debut this story has had me on the edge off my seat with all of it's twists and turns. Abi is such a strong character her shear grit and determination really shone through. Adam is the type of gentleman that every woman dreams of he's kind, gentle, patient, loving and caring.'

'It was an awesome read. Exciting and thrilling, indeed. The pain of Abi was detailed that I felt it through my bones. But her determination and willingness to live was on point.'

Persecuting Abi

Persecuting Series Book One

J M Ralley

Cover design by J M Ralley
Image courtesy of Chameleons Eyes
From Shutterstock

Persecuting Series

Persecuting Abi

Persecuting Adam

Chapter One

Police Officer Adam Leroy headed towards his locker. It was Friday, his shift had finished, and he had a couple of hours before meeting his girlfriend and her father for dinner. He figured he was the luckiest guy in the world. Abigail Lawton, another police officer, was the light of his world and the woman he was going to marry. Originally from New York, Adam had transferred to LA only eight months ago, and it was the best decision he'd ever made. They had paired him with Abi. At twenty-six she was a few years younger than him, but six years difference was nothing to worry about. They had hit it off at once, and he'd asked her out within the month. When their relationship had blossomed, they'd been separated and had been given new police partners, and six weeks ago they had moved in together. He pulled the ring out of his locker. Abi wasn't a fan of yellow gold, so he'd saved up and bought a white gold engagement ring. A 9ct ring with a twisted band of brilliant cut diamonds, around the central strand. Expenses weren't a problem when it came to the love of his life. Tonight, he would be asking Jack, her father, permission to marry his daughter. Heading home, he dug out one of his best suits and got ready. He hoped Jack said yes. Prayed he did.

Adam entered the restaurant. Italian, Abi's favourite food, and he noticed that Abi and Jack had already arrived. She looked up at him, as he walked towards them. His girlfriend was so beautiful, he thought. With long golden blonde hair, nearly the full length of her back and bright blue eyes, she looked terrific. Abi smiled back at him, not realising how nervous he was.

He joined them, and it wasn't long before their meal was finished. Abi went to freshen up, this was his chance. He looked over at

Jack. "Jack, I love Abi, and I wish to spend the rest of my life with her."

Jack looked back at him, as a smile formed. Finally, he thought. "You're good for her, make her happy, and I know she loves you back."

"I'm asking your permission to marry her." Adam looked nervous, this could go wrong. "I'll never hurt her. Your daughters' the light of my world."

Jack remembered his wife and the day she had asked him to marry him. The problems they'd had to overcome and probably the same thing, that Adam would need to deal with. He hoped he was wrong. His daughter deserved this happiness. "Adam, I know she is, it's obvious to everyone who looks at you two. I'll happily give you permission, but if you ever hurt a hair on her head, it'll be me you have to deal with." He warned. Jack's voice hardened. "I'll be handing her over to you. It'll be up to you to protect her and to keep her safe, no matter what happens in the future." With a bit of luck, he prayed that warning would never be needed.

Adam already knew how protective Jack was when it came to his daughter. He'd raised her single-handed when his wife had died. Abi had only been a baby and had never known her mother, but he'd heard the undercurrent in her father's voice. It had been more than a warning, and his cop instincts had kicked in. He had seen the old marks on her wrists and the other scars on her body. Some looked serious. When he'd asked her about them, she'd passed them off as an old accident, but he hadn't been fooled. He'd recognized the scars on her abdomen as old stab injuries, but he hadn't pressured her for an answer. He would wait until she was ready to tell him, but Jack's words had worried him. What were they hiding and why would she need so much protection? He remembered their first date, he was sure they'd been followed. Their Captain had also warned him, not to hurt her. Adam decided he would speak to Nat, the first chance he got. Force her to tell him, if necessary. If Abi needed protection, he'd supply it, that wasn't a problem. But he needed to know why.

"Have you decided how to propose yet?" Jack broke him out of his thoughts.

"I've arranged for both of us to have a long weekend off next week. I'm taking Abi to New York. I think it's time to she met the family. I'm thinking of doing it there."

"Make it romantic, something she'll remember and will make her happy." Jack motioned that Abi was heading back and they changed the subject. Jack stood. "I'll leave you two lovebirds alone."

Abi looked over at Adam, she was so lucky. The man was perfect, and she was madly in love with him. His short dark hair was set off by his dark, smoky brown eyes and being a few inches taller than her, at five feet eleven, it made him the perfect height for her. As neither of them was driving, Adam ordered another bottle of white wine. Abi looked at him in surprise, as he passed her an envelope. She opened it. "New York?"

"I thought it was about time I showed you where I grew up and meet the family." He thought of his brothers. "I can't promise my brothers will behave, but I'm willing to give it a try."

Abi laughed. "Sure."

They stayed for another hour and nattered away. Adam wondering what he had done to deserve Abi.

*****

Their long weekend came around quickly. The couple flew to New York, and they went straight to the hotel. The following morning Adam had arranged for them to have brunch at his parent's house. He was nervous, and he hoped they liked Abi.

Adam's brothers were already at their parent's house. Andrew was two years older and a police officer with the NYPD, along with his long-term partner Crystal, who was a nurse. Her naturally dark skin was highlighted by her dark brown hair and brown eyes. And Anthony, who was seven years younger and ran a security business with an old school friend. Both followed their father, with their brown hair and brown eyes. His parents stood to welcome her.

His mother, Martha hugged Abi. "Welcome to the family."

Abi noticed how Martha's ash-grey hair shone in the light, and her blue eyes twinkled with delight. Martha knew instantly Adam had chosen well. Abi was beautiful, and you could see immediately that they belonged together. His father, Samuel, welcomed his girlfriend too. Both noticed how nervous Abi was. Adam had told them so much about Abi, that she already felt like a daughter. They would soon have her at ease.

Brunch went well. Martha had made a lovely brunch casserole, and Samuel had opened a bottle of champagne. He made a toast to Abi welcoming her to the family, which made her blush.

Abi liked his family, and they got along brilliantly. The conversation was kept light. Abi was only asked a few questions, as Adam had already filled everyone in on Abi's family. She helped Martha clear up and followed Martha and Crystal into the kitchen. "It was a lovely brunch, thank you for having me."

Martha's smile grew as she glanced over at Abi. "Of course we would. We've been looking forward to meeting you for ages. I've told Adam several times to bring you. Have to meet the girl that's stolen one of my sons' hearts. I can feel the love in his voice, every time he mentions your name."

Abi blushed. "He's a loving man, I can see where he gets it from. Adam follows his father, obviously."

"He sure does, right down to becoming a cop. Samuel's now retired from the police force, and he was glad one of his sons followed in his footsteps. Let alone two. Three if you count Anthony's security company."

Martha and Crystal began to laugh. Abi looked at them confused, then realised she must be missing something.

"Sorry." Crystal said. "It's just that Adam's always said his first love was the job, but the way he looks at you, he's obviously changed his mind. You've managed to completely hook him. It's obvious he's devoted to you. In the time I've known him, he's never looked so nervous. I wasn't even sure he knew what the word meant. He wants you to fit in and to get along with us, but I get the feeling if you didn't, it'll be his family that he divorced, not you."

"There's no worry there, I feel like I belong here already. It's obvious Adam loves you all and gets on wonderfully with his brothers," Abi replied. They were a close family, and she hoped she'd fit in.

Martha smiled. Abi was perfect for Adam, and they made a good couple. More importantly, Abi would be an excellent daughter-in-law. Adam had better not let her slip away.

Meanwhile, the men have moved into the lounge. "So," his father said. "Have you proposed yet? I didn't see a ring."

"No, I hoped to do that this weekend. I have the ring already." He pulled it out of his pocket and showed them.

Andrew looked at it. "Wow, it's stunning. That must have cost a fortune. How are you planning to propose?"

"I've arranged a table at a restaurant tomorrow night."

Anthony had other ideas. "That's not good enough. Abi deserves better, and I'm sure we can come up with a better idea. When are you leaving?"

It was their long weekend off. Technically, Adam and Abi should be back on duty Tuesday, but he'd arranged a couple more days. "We fly back Wednesday."

Andrew took over. "Right, that gives us a few days, so leave it with us. We'll make sure she gets the perfect proposal, one she'll never forget." They changed the conversation, as the women re-entered.

Later in the evening, Samuel managed to get Adam alone. "You really do love Abi, don't you? She's a good catch."

Adam looked over at his dad. "Yes, she really is the one for me. I'm so glad I transferred and found her. Abi's the one I was meant to find."

Samuel couldn't help but notice the old scars on Abi's wrists. She didn't seem bothered by them, but something about them wasn't right. "Adam, her wrists. What happened?"

Adam exhaled slowly, he knew this would come. "I don't know. I've asked, but all she says is that they're from an old accident. I'm not pushing her for answers. Whatever happened, she'll tell me when she's ready."

Samuel was a retired police detective. He had a good idea what had caused those scars, and it wasn't from an accident. Someone had intentionally harmed her, and it must have been painful, considering how severe those wounds must have been. He hoped Adam knew what he was taking on. A woman with that type of injury always carried the memories with her. "Whatever it was, she isn't bothered by them. Keep her safe Adam, whatever caused those injuries must have been serious. Let's hope it stays in her past."

Adam looked back towards Abi, as she laughed at whatever Andrew was saying. He hoped it wasn't more stories of him from when he was younger, he'd been embarrassed enough as it was today. He thought of what his father had said. Another warning to keep her safe. He needed to speak to Nat and to get whatever it was, into the open.

*****

In the morning, Adam got a call from Anthony. "You able to talk?" He asked

Abi was in the shower. "Yeah."

"Good, I've pulled a few strings. Be ready Monday evening at 6pm, a limousine will pick you up. You'll be driven over to the Key West Bight Marina. I've got you a sunset cruise on the Schooner America 2.0. Champagne and nibbles included. It's just the two of you. I've checked the weather, and it's looking clear, so should it should be perfect. I'm sending one of our surveillance photographers, Steve, to record the event. Abi's going to love it."

12

Adam was gobsmacked. Anthony must have called in a lot of favours, to pull that off. "Thanks, for once I don't know what to say. I really owe you."

Anthony laughed. "That'll be a first, Adam, out of words. I'll have to record the event because it'll never happen again."

Adam heard Abi has she moved around the bedroom. "I need to go, I'll speak to you later."

As she entered the room, Abi asked who had rung.

"Anthony, he always was one for early calls. Wants to know if we're free tomorrow evening. He'll pick us up at six." He would be looking forward, to her reaction.

"What's he up to?"

"Taking us for dinner. Anthony wants to get to know you better, without everyone else being around." Adam was glad to have his back to Abi, she could usually spot any lies. A point which made her such a good cop. "No doubt Andrew will do the same at some point. He won't want Anthony to get one over on him."

*****

The day of the proposal arrived, and Adam couldn't be more nervous. What if she said no? He would never live it down. Plus, he'd be heartbroken. He had everything crossed, prayed it went to plan. Abi had to say yes.

Abi had never been to New York, so he spent the day showing her some of the sights. They ended up at Central Park, and he treated her to a horse-drawn carriage ride. Abi's face was a picture as she leaned into Adam, and he placed an arm around her shoulder. After they had grabbed a snack, they headed back and arrived back at the hotel mid-afternoon.

"Any idea where Anthony's taking us?" Abi asked

"No. All he said was to wrap up in case it gets chilly. Why not wear that dress you brought this afternoon? You have that wrap, which will go lovely with it." The dress was gorgeous. A pale silver blue, that really set Abi's eyes off. Straight with a slight waistband

13

and three-quarter length sleeves. Lengthwise, it went slightly below her knees, so getting on the boat shouldn't be too awkward. He pulled out his suit, hoping for the best. Tonight, needed to go to plan.

Six came around quickly. Adam glanced at Abi, she was stunning, and he still had problems believing she was his. Hopefully, it would be forever. They waited in the foyer until the limousine arrived. Thus was it, he thought. "Abi, are you ready? The car's here."

As he opened the door for her, Adam heard her breathe as it caught in her throat when she spotted the limousine. "Anthony's gone all out hasn't he?"

The driver opened the door, and the couple settled in. Soon they arrived at the marina. When they headed towards the dock, Adam's phone rung. "I need to take this." It was a setup, he knew Anthony would ring to supposedly cancel. "Anthony can't make it, he's stuck in a job and wants us to carry on without him." Abi nodded and thought Adam sounded nervous.

The Captain of the Schooner America 2.0 met them personally as they boarded. He led them to a unique table that had been arranged on the deck. He handed each of them a glass of champagne. "Enjoy the sailing. The weather report looks good, and it should remain clear."

Adam held out a chair, and Abi sat. He sat next to her, both had unobstructed views over the ocean. So far, so good, he thought.

Shortly after they had set sail, a waiter appeared with a tray of hors-d'oeuvres and refilled their glasses. The sky remained clear, and the sunset was stunning. They'd moved to one the benches, and Adam put his arm around her. She snuggled into him. "Adam tonight's perfect. Anthony must have pulled in a lot of favours. I'll have to repay him at some point."

"That's Anthony for you. Always pulls out all the stops, guess that's why he's so good at his job. You warm enough, sweetheart?"

Abi nodded. There was a slight breeze, but not enough to cause her to get cold. A pod of dolphins swam past, and Abi leaned

14

against the rail for a closer look. Her face lit up with joy, and her hair was blown behind her in the wind. Adam couldn't help but wonder if Anthony had set that up as well. As the sun began to drop, he decided it was time. Abi was still leaning against the rail. He nodded towards Steve, pulled out the ring and got down on one knee. When Abi turned around, the sunset would be a great background. "Abi," he said softly.

She turned around, saw Adam on one knee, then the ring. Stunned, she looked at him. Steve got the perfect photo, Abi had no idea.

"Abi," Adams' mouth went dry. Please say yes, he prayed. "I've loved you since we met. I never want to let you go. Please, will you do me the great honour of becoming my wife?"

Chapter Two

bi was stunned, she didn't know what to say. Suddenly, everything made sense. Adam's nervousness. The way Anthony had cancelled. The evening had been perfect, but she'd never expected this. It must have cost a small fortune, she really had snagged someone special. She closed her eyes and hesitated in her answer. She loved him, knew deep down how much he loved her back. There really was only one answer, but her past? He wasn't aware of her history. He'd asked about the scars, but she had never told him the truth. But she needed to. She rubbed at her wrist, a habit she still did when nervous. No, she told herself. No, he wasn't going to spoil tonight. He was going to stay in her past, where he belonged. She'd stopped living for so long, never thought she'd find a man she could fully love, without any doubts and had given up. But Adam had made her feel alive, made her feel special and wanted. She'd known he was the one for her. That's why she'd agreed to that first date. Oh, she knew Nat had followed them, knew she had been ready to intervene like she had done so many times previously. But Adam had been the one. The one who helped her heal, to help her forget. The one who taught her how to love. After everything she'd been through, she deserved someone to help her forget what had been done to her. The one who had hurt and damaged her. No, he wasn't spoiling this. She wasn't going to let him win and ruin her life. He was nothing to her now, and it would stay that way.

Steve slightly lowered the camera. He'd noticed the look of sorrow cross her face. This didn't look good, Steve thought. He had to send a report directly back to Anthony, as soon as they docked and at the moment it seemed like she was about to say no.

Adam began to think the same thing. He'd seen that look of sorrow pass over her face. His smile faltered, as he closed his eyes. Please Abi, he prayed again. He heard a quiet yes and looked back up at Abi. Did she?

"Yes." This time he heard the excitement in her voice. Abi held out her left hand, and Adam slid the ring onto her finger. A perfect fit just like them. He stood, picked her up, twirled her around and kissed her fiercely on her mouth. She said yes!

The rest of the sailing soon passed, and they disembarked. The limo was waiting for them. Abi snuggled up to her new fiancé, her head was on his shoulder. Her eyes drifted closed, and Adam heard her breathing settle, as she drifted off to sleep. She said yes, it still hadn't sunk in. She looked so beautiful, the evening went perfectly. He needed to make sure he thanked Anthony because he owed him big time. Steve had rung him the moment they docked and no doubt the whole family knew by now. With a bit of luck, they would leave him alone tonight. He kissed the top of her head, she was now officially his. Adam remembered how she had reacted, how she'd rubbed at her wrist, and that look of sorrow. He'd noticed that she always rubbed at her wrist, when nervous. She'd done it the first time they'd kissed. Something wasn't right. It wasn't an accident that had caused those scars. No, there was something else she was hiding, but he couldn't figure out what, nor why she hadn't told him. He would speak to Nat before he'd talked to Abi. He couldn't help her if he didn't know what the problem was. And whatever it was, she needed to know she no longer had to face it alone.

When they arrived back at the hotel, they had discovered that Anthony hadn't quite finished. He'd arranged for them to have the wedding suite for the rest of their stay. As they arrived at the door, Adam stopped Abi from entering. She glanced back at him puzzled.

"I need to do this right." He picked her up and carried her over the threshold.

Abi laughed. "Practicing, are you?"

"No, just checking I can lift you. Might have to change my mind if you turn out to be too heavy." He dropped her on the bed, both were laughing loudly. "Abi, I meant what I said, I am never letting you go. I've got a pair of handcuffs to make sure." He kissed her, with hunger he couldn't contain.

"Take me," she said breathlessly. Adam started to remove her dress, tonight he would make sure she knew exactly what she meant to him.

******

After a somewhat energetic night, they finally headed down to breakfast and followed a waiter to a table. Adams' whole family was there, at least they were left alone last night. Abi blushed as she remembered how little sleep they had got. Adam spotted Jack amongst the crowd, Anthony had thought of everything. Abi noticed him too. "Dad, what…" She trailed off in surprise.

"Did you think I'd miss this," Jack pulled her into a hug. "My baby gets engaged, and you expect me to stay at home. No way. I flew in yesterday."

"Yeah," Anthony said. "You two spent so long wandering around New York, that it was difficult to get him to the hotel unnoticed. I had no idea which route to take, so you didn't spot us."

They all laughed. Abi hugged Anthony. "Thank you, the evening was perfect, I never suspected a thing."

"Glad to be of help." Anthony looked over at Adam. "Heard she nearly gave you a heart attack and nearly said no." He held up a folder. "I've got the photos to prove it."

Adam laughed. "Yeah, thought she was. Maybe a boat wasn't such a good idea, I could have thrown myself overboard in sorrow." They all laughed again. He got out the photos that Steve had sent over last night, and everyone commented on how lovely they looked.

Abi saw the manager walk towards them. "I'm sorry Miss Lawton, but there's a call for you."

She followed him to the phone. "Hello."

"Abi," It was Captain Dalton. "I hear congratulations are in order. Sorry, I couldn't get down there, but you know how busy it gets here."

Frank Dalton was an old family friend and their police Captain. "Thank you, but we are coming back, you know."

"Yeah, but I sent you a little something, and I've extended your leave, call it an engagement present. You're not back on duty until Monday."

The manager walked back towards her, with an enormous bouquet. "Frankie, they're lovely and thanks."

"Take care Abi and say hello to Adam for me."

She hung up, took the bouquet, and smelled the flowers. The fragrance was gorgeous. A mixture of red roses and white gypsophila. As she walked back to Adam, she felt happier than she ever had before.

Breakfast was lovely, and Abi spent ages showing everyone the ring. She grabbed a quiet moment and wandered out into the garden. Her dad followed her out. "Abi, you are happy, aren't you?"

"Yes, Adam means the world to me. He really is one in a million, and I'm lucky to have found him."

They found a bench, Jack took her hand, and rubbed her wrist. The old scars were barely visible. "Abi, I worry about you. Have you told Adam yet?"

"No." She paused, knew what her dad was hinting at. "I know I need to before someone else does, but it's hard. How do you tell someone, who absolutely loves you, that your uncle tried to kill you? How do I tell Adam what happened, what he did to me? That he'd do it again, given half a chance."

"He needs to know Abi, Michael's still out there. God forbid that he ever comes back, but if he does? Abi, Adam will need to protect you. He'll be the first one there now that you're moved in with him. He needs to know what could happen. That your uncle may still be a danger to you."

"I'll tell him, but not yet. Let us be happy for a bit first. He's likely to get Anthony to investigate." Abi didn't want to tell Adam but knew she must. When he found out the truth of what happened, it would test them. "I'll do it before the wedding."

"Sooner rather than later. Abi, don't leave it too late. He's not going to walk away, he loves you too much. Trust him. If it's easier, I'll be with you when you do, and I'll even dig out the police reports. You don't need to do it alone but tell him. If you don't want me there, Nat can be with you."

Abi knew her dad was telling the truth. Adam did love her but was he strong enough to handle it. "Give me a few weeks, please. Just a few weeks to be happy. I could lose him. After all this time Michael could still ruin my life. Dad, I couldn't live if that happened. If I lost Adam, my life would be over." Her eyes shimmered in tears.

Jack wiped away a tear that escaped. "Abi, you were badly injured, and he needs to know. He must have seen the scars, asked about them. He's a cop, and he's going to recognise stab wounds."

Abi knew her dad was right. Adam had seen the scars, but she'd passed them off as old childhood injuries. "What if I can't give him children? He wants them." She felt the tears, as they threatened to fall again.

"Oh Abi, you need to talk to him and tell him your concerns. As far as you're aware you can have children, but I'll speak to Julian. He can arrange for you to be checked over and put your mind at ease." Julian was the police medical officer and another close family friend. He'd been the one to help Abi recover and had arranged for her to have plastic surgery on her wrists, so the scars were less visible. She needed to talk to Adam and do it quickly. "Adam will understand Abi, just talk to him. Please." He pulled Abi to him. "I'm sorry, I didn't want to upset you. Today should be happy for the both of you. I just worry, and I hope it's for nothing. Do you still carry your ankle strap and gun?"

Abi pulled back and lifted one leg of her pants, which clearly showed her small ankle weapon. "Yes, even now. Dad he wouldn't be stupid to try again, surely?"

"I hope not but take care." Jack was concerned. It was Abi's chance at happiness and Michael wouldn't like it. He hoped his gut feeling was wrong, but it was the perfect time for him to reappear.

*****

Adam walked into the garden when had begun to wonder where Abi had gone. He spotted them as they sat on a bench and noticed the expression on their faces. Adam didn't miss the small gun, she had got strapped to her leg. He remembered that she always went to the bathroom before they made love and had found that gun under her pillow, on more than one occasion. Whatever they were discussing, it was serious. Abi seemed so happy with the engagement, so did Jack. That couldn't be the problem, so what was? He'd noticed the way Jack rubbed her wrists, the fact that Abi had been crying. He narrowed his eyes, just as his dad walked up behind him.

"Son, I think you already know those scars aren't from an accident. You need to talk to her and get her to tell you. Don't start your life together with a lie. I know you love Abi and will stand by her, but does Abi know that." Samuel stopped and studied his son's fiancé. "It looks like her father's telling her the same thing. Adam, those scars, if I had to hazard a guess, I'd say they're from wire."

Adam looked sharply round at his father. "Wire?" he said confused.

"Yes, of the barbed variety. Whoever did that must have been one evil, sick bastard. Has Abi got any other scars?"

Adam nodded. "Several, all over her. Including two stab wounds to her abdomen."

Samuel shook his head slowly. "She looks so happy, but she's obviously suffered. Get her to talk to you. It'll be better out in the open. Make sure she understands that you won't walk. She's probably thought it."

He would, but not now. Let Abi have some happiness. It could wait until they arrived home and he wanted to speak to Nat first. He

21

had a bad feeling that the threat was still out there, and it was severe enough that Abi was armed, at all times.

Chapter Three

They stayed in New York until Wednesday and decided to keep their original flight back. Abi had arranged to meet her best friend and Frankie's daughter, Michelle, for lunch on Thursday and she was barely able to keep the happy news to herself. She ordered champagne for them both and told the waiter they would both have the house specials. Michelle studied Abi. It was unlike Abi to drink champagne, apart from special occasions. "What are you up to?" She asked.

Abi knew Michelle hadn't spotted the ring yet. She'd tried to keep it hidden. As she picked the glass up in her left hand, she let the light hit the diamonds. "Nothing, Michelle. What makes you think I am?" She answered innocently.

Michelle's face lit up. "He proposed!" She squealed. "How? When? Abi, details!"

Abi told her everything. How perfect it was and how she was so lucky to have found Adam. Michelle was so excited for her, but Abi noticed a brief look of sorrow on her face, as Michelle asked. "Have you told him?"

Abi shook her head. "Not yet, I've had the same conversation with dad. He loves me Michelle, but it's going to hurt him so much. I'm scared I'll lose him." She took a deep breath. "I don't know how to."

"Abi, I've seen the way he looks at you, and there's no way he's leaving. Tell him before he finds out. It'll be a lot harder if he hears it from someone else. I know it'll hurt, bring it all back, but it'll be better out in the open."

Abi knew her best friend was right, but how?

*****

23

Abi returned to their apartment. She needed to tell him, *must*, but just not yet. In a couple of weeks, she thought. She just wanted a couple of weeks of happiness. A bit of time so they could enjoy their engagement. Abi had buried the memories deeply, and she really *didn't* want to bring them back up. But she knew she had to. It was unfair on Adam to not be told. He needed the chance to walk away if he wanted too. He may not want to take on a woman with her history.

Abi had spent the rest of the afternoon with Julian at the hospital. She needed to know if she could have children, or whether Michael had taken that away from her. She had been examined thoroughly and was waiting to hear back. She wanted all the information at her fingertips when she spoke to Adam. Needed to be able to answer his questions and he would have loads. She snuggled next to Adam on the couch. "Good lunch?" He asked.

"Yes, Michelle's happy for us both. I've already asked her to be my bridesmaid."

Adam noticed she was slightly tense. "You okay?" She didn't sound incredibly happy. Her tone had been flat.

"Fine, just tired."

"Abi, you're happy about the engagement, aren't you?"

"Of course, I am. Today's taken a lot of out me, that's all. I'm probably still suffering from jet lag."

Adam wasn't convinced but let it go. Whatever was wrong, she would tell him when she was ready, but he's worried. Abi's been slightly quiet since they got back. He kissed the top of her head. He could wait.

Abi let a tear fall. Oh God, she thought. How do I tell him?

*****

Monday came around quickly, and they were back on duty. As they entered the station, everyone cheered and congratulated them.

Detective Natalie Nathaniel walked up to them. "Adam, you kept that quiet. Congratulations." She hugged them both and whispered in Abi's ear. "Don't let him go." Abi instantly tensed. Nat looked at her, as worry creased her brow. "Abi?"

Abi shook her head and mouthed later.

Adam caught up with Nat before she could speak to Abi. Nat noticed how worried he looked. She waited for him to begin, but had already guessed what was coming.

"Nat, what's going on? Abi's not her normal self. I saw how she tensed up earlier. I'm worried there's something wrong, and that she's having second thoughts."

Nat looked at him. Knew that Abi needed to speak to her fiancé. "Adam, I can honestly say it's not the engagement, she's madly in love with you. However, she does need to tell you something, but she's not sure how. Give her chance. It won't be easy for her to say. Just listen when she does open up and let her get it all out."

He remembered what his dad had told him. "The scars on her wrist, are they from barbed wire?"

Nat tried to keep the shock from her face, but Adam saw it. "I'll take that as a yes. I also recognise stab wounds. Nat, what happened?"

Nat shook her head slowly and sighed. "Adam, it's not for me to say." She narrowed her eyes at him. "Does it make a difference to how you feel about her, knowing what you already know?"

"No, not a scrap. I just wish Abi would talk to me. Jack told me that he expected me to protect her, to keep her safe. Whoever did that to her, he's still out there, isn't he? I know she carries an ankle strap, at all times. She isn't confident that she's safe. Whoever it was, must have seriously hurt her."

Nat nodded in agreement. Adam was figuring it out. Abi needed to talk to him and soon. "Unfortunately, yes. He's not made a move since. In fact, we haven't heard from him. Abi recovered from it, and I hope he doesn't return. Adam, you two getting engaged, may be enough to bring him back. He won't be happy and certainly doesn't want Abi to be happy. We are all hoping he's dropped dead."

25

"Why? What's he got to gain by it?"

"Talk to her, then talk to Jack. He's not joking when he's asked you to protect her. If he does come back, she may not survive a second time. In fact, I know she won't. She barely did the first time."

Adam agreed with her. He would speak to Abi in the next few days. She needed to realise she could trust him. Now he had figured some of it out, maybe it'll be easier for her to fill him in on the rest. He considered searching the police records but didn't want to go behind her back. That certainly wouldn't be the way to prove to Abi, she could trust him. His gut feeling had warned him it was serious, but what Nat had said, it had been life-threatening. She must be terrified whoever it was, would come back.

Nat caught up with Abi when she arrived back at the station for a break and dragged her into the restroom. After checking no one else was in there, she asked. "Abi, what's going on?"

Abi placed her hands on a sink, her back to Nat. "How do I tell him?"

"Oh Abi, is that what's worrying you?"

"I know I need too, but I just don't know how."

"Abi, Adam caught me earlier. He's already figured some of it out. He knows about the stabbing and the use of barbed wire. Knows the threats still there and that you carry a gun always. You need to talk to Adam. If it's easier, I can dig out the case files from the records. Tell him the basics and let him read the rest. But you have to tell him."

Abi turned around and leaned back against the sink. He tears shone in her eyes "What if he can't cope with knowing? Walks away. I fought to stay alive Nat, but I could still lose everything."

"He loves you Abi, truly loves you. Adam won't walk. If anything, he'll be more protective of you."

Abi tried to believe Nat, but it was hard. Adam did love her, she knew that, but the cop in her knew traumas like this could split relationships up. The partners couldn't always cope with it. "Nat," she began quietly. "If he returns, abducts me again and I don't come back, look after Adam. It'll break his heart." A tear slipped out.

26

Nat now knew the real reason Abi was upset, and it wasn't about Adam at all. "Abi, it's been eleven years, he's highly unlikely to attempt anything again. You fought and won against him once. Now you're a cop, he'd be stupid to try again."

"But he might, we both know he's capable of it. Now I'm engaged, happy. Nat, I have a bad feeling. Sometimes I think I've got a stalker. I know, I'm probably stupid, but I just can't shake the feeling. What if he is back?"

Nat pulled her into an embrace her. "Abi, I'll look into it. If he's back, I'll find out. He *won't* get to you. There's a whole station that will watch your back, keep you safe. Hell, Adam would shoot him on sight."

Abi washed her face and composed herself, ready to go back out. Nat stopped her. "Take the rest of the night off. I'll square it with the watch commander, tell him you're sick. Give yourself a bit of time before Adam finishes, then tell him."

Abi shook her head. "Not tonight. We only have one more night shift to get through and then we're off for the weekend. I'll tell him Saturday. I promise I will." She was also speaking to Julian tomorrow, her test results should be back, and if she wanted to be upfront with Adam, she needed to know all the details.

"I'm sending you home anyway. You're in no position to work tonight."

Abi headed back to her locker and went home, but Nat made her way to the Captain's office.

"Nat, how can I help you?" Frankie asked.

"It's Abi, I've sent her home."

"She's upset," Nat paused before she continued. "She needs to talk to Adam about Michael, but doesn't know how to start, but that's not the main reason. She's convinced he'll come back, try again. She already thinks she has a stalker."

"Christ. Nat look into it. I'll get a tail on her when she's not at work. She should be fine while on duty, there are enough cops around to stop him making a move. But we'll cover all the bases, just in case. If he thinks he can come back and try again, I'm not making it easy. God, I hope he's not. What he did before she was damn lucky to survive. She won't be so lucky a second time. He'll make sure of it, as well as making it worse for her."

Nat stood and got ready to leave. "Frankie if he succeeds, grabs her a second time, I want to kill the bastard myself."

"Get in the queue. I think Adam will want the pleasure."

Jack had already spoken to Frankie. They knew Abi was worried about telling Adam, but neither of them knew about the last bit. "Michael would be stupid to try again, but I'll put the word out. Speak the officers who know what happened and get them to keep an eye out for him. If he tries anything, we'll get to him before he gets to Abi. She won't go through that again, not if I can do anything about it."

"I just hope we're wrong, that Abi's worrying over nothing, but my gut feeling says differently. Frankie, I think he's back, and it's just a matter of time. She's telling Adam the weekend. I've said I'll get her the case files. It'll not be easy for her, but when Adam sees what Michael did, he'll be fuming."

"I'll look at their rota's. I'll put Abi back on desk duty for a few weeks until she's more settled and I'll make sure Adam works the same shifts. That way he can be with her when off duty. He'll want to be once he founds out."

"Damn it. Frankie, she's just got her life back. It's taken her a long time to trust another man, to let him get close enough to begin a relationship. Michael can't be allowed to prevent them being together. She deserves this chance at happiness. Bloody well deserves it."

*****

Abi was in bed when Adam finally arrived home. He'd be held up on his last call out when he'd heard Abi had gone home early. He'd tried to phone her, but she didn't answer. Adam was worried, hoped she was alright. He couldn't understand why she wouldn't talk to him. He crawled into bed. They were off the weekend. He would take her out and cheer her up. Then he would get her to talk to him, and find out what the problem was. Once and for all.

Abi woke up early and left Adam in bed. She had to speak to a Julian, and then she would talk to Adam tomorrow. Julian was waiting for her at his home and handed her a cup of coffee. He had her test results and prepared to tell her. "Abi, I rushed your tests through and have the results. You know that you were severely injured." He stopped, and Abi nodded. "You were stabbed twice in the abdomen, and both wounds penetrated quite deeply. The scans show that the internal injuries have healed, but there is a lot of scarring around your uterus and ovaries." He paused and held her hands. Knew this wasn't what she wanted to hear. "Abi, it's possible that you won't be able to conceive, if you do, you may not be able to carry full term. We can do further tests if you want, but we'll need to test Adam as well, just to make sure he's okay. It may be possible to have surgery to remove the scarring from your uterus and supplements to help support the pregnancy. You need to discuss this with Adam. Let me know if you decide to go ahead and try."

Abi knew it was a possibility, but hearing it said made it real. She had no choice and had to tell Adam tomorrow. She would speak to Nat later and get the case files. Adam would want to know everything, so she would show him. She just hoped she still had a fiancé at the end of it all.

Abi went straight to the station, she wasn't ready to see Adam. She needed to get her head around all of this first. She knew Adam wanted children, and this would be a blow to him. She met up with Morris Knight, her partner and headed out on patrol.

*****

Adam had missed Abi. She had left before he'd woken up and left a note saying she'd got a few errands to do before their shift began. He had noticed how tired she had looked at the shift briefing, but she said she was fine. He headed out with his partner,

29

Charlie Butler. It was a quiet night, so he radioed over to Abi. "4-Adam-45 to 4-Adam-40, we're stopping for our break at Dunn's at 9:30pm, if you're free."

"4-Adam 45 this is 4-Adam 40, we'll try to make it. It's quiet tonight," replied Morris.

Adam smiled. Dunn's was a small cafe, that was a regular haunt for cops, and with it being cold and damp tonight, it looked like all the crazies had stayed at home. Only another hour to get through and he could have a little time with the love of his life.

Abi and Morris were already at Dunn's when Adam and Charlie pulled in. They grabbed a coffee and found a table. Adam sat next to Abi and pulled her close to him. He noticed she was tense again, and knew he needed to talk to her.

Morris broke the silence. "Had anything interesting, we've been dead quiet."

"Got called out to a code 30, looked like another hoax call," answered Charlie.

"Another one? We're getting a lot of them at the moment." Morris said. As he glanced at Adam and Abi. He motioned to Charlie. "Let's give the two lovebirds some time alone."

Adam watched them leave, Abi wasn't relaxing, and he's worried again. "Abi, are you okay?"

She sighed, not tonight she thought. "Yes, just tired."

"You've been tired a lot recently. Abi, please talk to me."

"Adam, I'm fine."

"Abi, *please*, I'm worried." He noticed she began to rub at her wrist again, and he took her hand. "Abi, whatever it is, just tell me it's nothing serious. That you aren't ill."

"Not tonight, Adam. Wait until the end of the shift. I do have something to tell you, but it's nothing we can't sort out, and I'm not ill, promise." She hoped she was right, prayed they could work through this. She didn't want to lose him, but she knew she could. She vowed that if he walked, she would hunt Michael down, make him pay. Anthony would be happy to help her. She was sure if it.

Adam gave her a quick kiss, as her radio crackled to life.

'4-Adam-40, please respond to a code 30 at the old miller's warehouse, by the marina.'

"See you later." Abi gave him a quick peck on the cheek, as she left.

Abi picked up the radio, as Morris and she got back into the car. "Roger," she responded.

They made excellent time, and as they headed towards the entrance, a hooded man ran out and continued around the corner. Morris gave chase while Abi headed back towards the car. She hoped to block the hoodie off at the road. Morris glanced over his shoulder as he turned the corner, and saw Abi as she got back into the patrol car.

Suddenly, he heard a loud explosion. He turned back, and as he ran back around the corner the shock hit him. "Abigail!" He yelled. "Oh, god no." He couldn't do anything but stare at their car. It was in flames.

Morris couldn't believe what he saw and called for Abi several more times. Finally, he had to admit to himself that she had been in the car and he collapsed back against the wall in shock. Morris couldn't do anything but stare at the fire. Eventually, he managed to pull out his mobile and dialed Lieutenant Green, back at the station.

"Green," he answered.

"Lieutenant!" Morris said. "There's," his voice began to shake.

"Spit it out Morris. Whatever it is, it can't be that bad."

"The car, it's…it's. Oh god, there's… There's been an explosion."

George became instantly on alert "Morris, are you trying to tell me the car has exploded?"

"Oh, god, yes. There's barely anything left. Abi…" his voice broke, as he trailed off.

George collapsed back into his chair, "Morris. Abi?" Concern laced his voice.

Morris hesitated. "I saw Abi, she…" He took a deep breath. "Oh god, she…she got into the car." As the shock set completely in, Morris slid down the wall and ended up sitting on the ground.

"Please god no." George closed his eyes in total disbelief and took a deep breath. Abi, a young upcoming officer, lost in such an awful way. "Stay put. I'll send a team over immediately." He hung up, and looked out of his office window into the foyer, as Adam walked past. "How do I tell him?" He muttered to himself. There were times he hated this job. Telling someone their loved one had died was always hard, especially if they were another officer.

Adam chose that moment to glance towards the office. He noticed how pale Lieutenant Green looked and Adam felt a knot in his stomach. Somethings happened, he thought, and it was grave.

George opened the office door. "Adam," he said quietly. "I need to speak to you. You too Captain Dalton." Who leaned against another desk.

They all returned to the office. George closed the door and asked Adam to take a seat. Oh god, he thought again, how do I tell them?

Abi's fiancé looked at him, the sick feeling he had was getting worse by the second. What's happened? Adam thought again. Adam's mind went to the last time he'd been called in. Abi had been injured after a bank robbery. Why did he think it was more serious this time?

George looked directly at Adam. "There's no straightforward way to say this. There's been an explosion, Adam-40 has been destroyed."

Adam glanced back in shock, he felt faint but had to ask. "Abi?"

"Adam, I'm so sorry," Lieutenant Green stopped, he still couldn't believe that he needed to say this. "They were called out to a code 30. Morris is still in shock, so I don't have the full details yet, but..." George paused and took a breath, which seemed to have suddenly become difficult. "He saw Abi getting into the car, before the explosion."

Frankie stood behind Adam and placed a hand on his shoulder. "Adam, there will be a full investigation. We'll find out what's happened and why. I'll get someone to take you home."

Adam stood up, walked over to the window, and stared out. His only thoughts were on Abi. How he would never see her again, never see her laugh or smile. His world that had seemed to be so perfect, now shattered apart.

*****

After Adam had left, Frankie turned to George. "What the hell happened?"

"I'm on my way over, coming? Because I don't bloody know."

They both headed out, and when they approached the scene, they saw what was left of the car. The forensic team were already there.

"She never stood a chance," Frankie spoke first. "There's nothing bloody left. It must have been one hell of an explosive? Someone knew what the hell they were doing."

"Josie," Frankie called, as he spied her.

Josie was their head forensic pathologist and if anyone could figure this out, she could. "Frankie, I don't know what to say. If she was in the car, it would have been quick. I'll know more once I get the car back to the lab. However, it was a high precision explosive, which only affected the car. Nothing else in the area. High temperature as well, due to the damage that's been done. This was someone with experience. There was no way it was an amateur. It looks like they thought it through. It was planned, there's no way it wasn't."

"Shit." He narrowed his eyes. "What do you mean, *if* she was in there?"

"As I said, I need to get what's left back to the lab. But with the amount of destruction, I don't know if there will be any traces of DNA, to prove she was. Saying that, it won't prove she wasn't."

"Are you saying that there's a slim chance she wasn't in the car?"

"Very slim. But if Abi wasn't, where is she?"

Damn good question, Frankie thought. "Where's Morris?"

Josie pointed to one of the patrol cars and Frankie headed over. "Morris, are you okay?"

33

Morris looked up at his Captain. "Abi," was all he could say.

"Let's get you in." He called over another officer. "Take him to the station. Morris go and make your statement, then go home. Take a couple of days off."

George walked back over. "Damn it Frankie, its bad. Who would want to do such a thing? It doesn't make any sense."

Frankie agreed it didn't, but he had one more job to do. "George, I need to inform Jack. I'll leave you here in charge."

He pulled up outside Jack's and sat there for a few minutes. Jack was one of his oldest friends. He'd watched Abi grow up, and now he had to deliver the worst news possible. She was his daughters best friend, only a few months younger than Michelle, and he had yet to tell his family. He hit the steering wheel in anger. God damn it. Of all the cops, why Abi? Oh hell, he didn't mean that. It shouldn't be any cop, but sweet Abi? Everything she's been through, for her to survive that and now this. Life was so damned unfair. He couldn't put it off any longer and rang the bell.

"Late night?" Jack asked as he let Frankie in.

"Jack, there's been an incident."

Jack swung round. "Abi? Michael?"

Frankie shook his head. "I wish it was. Jack, Adam 40 was destroyed. An explosion. I'm so sorry Jack, Abi was in the car."

Jack collapsed onto the couch. "No. Please Frankie, no."

Frankie let it sink in. There was nothing he could say or do. After a few minutes, Jack looked back at him. "Why?"

"We don't know. Abi and Morris were called out to a code 30. They saw someone running away. Morris gave chase, while Abi went back the car. Morris had just turned the corner when he heard the explosion. It was too late to do anything."

"Was she definitely in the car?"

"Morris saw her getting in. Josie has the remains back at the lab. She'll let us know if she gets anything. Jack, I....Oh god, I'm still having trouble believing it."

"Adam?"

34

"Devastated. I've arranged for someone to take him home. He can take as long as he needs."

Both sat in silence. Eventually, Frankie got up to leave. "I haven't even told my family yet. Jack, if you need anything, anything at all, ring me."

Frankie drove home. Tonight couldn't get any worse. His wife, Louise was still up.

"Hey, bad night?" She saw the expression his face.

Frankie poured himself a whiskey and sat down. "The worst."

"Frankie?"

He downed the whiskey in one and glanced over at her. "Abi's dead." His voice full of sorrow.

Louise went pure white. "What!"

Frankie told her, and she found it hard to take it in. "I've contacted Andrew's captain, and he'll let Adam's family know. He sure as hell needs them now."

"Come to bed, try to get some sleep. It'll just get worse tomorrow." Louise said.

Chapter Four

Adam woke up, stretched, and reached for Abi. The bed was cold, and his eyes snapped open. Last night flooded back. "Abi," he whispered as it sunk in. She was really gone. He reached over and hugged her pillow. It still held her scent, and he inhaled deeply. He thought of his family. A police officer blown up, it would make national news. He needed to contact them. They couldn't hear it like that.

Adam wasn't aware that Frankie had already spoken to his old Captain and his brother, Andrew, had been informed. Andrew had called his other brother, Anthony and told him to meet him back at their parent's place. The urgency in Andrews' voice had worried him. When he arrived, everyone looked at him. He wouldn't have called a meeting unless it was necessary. Crystal was with him. She was in bits and unable to control her tears. Andrew had to support her. They looked at each other as Andrew began to tell them what had happened. The shock hit them. All of them knew Adam must be distraught.

Andrews' captain had given him leave of absence, for as long as Adam needed him. Anthony had also arranged to fly down. Their brother would have all the support he needed, for however long.

Adam was still in bed as someone knocked on his door. He ignored it, they could leave him the hell alone.

"Adam," someone called. Andrew? He can go to hell too. Wanting to be left alone, he ignored Andrew for as long as possible, but after he'd threatened to break down the door, Adam decided he'd better let him in.

Andrew followed him to the lounge. "Adam, I'm…" he trailed off. "Hell, I don't know what to say." There was nothing he could say.

Adam looked shattered, Andrew doubted he'd slept much last night. He made them some coffee and sat next to him on the couch. "Anthony's gone straight to the station. We'll both be staying as long as necessary. We all loved Abi, and we're not letting you deal with this alone."

Adam stared into space, all he could think of is why? Why Abi? Why now? Everything was going perfectly for them. She'd agreed to marry him, and they had a wedding to sort. Now it was a funeral. Andrew placed his hand, lightly on Adams' shoulder. "We'll get to the bottom of this. Neither Anthony or I will let this go until we know what happened. We'll find who did this."

Adam stood and walked over to a photo. The one Steve had taken of their proposal. Abi was so happy and had looked so stunning. "Why? I don't know why anyone would want to do such a thing? I don't know how I'll live without her? If I even want to." She was going to talk to him today, tell him what was bothering her, but now he would never know. She died with a great weight on her mind. He should have forced her to tell him the other night, forced her to stay at home. She'd still be alive then, still be with him. He collapsed back onto the couch and Andrew held him while the tears fell.

Andrew knew Adam needed time but was right on one thing. Why and who? None of it made any sense, but he knew Adam wasn't going to handle it alone. No way. He would be investigating with Anthony, and they would get to the bottom of it. Find out who had planted that device and why. They couldn't bring Abi back, but they could give Adam closure.

*****

Anthony had gone straight to the station and entered the captain's office. "What the hell happened?" He asked.

Frankie glanced up at the stranger. He had no idea who he was but knew precisely what he was asking about. "If you're a reporter you'll have to wait for the press release, like everyone else."

Anthony realised he hadn't introduced himself. "Sorry, I flew straight in as soon as I heard." He held out his hand, and Frankie shook it. "Anthony Leroy, Adams brother. Andrews gone straight round to Adam, but I need to know what happened."

Ah, yes Anthony, Frankie thought, the brother that had the security firm. He was glad Adams' brothers had flown down. God knows, he needed all the support he could get now. "I'm afraid we don't know much. Abi and her partner were called out to a suspected burglary. On arrival, Morris chased a suspect while Abi got back in the car hoping to head them off." Frankie paused, he was still trying to get his head around it himself. "Morris heard the explosion. Abi had no chance, no chance at all." He stopped again and shook his head. "Anthony, we have nothing to go on. Forensics have extraordinarily little. Josie's worked all night, and I've sent her home." He had ordered her home. He'd called her back in as he had wanted their best person on the job, but she had little to go on. "There wasn't much of the car left. Whatever explosive was used it was powerful. It was quick, Abi wouldn't have known what hit her. Josie can't even confirm Abi was in the car. There's just not enough evidence to even start a proper investigation."

"Was she definitely in the car? Could Morris be wrong? Are you *sure* on the details?"

"Believe me, Anthony, I've thought the same. Considered all the what if's, but Morris saw her getting into the car. We've checked the timings, and there wasn't enough time for her to get out." He'd been at it all night, looked at every angle but just couldn't change a damn thing. "I've tried, really tried. I've had every available officer at it, but nothing changes. Everything points back to Abi being in the car. I can't get a different answer, no matter how hard I try."

"Anyone owned up?" Anthony asked. After something like this, someone usually admitted to it. Would want to gloat about blowing up a police officer.

"No. I've asked everyone to call in every favour they have, every informer. Anything to get a damn idea of what happened. Someone must know something. I've arranged a press release for this afternoon. We'll be asking for any information and I have set up a special phone number. I just hope someone can give us something."

Anthony nodded, the captain was going all out. "I'll be staying until we know what's happened and Andrew will help as much as possible." He handed Frankie a card. "I'll be on his number. If you get anything, anything at all. I'll appreciate a call."

Frankie nodded back at Anthony. "Certainly. To be honest, I'll be grateful for the help. I'll even send you the reports." Frankie watched him leave. Another two helping wouldn't make a scrap of difference if they couldn't get a breakthrough. They needed something to give and soon.

Josie walked into his office, complete with her report.

"Thought I sent you home?"

"Couldn't sleep." She sat and passed him the report. "It's not very useful. It was as I thought. A high precision, high temperature explosive. The type you'd find in the army. I expect you're looking for an ex-army person."

"Any idea how it was planted?"

"That's the problem. If it was connected to the underside of the car, as they usually are, then I'd have some connection on the frame that's left. There isn't. It looks like the explosion started inside the car. Somewhere on the driver's side. Abi would have seen it and wouldn't have gotten in."

"Doesn't make sense. Car bombs are usually placed underneath, so why inside and why didn't Abi see it? She wasn't stupid, would have noticed a bomb. Something wouldn't have looked right, and she certainly wouldn't have gotten into the car."

"That brings me to something else, that doesn't add up. I've checked the timings. There's not much time between them leaving the car and the explosion. Until they separated, both could see the car. There wasn't time for someone to place it. It must have been done *after* Abi was in the car."

"Are you saying she saw the person, saw it coming? Christ, she would have been terrified." But it still didn't make sense. She didn't scream or fight. For god's sake she was armed, why didn't she shoot? "Was she in the car?"

39

"Can't tell. As I said last night, there's not enough evidence left. I can't say whether she was in the car or not"

"It's down to Morris's statement then. Thanks, Josie, it's excellent work."

He watched her leave. Damn it, he'd hoped she'd come up with something useful. Abi saw it coming. He wouldn't have wished that on his worst enemy.

*****

Frankie's called in every reporter he could get in touch with. National and international. He hoped it would be enough. He walked to the microphone and saw it was a good turnout. He just wished it was for different reasons. Their press officer had already prepared the statement and advised everyone there would be no questions. They had no answers anyway.

"Thank you all for attending," he began. "We are appealing for any witnesses to an incident that happened last night, that caused the death of a young, upcoming officer. Shortly after 10 pm yesterday, one of our patrol cars responded to a code 30, a suspected burglary at the old Miller's warehouse. There was an explosion, and Officer Abigail Lawton was pronounced dead at the scene. This is a great loss, not just to her family, but to all the officers at the station and she will be significantly missed.

We are asking for anyone who may have any information, to contact us on the number provided. Members of the public are advised they can contact us anonymously, and all leads will be investigated." He paused, looked around and spotted Anthony in the crowd. He noticed that Anthony watched the reporters, their reactions, and expressions. Frankie couldn't help but think that he would make a great cop. Anthony was on the prowl, and if anyone here knew anything, Anthony would pick up on it. Frankie was glad to see him and hoped he could find something, which they were missing. "This is a direct attack on the police force, something we will not tolerate and the person responsible will be caught. As will

40

anybody else who may have been involved." He stood down and hope he could keep that promise.

Anthony hadn't spotted anything in the crowd. If anything, the reporters seemed upset at the news. He took one more glance around the room, and a man at the back caught his eye. The man didn't belong here, Anthony thought. But he couldn't place why, but something wasn't right about him. Anthony's always had a good gut feeling, and it was screaming out at him now. He needed to talk to that man. He made his way slowly over, so not to startle the person, and tried to catch Frankie's eye. The man spotted him and moved quickly towards the door. Anthony walked faster but couldn't get through the crowd quick enough. By the time he got to the door, the man was gone.

Frankie caught up with Anthony. "Spot anything unusual?"

"Nothing obvious, but there was this man. Had some reporters ID but looked out of place. Can't place my finger on why. It's probably nothing, I'm probably clutching at straws. I just hope this gets us somewhere, and hope there's a witness."

"I'll let you know if we get any decent leads."

Anthony nodded, as they went their separate ways.

*****

Detective Nathaniel was waiting at the call centre they had set up. The phones had gone crazy the moment the press release went out. She sighed, most of the calls were a waste of time, they usually were, but they might just get one that wasn't. The phone next to her rang. "Detective Nathaniel, how may I help you?" The person at the other end breathed heavily. It sounded like another time waster. She was about to hang up when he talked.

"Shame about the cop, pretty little thing. I'm sure her fiancé is so upset, and daddy dearest must be falling apart."

It's him. Nat knew it was the person responsible, but she needed to keep a level head. The calls were being recorded and could be tracked. She motioned to another colleague, as he looked up at her. "It's him," she mouthed, as she placed her hand over the

41

receiver. The other officer quickly began to track the call. She removed her hand and continued the conversation. "Did you see the incident? Can you help us at all?"

"Oh, yes it was a fitting end to such a bitch. I only wish she'd suffered more, knew what had hit her. Knew who had done it. Adam should have looked after her better, should have treasured her more, protected her just like daddy said." He laughed, and Nat was notified that they were close to getting a location. Finally, she thought. "Why? What had Abi ever done to you?"

"Lived," he answered. "Abigail lived when she shouldn't have." The man hung up.

"Got it," the officer yelled.

Nat grabbed the address and called Frankie. "He called Frankie, the bastard called. I'm on the way to his location. Meet me there." She gave him the details.

Half an hour later they reached the meeting point. It was a small motel on the edge of town. Frankie walked up to Nat. He'd heard a copy of the call, and knew it had been made from a public phone. "Nat, let's do this, let's get the bastard."

Nat nodded back. As they entered the building, they went straight to reception. When they walked up to the receptionist, Nat showed her badge and introduced them. "How many phones are there?"

The receptionist answered. "Just two. One here and one in the public area."

"We're looking for a male, one who made a call within the last hour. Did you see anyone, or have any CCTV?"

"Sorry, no to both. Anyone can enter and use the phone. They don't need to log it."

Damn it, Nat thought, he chose this place well. "Can I see the guest register."

The receptionist passed her the book, and Nat studied the last few guests that had registered in. Frankie' stood behind her when a name jumped out at him. "That one," he pointed towards a name.

Nat looked at the name. Jackson Hodge. She looked at Frankie. "Who is he?"

"It may not be the same person, but that name rings a bell. He sent threatening letters to police officers a few years ago. Always to their home addresses. When we questioned him, he admitted freely that he'd kill a cop before he was done, but I thought he was still locked up."

Nat decided it was good enough for her.

They found his room, and Frankie kicked the door open. "Police," he shouted.

Nat followed him in. The room was empty. She walked up to a table and felt a cup. "Still warm, so we haven't long missed him."

They looked around the room. Frankie picked up an envelope and pulled out a photo. "Nat, he was here."

She walked over to him, and he showed her the photo. It showed the patrol car in flames, and Morris was in the background, collapsed against the wall. "He's taunting us," she said. "Letting us know that he's watching us. Let's get Josie here."

An hour later they left. Josie was rushing the forensics through. All they could do now was wait. Nat's made arrangements to meet Anthony and Andrew at the hotel they were staying at.

She knocked on their door, and Andrew let her in. "We've had a break," she told them. "The bastard called the call centre."

"What!" They both replied, unsure if they'd heard her right. She told them about the call and the motel. "We just missed him, but he left us a photo." She showed them a copy. "He's taunting us, playing with us, wanting to us know he's watching our every move. It'll be his mistake. He'll slip up when he gets too cocky."

"That's excellent work," Anthony said. "At least it gives us a chance." Anthony's phone rung. "Yes," he went pale as he listened to the call. Andrew and Nat were instantly alert. He hung up. "Adam's had a call. It sounds like it's from our man. Let's go."

Adam was distraught when they arrived. "He called, the bastard called."

Nat got her notebook out. "Adam calm down and tell us what he said."

Adam sat down and couldn't look them in the eye. "He told me he'd done it, blew her up on purpose to get to me. It's my fault. Abi's dead because of me. Said he'd made sure she knew what was coming. He put the bomb in her hands and pushed her into the car." He broke down. Adam looked at them other in disbelief. "He said he'd given her a choice, rape or death and she'd chosen death. Why? Why did she choose that? She was in uniform, had her weapon. Why the hell didn't she fight back?"

Nat knew he was right and the caller had contradicted himself. The two calls were different.

She didn't fire her weapon, they knew that. Neither had she shouted out. Something wasn't right with this call. "Adam, he's lying. She wouldn't have chosen to die. Abi would have fought him, fought him all the way. She didn't fire or shout, she would have if she'd had time. We've considered it, there wasn't time for a conversation, even if he was there."

Adam lifted his head up sharply. "There?"

Nat knew she'd slipped up, but it was too late. She showed him the photo. "He was there Adam, but we don't know how long for. He's playing with you. This call proves it. He couldn't have done what he said. He's clever, thought it through, but he'll slip up. We'll get him and the truth." Nat left the boys alone. She needed to log this development.

*****

Frankie had gone to see Jack. He wanted to keep him in the loop and informed him of what had happened. "We'll get him, Jack. Now he's made contact he'll make a mistake. You know how it works, they get cocky and get caught because of it. You'll get your answers, we all will."

"I still can't believe she's gone. I wake up and hope it's a bad dream, then reality kicks in. I want the person responsible caught, I need to know why. The call just doesn't make sense. What did he

44

mean 'because she lived'?" Jack had a terrible feeling, a feeling he hoped was wrong. Surely if it were him, he'd admit to it. He'd want Jack to know what he'd done. He looked at Frankie. "What if it's Michael? He tried to kill her before, and she lived. What if he's back?" There, he had finally said it out loud. Finally admitted what he hoped he was wrong about.

Frankie had already considered Michael. He had gone after Abi once, and she'd won. But he had always sworn he'd come back, but it had been years. Maybe they'd relaxed too much, let their guard down. "Michael wouldn't taunt us, he'll make it obvious it was him. This isn't his style. Anyway, he'd want Abi alive. Want her to suffer. Blowing her up? No, that's the one thing he wouldn't do." The only problem was that if Michael had heard what had happened, and he surely would have seen the news, he would have been in contact. Would have gloated about it, even if he wasn't involved. Frankie wouldn't put it past him to use it to cause trouble. "We don't even know if Michael's still alive. No one has seen him, not since he kidnapped Abi. Whoever it is, we'll get him." Frankie said as he left.

*****

Nat returned home. It was late, and although she was tired, she was having trouble sleeping. She got up and switched on her laptop, then pulled up the transcripts of the two phone calls. They did contradict themselves. The call to her said Abi didn't know what was happening, it was quick. The one to Adam said he'd talked to her and had placed the bomb in her hands. Why? Why two completely different calls? It didn't make sense. She sighed. Abi. She can still imagine her face. She was so happy, engaged and everything to live for. Who could do such a thing? She'd considered all of Abi's recent cases, it there was nothing. There was no apparent reason for anyone to go after her. Nat couldn't shake off a feeling she had. She thought back to when Michael had abducted Abi previously. She shook her head, no, it wasn't his style. He would want her alive, want her to suffer. Blowing her up would be too quick. She went to switch off her laptop, just as her e-mail pinged. She opened it. Another photo, one of Abi with Adam. They're were laughing and looked so happy. She opened the second attachment, the second photo. She gasped, couldn't believe what she saw. A picture of Adam when he proposed, on his knee and when Abi looked stunned. How? How the hell had he got that one? My God, whoever this sick bastard was, he'd been following them for a while. She'd already ruled out Michael, she already knew he would play things differently, but someone possibly linked to Adam? Someone who wanted to get to him? Wanted Adam to suffer instead? She needed to figure out who the actual target was. Abi, or Adam. They wouldn't get a break until she did.

Chapter Five

The following day she heads over to see Adam. She's arranged for Anthony to be there, Adam would need the support. Anthony lets her in, and she sits opposite them. Nat decides it better to get straight to the point. She pulls out copies of the photos, she'd received last night and shows them.

"Abi," is all Adam can say.

Anthony looks up at Nat. "When did you get these?"

"Last night," she replied. "I couldn't sleep so I started to go back through the transcripts of the phone calls. He sent them by e-mail." She pauses, looked at Adam. "Adam, I need to ask if you've had any threats against you, since transferring to LA."

Adam shook his head. "No, nothing. I would have said if I had."

"What about Abi, has she received any?"

Again, Adam shook his head. "If she did, she never said anything." He paused and thought of how upset Abi had been recently. "Something was bothering her, she's been tense. In fact, since the engagement, then you sent her home early. She wouldn't talk to me but eventually said she'd tell me after that last shift. Now I'll never know. You said yourself she had something to tell me."

Nat knew what she wanted to say. Knew Abi was going to tell him about Michael. She'd ruled him out, so she didn't say anything. Adam would need to be told, but not yet, not like this. The funeral was in a few days, Nat would arrange for him to be informed afterwards. "What about in New York? Any threats before you came here?"

Again, Adam said no. Damn it, she thought, still nothing.

"Anything. Adam, can you think of anything at all? I'll be truthful, we're still stumped. We have no concrete leads to go on. He's been following the both of you for a while, even when you went to New York. Whoever he is he was after one of you, but we don't know who or why. Abi may have been the easier target, but it may have been to get to you. You're both cops, we make enemies, it's the way it's always been. I'm begging Adam, can you think of anything?"

Adam thought, he thought hard. Thought of the cases he had worked on recently. Everyone who's contacted him. "I'm sorry Nat. I'm trying but there's nothing, I can't think of anything. I've received no threats, no nuisance phone calls. There's no reason for anyone to target either of us. I don't understand why anyone would be following us, or what we've done to upset them."

"The two phone calls don't make sense, he totally contradicts himself. The one to you was without doubt a lie. Adam, I must think that *you* are the target and Abi was just a means to you. If you do think of anything, let me know. Even the smallest thing, may help." Nat got up ready to leave. "Anything at all Adam, just ring me."

Anthony watched as Nat left. The photos had upset him. Someone was following Abi and Adam, why? Nat may think she has nothing, but it was enough for him. Somehow the person responsible had gotten hold of a copy of Adam's proposal, it wouldn't have been easy to do. Anthony had sorted that out himself. Set it all up, so how had he gotten access? The only other people on the boat, were the captain, the waiter and Steve. Steve had worked for them for a while, he couldn't believe he would have anything to do with it. The Captain seemed genuine too, and besides, he had a good reputation and no reason to be blackmailed. That left the waiter. Andrew had gone back to New York. He was working from that end. He would ring him later.

*****

Andrew received a call from Anthony, who had sent him an email of the forensic photos. He was livid. Whoever had done this has been working on it a while. Planned it entirely, but why? They still didn't know why, or who the intended target was? He'd spoken to his Captain and been given permission to work on the case in New York and was about to interview the waiter.

48

"Can you please confirm your name?" Andrew asked.

"James Anderson," the waiter replied.

"Thank you for coming in. James, you're not in any trouble. I'm helping with the investigation into the death of Officer Abigail Lawton, from LA. Can you please confirm that you were the waiter when her fiancé proposed?"

James had heard what had happened and couldn't believe it. They'd been such a happy couple, and it was obvious they were meant to be together. "Yes, I was. It was a lovely evening and perfect for them."

"Did you notice anything out of the ordinary? Were there any problems with the sailing, anyone hanging around?"

"No, everything went according to plan. The caterers arrived on time, and we were ready well in advance. Once I arrived, I never left the boat. We spent the time preparing, moving the chairs and table. We wanted everything to be perfect, and it was. We couldn't have arranged it any better."

Andrew noticed James was beginning to sweat. He was holding back, he thought. "Are you sure nothing else happened. Abi was killed unlawfully; her fiancé is distraught. We won't stop until we find the person responsible and will take down everyone else involved." He looked directly into James's eyes as placed the proposal photo in front of him. "We need to know how her killer got this photo."

James panicked, he never meant to hurt anyone. It was just a photo.

Andrew noticed his distress. "James, if you can help at all, we'll be grateful. You aren't in any trouble, we just need your help. This information may make a difference to the case."

"He just wanted a photo," James finally said. "A man approached me that morning. He'd heard that there was a special sailing that evening and asked if I could place a camera on the boat. I said no, said it wasn't possible as it was a private sailing. He threatened me, said he knew how much I loved my wife and how would I feel if she disappeared for good. He forced me to place a small video camera on board, in a place where he could watch everything that they did. You have to believe me, I didn't know what he had planned."

Andrew could tell he was telling the truth. "Thank you for being honest, but why didn't you report the threat?"

Andrew could tell he was telling the truth. "Thank you for being honest, but why didn't you report the threat?"

"He told me he wanted to make a special video for the happy couple. It was going to be his engagement present to them. Said they were special friends of his. I didn't know he meant to harm them. If I'd known, I'd have stopped the sailing."

"Can you give us a description of the man?"

"Tall, nearly six-foot, dark blond hair and I didn't notice his eye color." James looked back at Andrew. "If I'd have known what he had planned." Tears watered in his eyes. "I would have told someone, called the police. She didn't deserve to die like that. To die at all."

Andrew thanked him, they had a lead at last. He typed up his notes and sent a copy directly to Anthony.

*****

Anthony went straight to the station. "Nat, we have a description," he handed her a copy of the waiter's interview.

Nat read it. "Andrew's done an excellent job. I'll get this circulated, we have a chance of finding him now." She was still concerned, which one he was after? The distress this was causing Adam, he still had to be the priority. "I can't help thinking it's Adam he's after. Wants him to suffer, but I can't figure out why?"

Anthony remembered what Adam had said about Abi being upset. "We need to know what Abi was worried about. What she was going to tell him." He glanced over at Nat and saw the look that crossed her face. He narrowed his eyes. "What aren't you telling me, Nat? Do you know what the problem was? Why she was so upset? Come on Nat, spill it."

Nat looked back at him and sighed. She had to tell him about Abi's past. "Unfortunately, I do. I'll tell you, but it's a completely different case. *Michael* isn't behind this. It's not his style, he'd want Abi alive. You can't tell Adam, not yet. He's not ready to hear it."

50

She paused and waited for Anthony's answer. "Okay, I'll keep it to myself, but if it becomes important to the case, I will."

If it became important, Nat would tell Adam herself. "Jack has a brother, Michael. Abi's uncle. When she was fifteen, he abducted her. To cut a long story short, he tortured her to make Jack suffer for something in their past. I was still in uniform and worked on the case. I helped her recover. It's how we became such close friends."

"What happened?" Anthony could hardly believe what he had been told.

"He tormented Jack. Sent him parcels and told him what he was doing to his daughter. It wasn't pretty. He never sent photos, never let us know where he was or where he was holding her. Made Jack fully aware that it was his fault. Abi would die because of him, because of what he'd done. Jack was distraught. We pulled out everything but to no avail. He'd buried her away too deeply. We finally got a break and found her." She hesitated, remembered how critically injured Abi had been. "He held her for three months. Beat her, kicked her, stabbed her twice in the abdomen. He had bound her wrists together with barbed wire, and she still carries some of the scars. She also had severe head injuries." She stopped again. Poor Abi, she'd fought so hard to stay alive and now this. Why? "The doctors didn't think she'd make it. She was barely able to breathe for herself and spent a few days being ventilated. She recovered, but it took a while. I never thought she would trust any man and I was so delighted when she fell for Adam. We all were."

"My God, the poor girl. Why didn't she tell Adam sooner?"

"She was too scared. Abi wasn't sure how to tell Adam and how he would react. We all told her to do it sooner. I even offered to give him the case files, to make it easier, but she wanted to do it herself. She finally told me that she was worried Michael would attempt to abduct her again. Had a feeling that she was being followed. That's when I sent her home early. Deep down I think she was nervous Adam would leave her. She had tests done a few days ago and found out that afternoon that the injuries he caused back then, had more consequences than originally thought. It was a hard blow to her."

51

"Nonsense, Adam loves her too much. He'd stand by her no matter what. Hell, he'd go all out to protect her. But you're right, this will destroy Adam. He needs time to recover himself before he's told. I'll keep it to myself, but thanks for telling me. Is Michael still alive?"

"To be honest, we don't know. If Michael is, he's never come back to LA and never contacted Jack. It's not him. As I said, he'd want Abi alive and would own up to what he's done. No this is someone else, but we need to know who his target really is. Was it Abi, or was she just someone he could use to get to Adam?"

"Trouble is we can't find any reason for anyone to target either of them and why did they video the proposal. Maybe it is someone that knows them, but I keep coming back to why? If we could finally figure that out, then maybe we'll have a chance."

Nat agreed. "Hopefully he'll contact us again."

"I'll be at Adam's if anything else comes up," Anthony said on the way out. Josie walked in as Anthony left.

"Good news Josie. I need good news." Nat told her.

"Can't-do. I've got DNA, but it's not in the system. No CCTV, so no footage of him. Whoever it is, he's a ghost."

"DNA not listed in the system? Great, just bloody great. An unknown, just what we need. He's probably laughing at us." Nat wasn't happy. She needed something to give and soon.

They both looked up as Matt entered. Matt was their head of digital forensics, and he appeared concerned.

"Problem Matt?" Nat asked.

"I'm not sure." He looked at Josie. "You've been running a DNA search."

"Yes. DNA from the motel, but it's not listed," Josie answered.

"I think it was at some point, maybe until recently. Your search jumped."

"Jumped?" Nat said.

"Yes. It may not be a technical term, but I say jump. There's a gap in the data. When you searched, it was ignored. Probably because there's nothing in the associated file. Whatever was in there, it's gone. I've run diagnostics to try and retrieve it, but no luck."

"Matt, any chance you can translate that, so I can understand it." Nat was confused.

"Right, the data was there. There is a file, but someone's emptied it. Whatever was in it, it's gone for good."

"Hacked?" This time from Josie.

"If I had to hazard a guess I'd say it was and by somebody good. There are no tracks, none of the security alarms was set off, and I can't retrieve it. Whoever did it is damned good with computers. It only got flagged up when you ran your search."

Nat didn't like where's this was going. "Let me get this right. We are looking for someone who can not only work with explosives but is capable of hacking into top security police computers and destroying information."

"Basically, yes," Matt answered.

"Are you saying that the bastard's known to us and we don't have a clue why? It's getting better by the bloody minute. I don't suppose anyone's going to give me any good news soon." Nat another thought. "Matt, he's contacted both Adam and me directly. Could he have gotten our contact details from our computers?"

"It's possible. If he can permanently wipe out information, then getting into personnel files would be easy. Makes me wonder what else he's been up to."

"Matt, can you set up a different system for me. I don't like the idea of him being able to hack in and to see what we are doing. Let's keep this investigation separate to the main computer."

"It'll be easy to do. I'll let you know when it's done. It'll be as secure as I can make it."

Matt and Josie left, but all they had done was to give her more questions and absolutely no answers.

Chapter Six

Jack stood in front of his mirror. He noticed how old he looked, but he never thought he would be burying his daughter. Hell, there wasn't even a body, but everyone needed closure, so he'd decided to go the full length and have a coffin. "Jenna," he whispered. "Look after our baby."

He heard the cars as they pulled up. This was it, he thought. How the hell am I supposed to get through today? He remembered to lock up, and they arrived at the church. It was full. There was a decent turnout, but then Abi was well liked. Not only by police colleagues and friends but by people who just wanted to pay their respects, to an officer lost on duty. Frankie walked over to him. "Jack, they're ready to start."

Jack took his place behind the coffin. Frankie was one of the lead bearers with Adam as the other. They began to move towards the church, and the air was full of sorrow. He knew everyone was thinking the same. Such a waste of a young life and they were no closer to finding out what had happened. Someone had owned up, but they still didn't have a clue who he was or why he'd done it. Josie admitted that there wasn't enough left of the car to do a full forensic report. There wasn't even enough to find DNA traces of Abi. The motel room wasn't much help either. The person had wiped away any traces of who the DNA had belonged too.

Before Jack had even realised everyone had taken their seats. Jack sat next to Adam. The priest began to talk but Jack was hardly able to listen, his head held low. Several people stood up and said how much they valued Abi, not only as a colleague and police officer but also as a close friend. Jack had been too distraught to even think about making a speech, so Frankie had agreed to do one.

"Abigail has been taken away from us to early, but in her brief time as an officer in the LAPD, she made a significant impact. She helped so many people, some of whom are here today, and she went out of her way many times. When she was paired with Adam, no one realised how close they would become, and it was a joyful day indeed when they announced their engagement.

Abi was well loved from the moment she was born and spent many a holiday at the station, with her father. It was no surprise when she finally put on the uniform, and it suited her. She's been through so much in her short life and will be sadly missed." Frankie moved towards the coffin, along with Adam and folded up the flag that was draped over it. Frankie handed it over to Jack then resumed his place, with Adam as lead bearers. They made their way out towards the graveyard.

Everyone gathered around as the coffin was laid to rest. Jack picked up one of the white lilies, they were always Abi's favourite flower and tossed it onto the casket. He watched as several others did the same, which included Frankie and Adam. Oh god, he thought again. How could this have happened?

Unknowingly to everyone present, another person had joined them at the graveside. Has he'd worn a wig, he knew there was truly little chance of anyone recognizing him. Anyway, they were too upset to notice everybody who was present. He saw how distraught Jack was and a smile appeared on his face. Perfect, he thought. Bloody perfect.

The stranger headed back towards an abandoned warehouse. It was dark and dismal, and it was the perfect place for what he needed. Derelict and out of the way, barely anyone came past. "Couldn't have planned it better," he said when he entered. He bent down and grabbed his victim's hair. As he pulled her head up he continued sarcastically. "Daddy dearest was so upset, and it was such a lovely funeral, it's same you missed it. But then, you'll get another one when your battered, dead body turns up. But I'll have some fun with you first."

Scared, gagged and bound, Abigail stared back at Michael.

55

2 weeks earlier

Abigail regained consciousness. Her wrists were bound with rope in front of her. She was gagged, a rag was tied around her mouth. It was dark, damp and she had no idea where she was. Her last memory was being pulled out of the car, right before it exploded. She'd heard Morris calling her name, then everything had gone black. She moved her arms and realised that the rope on her wrists was covering something sharp. Some sort of wire? The rope was tied to something. She could stand, but the rope didn't let her go far. She managed to get her hands to her mouth and pulled the gag out. "Help!" She screamed but knew no one could hear her. She had a bad feeling as a chill crept through her. The last time this had happened, Michael had been involved. Oh god, she thought, not again. She wouldn't survive a second time. He had nearly succeeded in killing at their last encounter, she still didn't know how she had survived. "Dad," she whispered. He must be going out of his mind with worry. Her thoughts turned to Adam. Why hadn't she been braver? Told him and arranged some time off? If she got out of here, she would tell him everything. There would be no more secrets, no more lies. If he walked then he wasn't worth it, but she was sure he would stand by her. Were they even looking for her?

It smelt musty. Where was she? How long had it been? There were no windows, so she couldn't even tell what time of day it was. It was night-time when the car had exploded, was it still the same night? She realised she was still in her police uniform. That was good, right? Maybe not. She was missing her belt, tie, and badge, so she had no possible weapons. Her police training started to kick in. "Come on Abi," she whispered to herself. "You're a police officer first and victim second," she tried to convince herself. "There *has* to be something you can use as a weapon."

She looked around as her eyes started to adjust to the dark. There were no windows and only one door, by the looks of it, so only one entrance and exit for her kidnapper. Hopefully, that would make it easier, but even if she disarmed her attacker how would she get out of the rope? It seemed to be tied to a metal pipe. She knelt and realised the floor was wet, at least a couple of inches. Where was she? She wondered again.

She felt along the floor the best she could, and tried to find something she could use as a potential weapon. No luck so far, just dirt and water. She moved forward a bit, still no luck. After what seemed like hours, she had covered most of the floor that she could reach. So far nothing. She began to feel deflated. "Abi," she whispered as she tried to keep her hopes up again. "There's a way out, there has to be. Come on girl, you have to get back home to Adam."

She sat back down against the wall and started to feel cold. How long before her captor decided to return? Would he return, or did he plan to just leave her here to wilt away? No, after all the trouble to grab her, he'd be back, she just needed to be ready for him. Her eyelids began to droop. She was tired from the exertion of trying to find a weapon. She shook herself awake and wait, what was that? There was a glint of something near the corner. She got up and moved as close to where she thought she saw it. As she knelt, she reached out into the water again. Stretched as far as she could and something sharp pricked her finger. Bullseye, she thought and picked it up. It was a small piece of glass approximately four inches long. It certainly wasn't big enough to injure her attacker, but maybe, just maybe, it might cut through part of the rope. She managed to hold it like a knife. It was hard with her wrists tied, but just about doable if she twisted her wrists a little bit. The wire dug deeper into her skin, but if she could weaken the ropes, she could cope with the pain.

Suddenly, she has hope. She started to saw at the rope as close as possible to her hands. It took a while, but it was fraying. Every so often she stopped and pulled on the rope, but there was no give at all. She carried on. Slowly it began to thin. She could feel it weaken. Her hope flared once more. Whoever had her would be in for a shock when they returned. She started to hum, even though there was blood running down her arms from moving her wrists so much, and her hands were sore and bled from the glass. Suddenly, the rope snapped. She was free!

Abi knew she still needed the element of surprise, so she sat down with the pipe behind her. The frayed rope hidden between her legs and waited.

A short while later Abi heard a noise and became instantly alert. The door opened, and she saw a shadow of a man enter. She had put the gag back into her mouth and hoped he didn't notice anything different. He walked towards her and had left the door slightly open. As it was dark, she can't see his face. This could be her chance. She lashed out with what was left of the glass and caught his cheek. He was taken surprised. Abi took her opportunity and made a dash for the door. Her tied wrists made it challenging to run, so she looked for a hiding place. There was nothing obvious, and she could hear him as he got closer. She tried to run faster, but tripped and then he was on top of her. Oh god no, she panicked, not again. Memories flooded back from when she was fifteen. She struggled, but he was just too powerful.

"Bitch," she heard him say.

"No," she muttered through her gag. Fear ripped through her, and her breathing increased. She recognized that voice. It was him, he was back. It was then that all her hope faded away, as she remembered their previous encounter. There was no way she was escaping. The only way he would let her go, was when she was dead.

He pulled her up. A hand was wrapped tightly around the back of her neck, and he pushed her back towards the room. They entered, and he shoved her to the ground. Abi raised her head, and he backhanded her around the face.

"Bitch," he repeated, "Did you think it'd be that easy. Did you really think you'd be safe? No, I still plan on making Jack suffer and suffer he does. Don't expect anyone to come to your rescue, Morris has told everyone you were in the car." He grabbed her wrists, and pain rips through her, as he tied her back to the pipe. "Even now they're planning your funeral. No one's looking for you."

He paused and looked down at her scared face. He sneered at her. "I have a whole heap of time to torture you. Shame that you don't." He laughed as he walked out.

Abi let the tears flow. Why now? Deep down she knew. Adam meant the world to her. He was the first man she had trusted, the first she could let get close. She was happy, extremely content and engaged. Her life was back on track. She never thought that she would ever get married, not until Adam came along. She'd been scared, he hadn't known her past. He'd thought she was a virgin with how tight she had been. If only she'd told him the truth. Now she wouldn't get the chance. She'd known everyone had warned him, but not why. Why? Why hadn't she told him? Please let my death be quick this time, she prayed. Don't let me suffer again. But she knows it was in vain. Michael would have every plan to make it painful. Extremely painful.

Present day

Michael let her go, pulled the gag out of her mouth, and sat down on a stool opposite her. "How does it feel to be a ghost?" He had left a couple of biscuits and a bottle of water on her lap. He visited every couple of days, but so far, he hadn't really harmed her. He'd left her hands bound in front of her on purpose. She could still eat and drink to a degree but had to twist her hands to do so. They were tied with wire under the rope, and he knew it was painful every time she moved them. "Not a single one of them has figured it out, I think I'm going to have to leave them a message." He watched her eat, and an idea formed in his head. Jack needed to see exactly what he was doing. Leaving her dead body for her father won't be enough. Torture, that what he needed to do. Abi had to be tortured, again. "I'll make you a deal Abi," he said, and she looked back at him. "I'm not going to kill you."

Abi breathed a sigh of relieve. Maybe Michael had changed his mind, perhaps he would let her go.

"Nope, it didn't work the last time. I left you close to death, and you still survived. No, this time I'll play it differently."

Abi's heart fell, he wasn't letting her go. Fear shone in her eyes, she dreaded what he had planned.

"You proved the last time you have what it takes to survive, fought me and won. But what about dying? Do you have the strength to accept your own death?"

What? Abi thought. He's lost it. I'm *not* planning on dying, not if I can help it. I have too much to live for. Adam, I'm *going* to live for Adam. I'm getting married, and Michael's *not* going to stop me.

Michael lifted her up, slammed her against the wall and slammed his fist into the side of her face. She screamed out in pain, but he hadn't finished. He punched her in the stomach, not once but twice. He winded her, and she collapsed gasping for breath.

He bent down, grabbed her by the hair again and put his face in front of hers. "How much can you take Abi? How much is too much? How long before you beg me to kill you? I had you for three months of fun the last time. Can you hold out longer?" He stood as he let her go. Just before he left, he replaced her gag. "Yes, Abi that's the plan. I'll torture you until you beg to die and just to keep daddy in the loop, I'll send him the photos of everything I do."

Abi watched him go. Her fear turned to anger. Never, she thought, I'll never beg to die. So why did her heart say different?

*****

Michael returned a couple of days later. Abi lifted her head; the defiance was evident in her eyes. He bent down and tilted her head up. "Beautiful," he said as he dropped more food onto her lap. He sat back on his stool. "The bruises are just lovely." Her face was badly bruised from their last encounter, and her right eye was swollen. "Eat up Abi, or is it too painful? Want me to end it yet, or are you ready for more?"

Abi finished her bread roll and looked back at him. "*Never*," was all she said.

"Fighting talk Abi, be careful. I'll take up on that."

"I'll fight you all the way, Michael. I won against you before, I'll do my damned hardest to do it again." She thought of her Adam and dad. She would do her best to return to them and alive. After finding the love of her life, she was going to return to him, she vowed.

"Right then, if you're ready let's start."

He lifted her up and turned her face first towards the wall. He used his knee to separate her legs. Her breathing increased, please God, no. "Don't worry Abi, I'm not going to rape you, but my cock is eager to get inside of you again. You'll be very much reacquainted soon." He clenched his hand and struck her in her lower back several times. She cried out at with every punch. He released her, turned her back round he slammed her against the wall. He kissed her roughly on the mouth. She gagged as he forced her mouth open and pushed his tongue in. He kneaded one of her breasts and then moved his hand lower down. Abi tensed as he pulled out her waistband, his hand was now between her legs. He pushed a finger inside of her and wiggled it deep inside. "So wet Abi, so bloody wet." He looked her in the eyes. "So, it's true then. You *are* finally letting someone else fuck you. I'm surprised after what I did to you. Is he as good as me? Abi, you know I don't like sharing, does Adam?" He saw the surprise in her eyes. "Oh Abi, I've been following you all of your life. Kept close tabs on you. You told Nat that you thought you were being followed. Guess what, it was me. I phoned the call centre after the press release, and they came close to getting me, but I got out. They got my DNA, but I hacked their systems and removed all traces of me. They don't have a bloody clue."

He continued to stroke her pussy and clit. He rubbed and teased, then pulled out just before she came. "Not yet Abi, not yet." He licked her juices off his fingers. "You still taste good. I'll have my mouth sucking on you soon." He replaced her gag.

Abi slid down the wall, and as she hit the ground, Michael called her name. As she looked up, he took a photo and left.

*****

It's been two weeks since Abi's funeral, and Jack still visited the grave daily. Every day, fresh flowers or cards appeared. He was

61

still a few metres away, but already he can see a new envelope attached to the grave. He'd made it a vow to read every one of them. Not all were from friends, but people she'd helped as an officer. He knelt in front of her gravestone, still had trouble believing she was gone. After he had picked up the new envelope, he pulled out a photograph and stopped breathing. Shock and horror passed over his face. No, he screamed internally. Oh god, no. He's gone pale, and his hands began to shake. He closed his eyes briefly and then stared back at the photo. He couldn't believe what he was seeing. Abi bound and gagged was staring right at the camera. Fear shone in her eyes. Bruises marked her face, and one eye was slightly swollen. "Abi," he whispered. "Oh god, Abi." Tears threatened to fall. He still knelt, and stared at a photo he prayed was untrue. His heart raced, and his stomach began to knot.

Abi? Alive? He could think of only one person who could pull this off. He slowly turned the photo over. There was a handwritten message, in handwriting, he hoped to never to see again.

'I have something extraordinary of yours. Your daughters not quite so beautiful now is she, but still has spirit. I must wonder what will break that spirit. I'm going to give it a go. She'll beg me to kill her by the time I'm finished. Tell Adam, I'll show her what a real man is before I'm finished. Tell him I don't like sharing and she's the one that will suffer. My finger has already had a good feel, my cock will be next.
Your loving brother'

The tears began to fall. "Oh Abi," he cried. "I'm so sorry." All the memories he'd buried from when Abi was fifteen came flooding back. God, she must be terrified. She had barely survived the last time.

He stayed there for a few more minutes, then he started to feel the anger build up. How dare Michael do this. Abi was recently engaged, and her whole life was in front of her. A fiancé that was perfect and would do anything for her. No, Michael wasn't going to win, not this time. He was damn well getting his daughter back. And alive!

Chapter Seven

Adam entered the station ready to start another shift. The grief hit him, it was the same every day. There were too many memories of Abi here. He had thought about New York. He'd already spoken to his old Captain, and he was seriously considering about transferring back. He walked over to the reception desk. Nat leaned with her back to the counter and stared into Lieutenant Greens office. He turned to see what she was so interested in and spotted Lieutenant Green with the Captain and Jack in a heated conversation. "What's going on?"

"Your guess is as good as mine," Nat answered. "Jack stormed in and dragged Frankie into the office. They've been going at it ever since. Whatever it is, Jack's not happy. None of them are."

Adam wondered what had got Jack so uptight. Apparently, something must have happened. Something to do with Abi, it had to be, but what? The office door opened, Frankie came out and motioned to Nat to follow him. Adams' gaze followed them as they entered another empty office. Their Captain hadn't been able to look him in the eyes. He observed them and wished he could hear what was being said. He didn't notice Jack looking towards him. Didn't see the look of sorrow on his face.

Frankie walked over to the desk and sat on a corner. "Nat, you're to pass all your investigations to someone else, I don't care who. I'm making you lead in another case. It takes priority over everything else. You're to eat, sleep and breath this case." He hesitated before he continued and lowered his head in total disbelief. "Bloody hell, why didn't I see this coming? Damn well should have known he was involved. Shouldn't have ruled him out."

Nat went pale. Jack storming in began to make sense. "Frankie," she stopped and swallowed nervously. She couldn't believe what she was thinking, didn't want to say it out loud. She'd ruled him out too. Her mouth went dry, and she managed one word. "Michael."

Frankie lifted his head and looked directly at Nat. "He blew the car, Nat," he said softly.

She went even paler. Oh god no, she hoped she'd been wrong.

"Oh, it gets better." Frankie handed her an evidence bag.

Nat took the bag and noticed the photo inside. She collapsed against the wall. "Abi," she breathed out slowly. Bound, gagged, scared. Bruises covered her face. Then it hit her, and she looked over at Frankie. The shock clearly etched on her face. "She wasn't in the car."

Frankie nodded, he still couldn't believe it himself. He couldn't bear to think about what Abi was going through, and he was yet to tell Adam. "Read the back," he said quietly.

She turned the photo over and read the message. "Oh god no. Frankie she won't cope a second time. What he did..." Nausea washed over her. "He'll kill her."

"After he's ripped her apart again. Nat, he's had her for about a month already. By the looks of it, he hasn't seriously hurt her yet, but it's only a matter of time. Time, we don't have."

Nat turned the photo back over. "I'm getting her back. I'll do everything I can to make sure it's before he does anything serious." She hoped it was a promise she could keep.

"Pick your own team, you shouldn't have any problems. Everyone will want to help once this gets out. You can have access to anything you need, just ask, but not Adam. He's too close to this. Damn it, this is going to be a blow to him. It'll be best if he doesn't find out what happened before. He'll be going out of his mind as it is once I tell him."

Nat agreed and left the office. She remembered the first time Michael had kidnapped Abi. She must be terrified. Nat went to the records office and signed out the evidence so far. It wasn't much. Morris's statement, forensic report, photos from the scene and the photos their killer had sent. She then dug out the original file from when Abi was fifteen. Michael. It was Michael who rung, Michael

65

who had posted the photos. She returned to her detectives' desk and began to go through them.

Adam had seen everything. Nat's reaction, the way she'd collapsed. The shock was evident on her face. His heart raced, they had a lead. Nat couldn't look at him as she left, but Adam was going to damn well find out what had happened. He stormed into the office. "Frankie, what's happened? I know it's about Abi, so tell me." He said forcefully.

Frankie looked at him, this really was going to be hard for Adam. Hell, it would hit everyone hard. He prayed they could find her in time. Prayed she didn't have to go through it all again. Hoped she could hold on.

"Frankie," Adam growled.

Frankie took a deep breath. Adam was going to flip. "Adam, we have new evidence. Abi wasn't in the car, someone has abducted her." He showed Adam a copy of the photo, one without the message. Adam couldn't see that note.

Adam was stunned. "Alive, Abi's alive?" He sat down as he stared back at Frankie.

"Nat's lead detective and we'll do everything we can to get her back. We'll do our best to find her. Find Abi before he harms her anymore." He had intentionally left out Michael's name. That would open a whole assortment of problems that Adam wasn't ready for, not yet. Adam didn't need to know what Michael was capable of. What he was likely to do to Abi. What he had done before. He waited for Adam to get his head around this.

"Why? Why her? Frankie why?"

Frankie couldn't answer that one truthfully, not yet. "I wish we knew. Adam, he's gone out of his way, which wouldn't have been an easy abduction to set up. It would have taken time. The only question has been answered. Adam, I'm sorry, but Abi was the target all along. She never stood a chance against him. He was just too damned good." Again.

Adam glanced back at the photo. "What's he doing to her? Abi must be terrified." He looked at Frankie directly in the eyes. "I want to be included in the investigation."

"Adam you know you can't. I'll make sure you're being kept in the loop, but you can't be involved. If anything happens, I'll make sure you know."

"Frankie, *please*, I can't just sit back and wait. He could be doing anything to her. Frankie, I know what men like him are capable of. Abi could be in terrible danger." He glanced back at the photo. Looked at her wrists. There's something under those ropes. Probably wire again looking at the dried blood on her arms. Her face was swollen and bruised. At least her uniform was still intact. He looked back at Frankie. "Frankie, is he going to rape her?"

Shit, Frankie thought, the one question I hoped he wouldn't ask. "Adam, we don't know. Her uniforms still intact, so he hasn't yet. I'm hoping we'll find her before he does anything that serious. She's going to need a hell of a lot of help when we retrieve her, and we will. You'll need to be strong too, for Abi. She'll need you more than ever before. Whatever he does to her, it's you that she'll depend on the most. Adam, it won't be easy, just be ready for whatever state she's in." He tried to give Adam the heads up, without telling him anything. Wanted to warn him what state she could potentially turn up in. God, he hoped he was wrong. Prayed Michael didn't do what he did last time.

"A month, he's already had her a month. We weren't even looking for her. I should have been searching, should have known she was alive."

"Go home. Take some time off. Anthony's staying down here to help. Andrew's doing what he can in New York. We *will* find her, but it may take time." He just didn't know if Abi would still be alive. If she were, she would be emotionally damaged again. Could she recover a second time? Even Frankie doubted it. He watched as Adam left. Christ, he would find out the truth at some point. Hopefully, after they got Abi back.

*****

Michael returned, and after he had given Abi some food, he sat down again. "I left daddy a lovely photo of you, his face was a picture. He didn't have a clue I was behind it. The whole station is in chaos. No one was looking for you, yet now they find out you're alive."

Abi looked up sharply, her hope flared again. They would be looking for her. This could be over soon, and she would be back home, safe and sound. Back in Adams' arms.

Michael noticed her reaction and continued. "Oh Abi, think they'll find you? It won't be that easy, I've buried you deeply away. I'm *not* making it that easy for them, and I'll have loads of time to break you and break you I will. You'll be screaming to die *well* before they get anywhere near."

Michael stood and headed over to her. It was time to begin. He grabbed her ankles and dragged her to the ground, and she gasped as her head banged against the floor. He started to kick her in the ribs, several times, then placed his foot over her throat and pressed down. She panicked, tried to stop him, but he was too powerful. The pressure continued until she blacked out. Michael replaced her gag. He smiled as he left the warehouse. Unbeknown to Abi, he had set up a video link. He was filming everything, and he could send Jack full video footage of everything he did. Tomorrow was going to be fun. But not for Jack.

*****

Jack felt persecuted. Michael had Abi, and the photo he had sent hadn't been good. His baby tortured again. How would she survive? Could she, once more? He knew Frankie and Nat were doing everything possible, but Michael must have planned this for a while. It wouldn't be that easy. His phone beeped, and he opened the link but doesn't pay much attention to it. Then he heard screaming. His eyes focused, and his mind screamed. Abi! Michael had sent a video with full sound. He could listen to Abi screaming, as Michael kicked her repeatedly in the chest. He could see how much force

Michael was using, has Abi moved across the floor slightly which every kick. She then panicked as he put his foot on her throat and blacked out. There was a message at the end.

'Jack, she's putting up a good fight, I'll give her that. What about we make it more interesting. How about you decide when she's had enough. You tell me when to put her out of her misery. You tell me when to kill her. I'll contact you every few days with a new video, then I'll ring you. You just have to say the words; Jack and I'll stop.'

Chapter Eight

Nat wasn't getting anywhere fast. She's looked through the evidence so many times, she has it pretty much memorized but, she couldn't help feeling that she's missing something. Standing Nat stretched her neck and back, and it struck her. She snatched up Morris's statement and scanned it again. "Code 30, they responded to Code 30," she muttered.

Looking at the evidence gathered in front of her, she's realized there's no statement related to the burglary. Something nagged at the back of her mind. Hoax calls. She remembered the uniforms being sent out to numerous hoax calls, before the explosion, but didn't remember hearing of any since.

She headed towards the reception area. "Officer Henson," she called. "You had a run of hoax calls. Can you get me transcripts of all of them, and a list of the officers who responded and their statements, please? Leave them on my desk when ready."

Nat watched Henson as she walked off towards the records department. She found a free computer and searched the database for the address that the Miller's had moved to. After she'd grabbed her car keys, she headed out to her Sedan.

She pulled up in front of the new offices and when she entered, spoke directly to the secretary at the front desk. Nat showed her badge. "I need to speak to Mr. Miller urgently."

The secretary picked up the phone and speed dialed Mr. Miller's office. "There's a Detective Nathaniel here to see you." She waited for an answer. "Yes, sir," she replied. "Follow the corridor, and it's the second door on the right." She told Nat.

70

Nat thanked the secretary, followed the instructions, and knocked on the door. She entered when prompted to.

"Detective," Mr. Millar stood, and they shook hands. "How may I help you?"

"I'm investigating an incident that happened outside your old warehouse and had a few questions."

"Of course, anything to help. Please take a seat." He knew exactly what she was referring to and they both sat down. "I went to Officer Lawton's funeral. Couldn't believe what happened. Such a waste of a young life."

"Mr. Millar," Nat said.

"Zeus," Mr. Millar interrupted. He saw Nat's face and held up a hand to stop her from saying anything. "Blame my parents, they had a weird sense of humor when it came to naming me." They both laughed, but it was soon back to business.

"Zeus, do you mind if I tape this conversation?"

"Not a problem, go right ahead."

Nat set up a small recorder on the desk and continued. "Were you aware that someone had called and informed us that the warehouse was being burgled?"

"No. I'll be honest with you there's nothing worth stealing. All that's left there is old shelves and racks. Stuff that we no longer need and is no use to us. It wouldn't be worth the hassle."

"Can I ask why you moved?"

"Expansion. Our clothing lines are growing, and there simply wasn't enough space anymore. We combined the warehouse with our offices and moved here."

"Do you still own the premises?"

"Not for long, we're in the process of selling it to a developer. It's prime real estate being close to the marina. We expect the deal to be completed shortly."

"That may need to be delayed until our investigation is complete, as it's still a crime scene. I'm sorry if it causes any problems. Does the building have a burglar alarm?"

71

"Yes, but we had it deactivated when the move was complete. As I said, nothing worth stealing and it seemed pointless paying for security there any longer."

Nat remembered the phone call. The caller had said the alarm was going off. It was beginning to look like another hoax. "Do you mind if we have access to the building."

"Of course not, I'll get you the keys." Zeus left the room, and Nat stood and waited for him to return. He was only a few minutes and returned with a bunch of keys. He handed them to her with a business card. "Take as long as you need, I'll inform the developers that there'll be a delay. I'm sure they'll understand. If you need anything else, you can get me directly on my mobile." They shook hands again, before she left.

Nat found a spot to park as she arrived at the warehouse. As she approached the entrance, she remembered Morris's statement.

'A man ran out of the front door when they arrived.'

On inspection, the door wasn't damaged. Nat tried it, and find it locked. After she had unlocked it, she entered and wandered around a few of the rooms. Zeus was right, it was just junk left, nothing of value at all. She was now convinced it was another hoax call. Michael used to be a cop. He would know how to set this up and have the contacts to do it. It would have been easy for him. She went back to the car and started the engine. Something bugged her, so she decided to park where Morris had. There was a slight overhang over the doors. From where Abi and Morris had parked, someone could have easily have hidden there and run out when they heard the car. She pulled out her mobile and rang Lieutenant Green. "George," she said as soon as he answered. "Can you come over to the Miller warehouse."

He knew precisely where she meant.

"If he's available, can you bring Frankie too."

George agreed, and it wasn't long before they arrived.

"Nat," Frankie said. "What have you got?"

72

She informed them of what she had found out. "It's another hoax. I just can't work out, how he got her out of the car without any commotion."

"Let's try to re-enact the scene," George said. "Nat, you be Abi and Frankie, pretend to be Michael."

George took off his police belt and handed it to Nat. "Wear this. Let's make this as real as possible."

Nat went back to her car, opened the door, and began to get in. Frankie grabbed her from behind and pulled her out. Nat screamed and reached for the gun George had given her. Frankie let her go.

George walked towards them. He had noted some interesting points. "Morris only heard the car explode, Abi didn't scream or shoot."

Frankie had an idea. "Let's go again," he said.

Nat went to get back into the car, while Frankie stood behind her. He didn't want her to see what he planned to do, he wanted a genuine reaction. Frankie pulled a clean tissue out of his pocket and grabbed Nat again. This time he put one arm around her neck and the tissue, in his other hand, over her nose and mouth.

Instantly Nat panicked, she forgot all her police training. She couldn't scream, it felt like she was suffocating, and she had *totally* forgotten she had a gun. Her nails clawed at Frankie's hand and has he continued to drag her backwards, her heart began to race, while her breathing increased. God, she was so scared and had forgotten entirely that it was a re-enactment.

George saw precisely what was happening and motioned to Frankie to stop. Frankie steadied Nat as he released her. Knew he had an authentic and real reaction from her. They look at each other, now knowing what must have happened. Abi would have been terrified, forgot she was armed and panicked. At some point, Michael would have thrown the explosive into the car and blew it once they were a safe distance away. However, that didn't explain what happened next. According to Morris, no other vehicle was in the area. Michel must have stayed close.

Nat recovered and turned to Frankie with daggers in her eyes. "Some warning would have been nice."

"Sorry. Nat, I needed a real reaction. If you'd known what I had planned, you could have reacted differently."

"Abi would have been terrified. I forgot I was a cop, forgot I was armed. Hell, I forgot all my training. Frankie, she wouldn't have seen him. Wouldn't have known it was Michael, not at first. I hate to think when she found out. We *have* to get her back."

"And soon," George said. "Very soon. I was new to the station the last time, but her injuries? Hell, I remember what he did. If he does that again…" He broke off. He'd seen some cruel cases, but that? That had sent chills right down his spine. The fact that someone was capable of that type of damage. "Are you putting out an unofficial shot to kill order again?"

Frankie glimpsed at him. "Yes, but only to the officers that were around the last time. Nat, can you get them in for a briefing. They're all very aware of what happened before. Know what he did. I want to be sure that Adam doesn't find out. Not yet."

"No problems, I'll arrange it for tomorrow. Frankie, I told Anthony about Michael. Just that he'd abducted her, not what he did. I told him not to tell Adam. He's agreed."

"Good, but don't invite him to the briefing. If he finds out the truth, he won't be able to hide it. Adam will get it out of him."

"If he knocked her out," George finally said. "He must have hidden her close by."

All three of them began to look around. Frankie discovered a small alley at the back of the building. He started to go down and saw a door which was slightly ajar. When he entered, Frankie spotted something on the floor. As he knelt, he saw that it was a rag. He picked it up with a pen and placed it into an evidence bag. "Over here," he called.

George and Nat ran over. Frankie showed them the rag and explained how he found it.

"Christ, she was within reach of us all. We were so certain she'd been in the car that we never bothered to search. The bastard would have heard everything we did." Nat said.

"Michael pulled off the perfect abduction." Frankie shook his head. "Abi never stood a chance."

George pulled out his mobile and made a call. "Josie, get a team together and get back down to the old Millers warehouse. We've had a breakthrough," he ordered.

Josie arrived with a team in tow. "What have you found?" She asked.

Frankie and Nat had headed back to the station, leaving George in control at the crime scene. "We've figured out that Abi was knocked out, by something being held over her mouth. She must have panicked, which explains why she didn't defend herself." He showed her the room and handed her the bag, with the rag in it.

"She must have been terrified." Josie took note of the rag and the room it had been found in. She told her team to start in there.

George took her to one side and made sure no one could hear what he was about to say. Frankie had given him permission to tell Josie about Michael. "Josie, you need to know something but can't tell anyone. No one at all, but you need to know to help with the investigation. You weren't at the station at the time, but Abi was abducted when she was fifteen. The same man has her now."

"Christ. What did he do?" Josie asked with surprise in her voice.

"He held her for three months. Tortured, raped her several times and left her for dead. Josie, we need to get her back before he does the same. Abi barely survived."

"Thanks for telling me, I'll put everything into this. If there's anything, I'll find it." George knew that Josie would. He just hoped it would be enough.

*****

Nat returned to her desk. She'd arranged the briefing for the following morning, and Officer Henson has brought her the information she had asked for. She had brought the recordings of the calls too. Nat switched on the recorder and began to listen. Nearly an hour later she stopped for a break. She grabbed a notebook and started to cross-reference the reports. She made notes of the times, dates and who had responded. She paused, looked back over the reports, and referenced them to who was patrolling where. A pattern was emerging. Nat put a street map of the area on to the board and began to add colored pins while referencing back to the reports. As she sat back down back, she pulled out the recordings of the calls, that Adam 40 responded to. She closed her eyes as she listened. All the calls were made by a male. They were slightly different tones, but they all sounded similar. When she opened her eyes, she stopped the tape and took it down to forensics. She headed straight towards Matt, their head technology guy.

Matt looked up as Nat found him. "Nat, what you are doing down on these lonely levels?"

She held up the tape. "Recordings of some of the hoax calls, the uniforms have had. Can you clean them up and analysis the male voices?" She handed the tapes over. "Thanks. Can you bring the report up when you're done?" Nat turned to leave.

On the way back to her desk, she quickly texted Frankie and asked him to see her when he was free. She went back to the map as the pattern worried her. She was studying so hard, that she didn't hear Frankie walk in. "What have you got for me, Nat?"

She showed him the map. "The red pins are the station and Abi's apartment. Blue's where the car exploded. Yellows indicate where officers were sent to a hoax call and green where the corresponding calls came from. All the calls came in from phone boxes."

Frankie studied the map and frowned. As he pointed to the pins, he added. "The calls all come from a box close to where the same hoax code 30 is. This is excellent work, Nat. Michael would want to see the officers as they arrived."

Nat nodded. "It's not just that. There were twenty-three hoax calls in total. Abi and Morris responded to sixteen of them. I've marked those calls with black spots."

"That's more than half. Coincidence?"

"I don't think so. I've cross-referenced the reports, considered who was working when. The calls all came in between 9pm and midnight, so it was always dark. They happened over a two-week period, some nights had more than one. The darkness would have made it easier for him to hide, close to the property that was supposedly being burgled. He could see who arrived. But this is where it gets interesting. Abi was on night duties every time. In fact, she was patrolling the areas affected."

Frankie glanced over at Nat. "Had it all planned out, didn't he? All he had to do was to wait until Abi and Morris got separated. Easy when you think about it."

Nat hadn't finished. "The station's approximately three miles from Abi's apartment. All the calls happen in that radius. He stayed local to the marina." She glanced back at Frankie over her shoulder. "Abi thought she was being followed. It turns out she might have been right. Why didn't she come to us sooner?" Nat sighed. "Is it possible he's still in that radius, he'd want to be local. The photos arrive pretty quickly."

Frankie pondered this, Nat was right. Michael was using a digital video camera. All the photos are date and time stamped, and they arrive within a few hours of being taken. He must be able to check the video, chose the screenshot he wanted to use, print and get it delivered to the station quickly. The videos he sent to Jack happen a few hours later. "Nat, you're making great progress, quicker than I thought you would. This is a definite breakthrough." Frankie knew that area quite well, as it was his old patrol area. There were a lot of old, unused warehouse and factories, perfect places for hiding someone. Nat had given him a starting point.

*****

The following morning, all the officers that had been involved in the original investigation were waiting. Frankie walked in with Nat.

"Thanks for coming in. I've called you together because of what's happened. We kept the details quiet, mainly so Adam doesn't find out, but all of you were involved in the original investigation. It's been confirmed that Michael has Abi. We know how he did it and he held her in an empty room, in the back of the warehouse, while we were there. He's already sent a photo to Jack. Abi, bound, gagged and with a badly bruised face. Also, a video of her taking a kicking. He's had her over a month now, and we have no idea where she is.

I'm telling you this as you know what she went through, what happened to her and I'm concerned he's going to do it again. The message on the photo indicates that rape *is* on the cards, he's already been touching Abi." He paused, glanced around, and saw the disgust on everyone's face. He knew they would go all out to find her. "We think he's staying close to the area, possibly in one of the old marina warehouses. I'm asking for volunteers to search.

It's essential that Adam doesn't find out what he did before to her. He's going through it as it is and that *will* push him over the edge. If he needs to know about the abduction, we'll tell him, but details *will* be withheld. I've also informed Josie as she's head forensic on this and needs to know, what we are up against. Matt's been advised for the same reason.

I'm sure I don't need to remind you that we are up against the clock. Abi's life *is* in danger and knowing Michael her suffering *will* get worse."

I know I'm not the only who wants her back alive, but we need to be prepared that we may not. At best she'll be severely injured again.

I'm suggesting we speak to all of our informers and get it out there how determined are to get her back."

"Are you ordering a shoot to kill order again?" Someone asked.

"Not officially. We don't know where Michael's keeping Abi. If anyone spots him, consider him dangerous and call for backup. If possible and it's safe to do so, follow him and hope he takes you back to Abi, but if left with no option, then yes, shoot to kill. At least then he won't be able to harm her anymore.

Let Nat know when you can help with the search, she'll draw up a rota."

He left Nat to it and was glad to see everyone signing up.

Chapter Nine

A dam was going out of his mind. Being off duty, he wasn't aware of the breakthrough Nat had made. All he knew, was that it had been another few days that Abi had been missing for. All he could think about is how scared she must be, and tried not to consider what was happening to her. He'd seen the photo of his fiancé bound and gagged, an image he would never forget. He closed his eyes and thought back to the last few days they'd had together. Abi seemed upset and eventually said she had something to tell him. He didn't even have a clue what it was about. All he knew was that she had spoken to Jack, Michelle and Nat and she'd been upset afterwards. He was missing something, but what? Her father, a cop and a best friend, who had known her all her life and another officer, who had known her most of her life. He'd been warned several times not to hurt her and Jack had blatantly told him to protect her. Even his own father had recognized the scars and had warned him. With her injuries, something had happened to her. And it wasn't from falling through glass. Why hadn't he forced it out of her? Why hadn't she trusted him enough to tell him sooner? He didn't want to go behind her back, but now he needed to. He switched on his laptop and typed Abigail Lawton into the search box, pressed enter and waited. Most of the links related to her funeral. He scrolled down. An old newspaper headline caught his eye, and he clinked on it.

Police Sargent's Daughter Abducted from School.

The daughter of Sargent Jack Lawton has been abducted, after a man posing as a police officer took her out of the school she was enrolled at. Abigail Lawton was taken yesterday. Police are looking to question Michael Lawton, in relation to her abduction.

Anyone with any information, are asked to contact Lieutenant Dalton at the number below.

The report showed two photos. One of a young Abi and the other of Michael Lawton. He searched again and found another article, with a date three months later.

Sargent's Daughter Found Alive

Abigail Lawton has been found three months after being abducted. Her condition is listed as severely critical.
Police are still looking for Michael Lawton, in connection with this case.

Adam read the article several times. Abi had been abducted? The reports were basic but enough to finish adding it together. Michael Lawton had to be a relation. The scars indicated he'd been rough on her, but how rough? How far had he gone? Severely critical didn't sound good. Suddenly, everything made sense. Abi being upset. She must have been getting ready to tell him and worried about his reaction. He printed the articles off and headed straight over to the station. Frankie had a lot to answer for, and his captain was damn well going to tell him the truth.

Adam stormed into Frankie's office and threw the newspaper articles onto his desk. "Why the hell didn't you tell me," he yelled.
"Adam calm down, shouting won't change anything."
Adam briefly closed his eyes. Frankie was right, getting angry wouldn't bring Abi back, but he was upset that she hadn't told him. He sighed and sat down. "She'd been so upset and tense those last few weeks. At first, I thought she was having second thoughts about the engagement, but when she finished early, I was worried it was something else. Something more serious. I tried to talk to Abi,

but she just clammed up, said she'd tell me on Saturday. If I had known, I'd have made her stay at home that last shift."

"She wanted to tell you Adam, but I knew she was finding it hard. She was worried how you would react. It wasn't until Nat spoke to her, that we found out how worried she really was. Adam, she was happy, the engagement wasn't the problem, Michael was." Frankie stood up and walked to the window that looked out into reception. "Michael always swore to take away Jack's happiness, and we always knew that would be Abi. She was worried Michael would come back and destroy everything. Even thought she was being followed. It seems she was right. If only she'd talked to us sooner."

"I'm sorry Frankie, I guess I just needed to take my anger out on someone. Why though? Why go to all this trouble? He could have just killed her, not make her suffer, not again."

"Because he can, that's why. He won't stop, not until one of them is dead. Abi, Jack or himself. Finding Abi won't be enough, he must be taken out. Otherwise, he'll just keep coming back."

"Believe me, if I see him he won't be breathing for much longer," Adam growled as he shook his head. "I could have protected her if I'd known." Jack's warning made sense now. If only he'd asked at the time. He stood up to leave, but Frankie stopped him. "Adam, Nat's had a breakthrough. We've figured out how he set it up, abducted her. Even where he kept her." He filled Adam in.

Adam couldn't believe it. "She was that close?" He thanked Frankie and left.

Frankie could only sign in relieve, it could have gone a lot worse. Thank god, he hadn't asked what Michael had done.

*****

Abi had no idea Michael had changed his plan, or that he was recording everything. She dreaded every visit. She knew he'd broken some ribs, and only God knew what other internal injuries she might have. She just had to hold on. Every minute might be a minute closer to getting found. Frankie and Nat wouldn't give up, not until they knew where she was, whether she was alive or not.

Neither would Adam, he'd have his brothers helping him. She could hear Michael's footsteps. What would he do this time? Her uniform had begun to rip, and she was cold from sitting in the water.

Michael entered and put something in the corner, removed her gag and let her eat. The whole time he sat and stared at her. He knew she was in pain, could see how her breathing has changed. Good, he thought but hoped she didn't break too soon. The fun had only just begun.

Abi still has no idea how long it's been. "How long?" She asked.

"Abi, my dear. You've been in my tender loving care for six weeks. How do you like it so far? Had enough yet? What some more? Tell me Abi, what should I do next?"

"Let me go?" Abi praying with all her heart.

Michael laughed. "Oh Abi, I'll give you that, you just have to ask to die first. Two little words, kill me, should be enough."

Abi shook her head. "No, I have enough to live for."

Michael studied her. Yes, she does. A devoted fiancé, but what if she didn't. Maybe physically torture wasn't enough. He needed to add in some emotional abuse. Oh, this should be interesting. "Oh yes, Adam. Slight problem there."

Abi whipped her head up sharply. "Adam? What have you done?"

"*Me*, nothing. It's Adam who can't keep it in his pants. I've been watching him, seeing how he's coping and well, he's not really missing you anymore. You see, he's been visiting hookers, several of them. Looks like your fellow needs to fuck regularly to stay happy. I've probably saved you from marrying the worst loser ever. Maybe you should start spreading your legs too, get your own back."

Abi couldn't believe it. Not Adam, he wouldn't. "No, he wouldn't. There's no way he would do that. Your lying, your plan won't work. Adam's the perfect gentleman, he'll be waiting for me. He's healed me once, he'll do it again."

83

"Oh yes, he would and did, several times. Did you know he liked to spread it around before you agreed to marry him? Anyway, enough talk, I've got better things to do."

He pulled her to the ground and pushed his hand up her shirt. He squeezed both her breasts tightly, which caused her to whimper. "Your tits have developed lovely, I can't wait to taste them properly." He then put his hand down her pants and pushed his fingers back inside her. He pushed deeply, right up to her cervix and she gasped as he scratched her. He pulled out and licked his fingers.

Abi watched as he began to smile. "Abi, do you remember what I did, where I stuck my cock. How is your ass nowadays?"

She couldn't do anything to as he flipped her over and put his hand back into her pants. Abi felt him rub a finger over her ass and then he pushed a finger in. She whimpered as he drove it in deeper, a second finger joined in. She felt his second hand go under her pants and felt two fingers pull her anal ring apart. She felt the pressure as he stretched her, and she began to cry out as she felt herself tear slightly. He pulled out and wiped his hands on her.

"Beautiful Abi. You are so tight again; the surgeons did an excellent job. Shame I'm about to undo it all." He flipped her back over and noted the tears down her face. "Not enough yet?" He left her long enough to go to the corner and picked up the baseball bat that he'd left there. Abi's eyes opened wide. Michael forced her to stand, and before she knew it, he swung the bat towards her legs. She buckled as it hit them, once, twice, three times. He let her fall, and she thought he had finished, but he jammed the bat into her stomach, and she was winded. She leaned forward, and he hit her across the back of her neck. She toppled onto her side and blacked out again.

Michael was impressed with how well Abi had held on. The thought of losing Adam should have been enough to push her to her limits, but now she'd taken another beating, and he had really enjoyed touching her. He needed to up his game. She was still going to be a good fuck.

*****

84

Within the hour Jack had received the video. He felt physically sick as he watched what Michael doing, fully aware of where he was putting his fingers. He closed his eyes when he heard her cry out. It wasn't long before Michael rang.

"Jack, how's it going. Did you enjoy our little conversation? Abi thinks Adam's spreading it around. Fucking anything that moves. Oh, she's trying not to believe it, but she can't quite do it and that beating she took? Well, it would make a grown man cry. The surgeons did an excellent job repairing her, and I'll have lots of fun undoing it. I've already started to stretch her ass. Sweet and tight again. What do you say, Jack, has she had enough?"

"I won't say it, Michael. I won't let you kill her. As long as she breathes, we'll find her and bring her home."

Michael laughed as he hung up.

Anthony was there, and could barely believe what he had heard. "She won't believe him, she knows Adam too well."

Jack glanced over at him. "I hope you're right, if not she may give up. Adam's probably the only thing keeping her going."

"I'll get that sent to forensics and see if Matt can get anything from it. Jack, he didn't just rape her, did he?"

"No, and he's going to do it again." Jack hoped she could get through it, because the chances of finding her first were becoming slim.

Anthony headed back to the station, he had to speak Frankie.

"Frankie," he said as he sat in the office. "Here's the latest video and it's not pretty." He waited while Frankie watched, and noticed the look of anger that crossed over his face.

Frankie stood and walked over to the window. Michael had now made his intentions completely clear. He *would* tear her apart again. "She won't survive it again."

"He was rough with her, wasn't he?" Anthony asked.

"Too bloody rough. Anthony, she's now as good as dead. She may not beg, but she won't recover again. You'll need to be there for Adam, as I doubt he's getting her back. The longer he has her, the worse it'll get. Get that down to Matt."

85

Anthony headed down to forensics.

"Already have it," Matt said as Anthony entered. "I'll pull it apart, see if I can get anything." Matt had seen it twice already and knew exactly what Michael was doing to Abi. He hoped he would come across Michael first, as he wanted to be the one to kill him.

Chapter Ten

Frankie had been down to the town hall to get the maps of the area Nat had pinned on her board. He wanted the blueprints of the underground sewers and basements. He knew Michael would bury Abi deeply, and wouldn't just keep her in the main building of a warehouse. There was also the fact that they hadn't gotten any CCTV footage of Michael, as he approached the phone boxes. There were enough cameras, but he wasn't on any of them. They had no idea how he was getting around. He was now in Nat's office, comparing the two maps.

Nat walked in. "Frankie, what are you up to?"

"It's bothering me how Michael's getting access to the phone boxes. We should have him on CCTV, but we don't." He placed Nat's map on top of the blueprint. "These lines are the sewers, they run directly under the phones he's been using. I need to know if there are any manhole covers, in the near vicinity of the phones. Is he using the sewers to get around?"

Nat saw where Frankie was coming from. "I'll get a team out, get it checked. I'll also check if there have been any reports of damage to any covers. It's coming together. We have to be getting closer."

"I wish we were. Michael's been planning this for a long time. Worked it all out. Nat, have you seen the latest video?"

Nat had and couldn't believe it. "He's getting rougher. I'm not sure Abi will hold out much longer, and with what he said, he could be close to breaking her. Jack may not need to make the decision, Abi might."

Frankie feared that too. Abi could only hold on for so long. "She's a fighter, she's proved that, but can she keep it up?" Frankie continued to study the maps. "Nat, she's not coming back to us in one piece, he's made that clear. I've warned Anthony, now I'm telling you. You still have your trauma counselling, and you're going to need it. I'm asking you to be her counsellor again, to try and bring her back. It won't be easy, but if anyone can, you can."

"I'll give it my best shot. Let's hope we can get Abi back before he does tear her apart."

*****

Adam had no idea of the videos as they had kept it quiet, but Anthony did know. He'd spoken to Andrew, and he was flying back down. They had a grave feeling that it would be over soon. That Abi may not fight for much longer. Anthony arrived back at Adam's and let himself in. Adam was pacing, it was apparent something had upset him.

Adam peered over at Anthony. "Michael rung me. Said he'd messed with her head, that she was ready to die. That she'd begged to die. Anthony, what's he done? You must tell me. I know you're helping with the investigation, but they won't tell me anything. Please Anthony, what is it?"

Anthony knew he must tell his brother about the videos and the deal Michael had with Jack. Frankie had already agreed to it, but he'd held off. Adam was suffering enough. He got Adam to sit and sat next to him after he had grabbed his laptop. Anthony decided that showing him would be easier. "Adam he's sent videos, they aren't pretty but you need to see them. She hasn't begged yet, but this latest one." He hesitated. "This latest one might be too much. He's taunting her, telling her lies. He's made another deal with Jack. Said he'll stop when Jack begs him to kill Abi."

Adam startled at that. "Jack won't, he'll never make that decision."

"We all know that but," he paused again, this bit wasn't easy. "I don't think he'll have too. Adam, I think she might make it herself." He saw Adam's reaction. His brother was stunned that Abi might make that decision. "Watch the videos but prepare yourself." Anthony left him, went into the kitchen, and boiled the kettle. Adam would need a strong cup of coffee. As he heard Adam's distress,

Anthony's heart broke, as he knew that he couldn't do anything to console his brother.

"Bastard," Adam said, as Anthony returned with the drinks. "Find her. Anthony, you must find her. What he's threatening, it's not just rape. No woman can come back from that." He glanced at Anthony. "I've lost her, haven't I?" Adam was entirely downhearted.

"Adam, I'm sorry, but it's beginning to look like it. We simply aren't getting the breaks we need. Matt's torn those videos apart and got nothing useful from them. We still have no idea where he has her. Michael holds all the cards, and he's going to play them. We can't stop him. It's only a matter of time before he does what he is threatening to do."

"I love her so much, but I'm beginning to wish she'd beg. I'd rather Abi died then to know that he's going to hurt her like that."

Anthony already had an idea that she had been through something similar before and therefore, she probably wouldn't beg, but he couldn't let Adam know. "Adam, Abi's strong. I think she can cope with more than we think she can. Give her a chance. We might still get to her in time."

"I want her back so much. Whatever Michael does, I'll stand by her. Do whatever I can to help her recover. I'm not giving up on her. Not ever. Abi's too important to me."

Anthony was glad to hear it, and he knew that Adam meant every word. He merely hoped his brother wouldn't have to. Prayed they'd find her soon. If they didn't, there might not be enough of Abi left to save.

*****

Nat had returned from checking out some of the phone box sites. Frankie was right, every phone was near a manhole, and all seemed to have been recently moved. Her team had checked the others, and it was the same. The sewers, that's how he was getting around. Therefore, was it possible Abi was down there too. Michael was still using phone boxes, but not staying on the line long enough to always be able to track them, but the ones they had, were again near a maintenance hole. They were getting closer, she knew they were. It was only a matter of time, but did they have that time allowance. They were up to seven weeks. Seven weeks of Abi being tortured. Not just physically, but mentally too. The things Michael was saying, they had to be taking their toll. Abi would have to recover emotionally, as well as physically. Nat had been to church more times than she ever had before. Prayed for Abi, asked God to help them. Anything, to get her back. She looked back over to the board. They had a lot more information, maybe it was time for another press release. She would ask Frankie tomorrow.

Frankie agreed. They weren't getting anywhere fast enough, and Abi might be reaching her breaking point. Their press officer had called in the same reporters, and he began.

"Thank you all for coming in again. We are still investigating the incident that involved Officer Abigail Lawton. We have additional information stating she wasn't in the car when it exploded and is still alive. We know that Abi is being held against her will and we believe the man holding her, may be harming her." They had decided not to release all the information they had, just enough to hopefully jog people's memories. "The man we are looking for is Michael Lawton. We are publishing a picture of what we think he looks like. If anyone has any information on his whereabouts, we would be extremely grateful. We believe Abi's life in is danger and need to find her fast." He stopped. He had one last message. "Michael, if you are watching this, we will find her, and she'll be alive when we do."

The reporters began to ask questions. Frankie managed to field most of them, but one reporter asked the question he had been waiting for.

"Is this the same Michael Lawton who is her uncle? The one who held her before? The uncle who nearly killed her?"

Frankie looked straight at him. "Yes, which is why it's important we find her and soon," he walked away and prayed it was enough.

Nat was back at the call centre. She prayed that Michael had been watching and contacted them again. She didn't have to wait long. As she picked up a phone, Nat introduced herself.

"Nat, my dear, how's it going? Are you enjoying my entertainment so far? Abi sure is, her injuries are getting worse every couple of days. I think I need to up my game, she's strong and still holding on. I've had the most fantastic idea. Adam's spreading himself around, well Abi thinks he is. She's awfully close to breaking, but not quite there. Tell me, Nat, you know her so well. How's she going to cope with being raped again? My fingers have had a lot of fun inside of her. Yes, I think it's time my cock joined in, it's so hard and ready for her. Let's see if she still likes a real man. One who can keep going for hours." He hung up.

Nat glanced over at the Officer tracking the call. "Please say you got him." She begged.

The Officer shook his head. "Not long enough." The phone call had shaken them all up.

Nat hurried over to Frankie's office, he noticed how upset she was. "Nat, what's happened?"

"He called Frankie, the bastard called in again. He didn't stay on the line long enough for us to track him." She stopped, and Frankie saw a tear escape.

"Nat, sit down. Take it slowly and tell me what he said." Frankie knew this was going to be serious, it took a lot to shake Nat. It was what made her such a great detective.

Nat took a deep breath. "He said she's close to breaking but managing to hold on. He's impressed with how strong she is." She couldn't look him in the eye as she said the last part. "Frankie," her voice broke. "He said he was going to rape her, show her what a real man was like again. Said he could keep it up for hours. It'll be the last straw Frankie, she'll break."

Frankie didn't want to believe it, but the beatings were getting worse. "It'll test her. If Abi can remain strong, she'll make it. She survived it once before, let's hope she stay strong. Let's hope Adam can too."

"I'm not telling him about this call. Not yet. I'll let Anthony know so he can be prepared. God, I hope he doesn't send a video straight to Adam. That's all he'll need."

Frankie agreed, they needed to protect Adam from this as long as possible. "It'll break him too. Nat, even if we find her, Michael could still break them apart. Their relationship is strong, they love each other dearly, but rape? It'll be hard for her to bounce back from again, not if it's like before. There's a chance they may not stay together."

Nat raised her head. "We'll find her, no matter what. Like you said, I'll be counselling her myself, like before. I'll do everything I can to keep them together. To get her back."

Frankie nodded, it was their best plan. Nat had taken extra counselling training in rape, had helped many victims and had a high success rate of keeping couples together. "As I said before if anyone can, you can. Nat, when we find her, you can have extended leave for as long as it takes. Abi's our priority."

*****

Frankie headed over to Jack's. He'd called Anthony and asked him to meet him there. Jack let them in. Frankie looked directly at Jack as they sat. "Jack, what I have to say isn't easy, but you need to prepare yourself. Anthony, we aren't telling Adam, but you need to be ready too. Adam will need you in the next few days." Both men looked back at Frankie, both realised this was serious.

"Michael rung the call centre after the last press release," Frankie said. "He's impressed at how strong Abi's being, thought he'd have broken her by now. He's upping his game. Told Nat quite clearly, that he was going to rape her."

"No," Jack said. "It'll kill her, she'll beg. Frankie, he'll have won."

"How close are you to finding Abi?" Anthony already knew the answer but asked anyway.

"Not close enough, we won't get to her in time. Hell, I've spent most of my time off checking old warehouse, basements, and sewers, but nothing. So has most of the station. I've even put out an unofficial shoot to kill order. There's just no sign of either of them. We have no idea where she is. Damn it, he's planned this too well."

Jack didn't want to believe it. Raped again, his baby wouldn't cope, but he knew Michael was capable of it. "He's raped her before," he said quietly. "We know he's capable of it."

"I figured he was rough too," Anthony said. "How rough can he be?"

Frankie answered. "Very rough. I didn't realise anyone could be that rough, but she bounced back. Falling for Adam has proved that. We never thought she'd trust any man, let a man get that close to her. If she can remember that Adam's waiting for her, that he really loves her, it may be enough for her to find the strength to get through this."

"Adam's told me he'll stand by Abi, help her through it, no matter what's coming," Anthony said.

Frankie looked at him. "Good, that might be enough to keep her going. However, if it's like before, he may lose her trust. She may not let him near her, may not be able to allow any man near her, including us. Nat's going to counsel her again, try her best. I'm giving her extended leave for it. I just hope we get Abi back alive."

"She's good, and Abi trusts her. Nat will be her only hope." Jack agreed. But was worried himself. Would Michael stop at rape?

Frankie left, he needed to go back out and hunt for Abi. He still had a lot of places to check. Anthony stayed with Jack a while longer, didn't want to leave him alone, but eventually went back to the hotel. Andrew was waiting for him, having just flown in.

He saw the expression on Anthony's face. "What's happened?"

"He made contact again, you're not going to like it," Anthony told him.

"Shit," was all Andrew could answer.

93

Chapter Eleven

Michal returned, he'd given her a few biscuits this time. "Had a lovely talk with Nat, told her my future plans for you. She's already warned daddy, knows I'll do it. Can you guess Abi?"

Abi looked at him, dread filled her stomach. "Whatever it is, I'll not break."

"Are you sure Abi? Can you really be sure?"

"It can't be worst then the last time, I survived then."

"But this time you have a fiancé and a lot more to lose. Tell me Abi, would he cope with rape? Could your love be enough to survive that?" He moved over to her, grabbed her hair and pulled her up. He heard her cry out in pain. "Will he still want you after I've stuck my lovely, large cock in you and torn you apart? I can keep it up for hours now. Not just a few times like before, but a hell of a lot longer. I can rape you over and over, and you can't stop me. I'll keep going until I sag, and I'll send Adam the whole video."

Abi looked at him directly in the eyes. "I survived the last time, I'll do it again. Adam will care for me, help me through it, help me recover." Her voice sounded sure, but her mind said differently. She had doubts, would he? Could he? Rape broke up marriages. Would Adam really stand by her?

Michael saw the doubt cross her face. "Not sure, are you? Not sure at all. Something to look forward to. Tell me Abi, do you think it'll be as good as before?" He grabbed her ankles and dragged her onto the floor. She watched as he pulled out a penknife. He stabbed her in the right shoulder, then her left thigh and dragged the knife down as he pulled it out.

Abi whimpered, and he laughed as he placed the knife across her throat and applied enough pressure to draw blood. "Not yet, Abi, don't give up yet. I really do want to fuck you first." He stood and left after he'd replaced her gag.

Michael went back to his set up in another part of the warehouse. The place where his camera feed went to. Another video needed to be prepared, but first, he watched Abi for a while. She really had no idea he was filming all her torture. Maybe, once he had finished, he would make a loving film for Jack to treasure forever. Yes, he thought, why not. After all, his daughter would be dead. It would be the only thing left of her. A video of her demise.

He sent the video to Frankie, Nat, Jack, and Adam at the same time. The three of them watch it in horror but relax when he didn't rape her.

Anthony was with Adam and prayed with relief when Michael merely stabbed Abi.

Adam looked downhearted. Another torture, another painful day for Abi. How much longer before they found her? He'd heard the conversation. "Rape, he really is going to rape her," Adam managed to whisper.

Adam remembered the last time Abi had nearly been raped. She'd been in an armed robbery at the bank. Off-duty. They'd discovered she was a cop and took her as a hostage. He'd been in a police car with Nat driving. One of the men had pinned her against the side of the van, the back doors open. Adam had seen it all. The man pulling himself out, then Abi being shot. She'd told him that all five men planned on having her. It had come close to nearly broking her. But they'd stayed together. Abi had continued to trust him. But this? This time it was different. She couldn't defend herself. She was tied up.

Anthony closed his eyes in sympathy, Adam was beginning to lose it. "Adam," he said as he opened his eyes. "Listen to Abi, she's not given up, she's giving as good as she gets. She's answering him back. That's not the sign of a victim, but of a survivor." He needed to tell him, now was the time to come clean. "Adam, I need to tell you something."

95

Adam glanced up at his brother, the sorrow plainly in his eyes. "Abi can't fight much longer, it's been two months now. He's going to win. I'm never getting her back. He'll rape her. She'll beg. It's over."

Anthony sat down next to Adam. This was going to be hard, but Adam needed to hold it together for both their sakes. "Adam, you know he's abducted her before, but you don't know what happened."

"You know, don't you?"

"Yes. It's not pretty, but it's the right time to tell you. Adam, she fought him once, she has it in her to do it again. I'll tell you, but only so you know how strong your fiancé really is. What a fighter she is." He stopped to prepare himself, this would hit Adam hard.

"Michael took her out of school. He told the headmistress that Jack had been injured and was unlikely to survive. Said he needed to get Abi to the hospital quickly. They let her go, didn't know that Michael was lying. That he wasn't even a cop. He held her for three months. Adam, he repeatedly kicked her, beat her, just like he's doing now." He noticed the tears that Adam had let fall. "He stabbed her twice in the abdomen. They penetrated quite deeply, and she lost a lot of blood, but she held on. He hadn't finished. Michael eventually raped her, multiple times. Nat's told me everything." Or so he had thought. Nat held some details back. "He was rough." Adam broke down completely as he heard this, but Anthony hadn't finished. "When they finally found her, she was barely breathing and had severe head injuries. She spent a few days being ventilated. Jack was prepared to let her go; the doctors didn't think she'd make it."

Adam shook his head. "How? How could she possibly recover from that?"

"It took her four months, but she did. Adam, it shows her spirit, how strong Abi is. If anyone can survive this, Abi can. You'll get her back but be prepared for her to need time to recover. Be there when she needs you. You'll be the key to her survival. Your love for her will keep her alive."

Anthony stayed with Adam overnight. When he had finally fallen to sleep, Anthony rang Nat. "Nat, I've had to tell him. Michael sent a video, confirming he was going to rape her. Adam was in bits, knew he'd lose her. I had to tell him about the last time, all of it. It's the only way he'll survive this."

"Thanks for letting me know. Michael sent the same video to the station and Jack."

"Has Matt had any luck on tracing the feed?" Anthony asked.

"No. Every time he thinks he has it, another firewall pops up, but he's still working on it. Michael's apparently still good with computers."

They hung up. Maybe tomorrow they would get a break.

The following morning Matt rushed into Nat's office. "I've got it," he said.

Nat looked over at him as he continued. "The video location, I have it."

Nat was up like lightning. "Let's go."

She called a team in and met everyone, including Frankie, at the site. It was an old derelict warehouse, not far from the marina. It's not very secure, and the door only had a bolt. As they entered, she noticed the monitor. Nat and Frankie walked over to it. "Abi," they both said together.

It was a direct video link of Abi, who sat up against a wall. They can see how bruised and battered she was.

"She looks exhausted," Frankie said. "But she's staying in there."

They both gasped in surprise as Michael entered the room. Abi looked up, and they can see the dullness in her eyes. Could see she was getting close to breaking. They watched as Michael removed the gag and offered her a bread roll and a bottle of water. Abi accepted it and began to eat.

Nat noticed how she had to twist her hands to hold the food. "That must be hurting, there's fresh blood on her arms. It's not just rope that he's using. It looks like he's using wire again."

Frankie glanced around the room. "Wireless. She may not be close to this warehouse, but at least we have Michael's set up. We

97

can control what happens here. I want Matt over here, with a team, to monitor this twenty-four-seven. If we can see what's happening all the time, we might just get a location. Something to find her with."

Nat nodded back and contacted Matt. "He's on his way, so is Josie. If there's anything we can use here, they'll find it." She looked back at the monitor. Michael was sitting, looking at Abi. What was he up to? "He's feeding her, keeping her alive. We didn't know that before. The videos he's sent hasn't included this. He wants her to live as long as she can. Wants the pain he's causing to continue. It's something we weren't sure of before. This could be useful, something to work with, maybe bargain with. He'll keep her alive while he's enjoying this. It'll give us more time to find her."

Frankie agreed, but he was concerned. "Look at her eyes Nat, they're dull. The spark has gone. She's still holding on, but he's wearing her down. The videos he sends have never been this clear. He's amending them, so we only see what he wants us too. He's not feeding her enough, look at her weight loss. She'll lose her strength and maybe her will to live. She could die on her own accord. Just fade away. We need to find her and soon."

*****

Michael knew they had found his video set up. He'd only just got out in time. Nat was excellent, got close to him again. He'd let them have that feed. He smiled as he knew they were watching him right now. What could he do, to make it more exciting for them? Abi had no idea how close they were. Hell, they didn't know. The game heated up. He couldn't help but smile.

Abi saw the smile on his face, now what? What was it going to be today? She'd lost track of time. "How long?"

Michael looked towards the camera and grinned, as he knew they were being watched. "It's our two-month anniversary, Abi my dear. How should we celebrate? A romantic meal for two, a good fuck? Maybe a murder? What would you like?" He asked sarcastically.

Abi let her head hang. Two months. Would Adam still be waiting for her?

"Oh, I forgot, I have a little something for you to hear." He got his phone out and made sure the sound was turned up to full. He wanted to make sure, that his little followers could hear what was said. It was a masterpiece. He'd managed to get a sample of Adam's voice. This was going to be fantastic, and he pressed play.

'I don't know if I still want her. If Michael's raped her, she's spoilt goods, broken. I won't be able to love her anymore. I've arranged to transfer back to New York. I'm not hanging around to pick up the pieces. Our engagement is officially over. She's not my problem anymore. If I'd known about her past, I would have left her the hell alone. He's welcome to the bitch. It's obvious she spreads her legs for anybody.'

Abi couldn't believe what she had heard. It couldn't be Adam, he'd never say that. He loved her too much.

Michael sneered. "Guess now you have nothing to live for, so what do you say? Ready to give up? All you have to do is say the words Abi, I'll make it quick, and you'll suffer no more."

Frankie and Nat were shocked. They knew Adam had never said that, knew he was waiting for Abi to return to him.

"Abi, no," was all Nat could say. "Please god no. Believe in Adam, *please* just believe in him."

"Come on Abi," Frankie joined in. "Don't let him win, he's playing with you. *Don't* let him win."

Abi shook her head. "No, Adam's not like that, he's waiting for me, I know he is." He had to be, she thought, I need him too much. He's the only thing that's keeping me going. Abi knew Michael was paying with her mind. "And I'll get back to him. Whatever you do, you won't break us up."

Michael was glad she's not begging to die just yet, he had become quite fond of her stubbornness. This could carry on for quite a while longer.

Frankie and Nat could only continue to watch. Abi was defying Michael and holding out against him. She wasn't finished yet.

Michael moved towards Abi. Grabbed her wrists and twisted them. Abi let out a blood-curdling scream. Nat gasped, and Frankie steadied her, as she heard Abi's scream.

"My god," Nat said. "Even I felt that. There has to be wire underneath. That must have done some serious damage to her wrists."

Nat had to be right, even Frankie can see the blood pouring down Abi's arms. He also noticed how every officer in the room, had stopped and winced at Abi's scream. "He's getting rougher and knows we are watching them. It's going to get a lot worse for her now. Damn it, I hope she's not losing too much blood. With her weight loss, she really could just fade away."

Michael replaced Abi's gag and smiled up at the camera. He rubbed his groin and sneered at them. Made it clear how hard he was. He turned back to Abi. "Sweetheart, I'm all hard. Are you wet for me, shall we check?" He pulled her down onto the floor and ripped her pants along her groin. They could do nothing but watch, as he put his hand between her legs. Abi winced as he pushed two fingers deep into her and knew how bruised she already was. As he scraped her with his nails, Abi cried out. When he pulled his hand out, the blood on his fingers was clear. He turned back to the camera and licked his fingers. "She still tastes so delightful. I'll see you all soon."

Matt and Josie walked in during the last part. Josie paled drastically when she realised what Was being done.

"Bastard," Matt said. He knew he was only voicing what they all thought.

"Frankie she's not coping, look at her," Nat said the obvious. "She's badly beaten and already has internal injuries. She's going to break, and soon by the looks of it."

"Matt, I want Abi monitored twenty-four-seven. She's not to be left alone." He turned as Anthony entered.

"Holy shit," was all he managed to say. He may have seen the photos and videos, but seeing Abi in real life was different. "Please tell me she's not as bad as it seems." When no one answered, Anthony's heart fell. Hell. "Oh, Abi," he sighed. "We have to get her out of there."

Frankie left them to it. He still had to inform Jack and wanted to do it in person.

*****

Jack let him in. As soon as he saw Frankie's face, he went stone cold. "What's that bastard of a brother done now?"

"There's a bit of good news." If you can call it that, Frankie thought. "We have the location of where he's sending the videos from. Jack, we have the live feed. We can see Abi. Matt and his team are going to monitor it and hopefully, track the camera."

"How's Abi looking?"

Frankie heard Jack's heartache. "Jack I'll be honest, she's not brilliant." He told him what they'd seen.

"She's not coping, is she?" Jack took a deep breath. "Frankie, I've made a decision."

Frankie didn't like the sound of that but waited for Jack to continue.

"If he goes too far, does what he did before." Jack's voice cracked. "I can't watch her go through that again, can't expect her too." He looked up at Frankie, tears shone in his eyes. "I'll let her go. I'm not having her suffer, not through that. It'll be unfair to her."

Frankie fully understood where Jack was coming from, but it was still hard to hear. He thought of Michelle, his daughter. If it was her, could he just sit and watch? He doubted it, doubted it very much. The chances were, he'd do the same thing. "Jack, I understand, really I do. But let's give her a chance first, she could surprise us all again. If it gets too much for your daughter, I'll stand by you." Adam would probably kill him though. If there's any God up there, please help her, he prayed.

Chapter Twelve

Anthony had spent the last few hours with Matt observing Abi. She had slept for the last hour, at least she was trying to get some rest. When she woke up, they watched as she shook her head and tried to stretch. Come on Abi, you can do this, she told herself. Her gag felt loose, and she managed to remove it. "Adam," they heard her whisper. "It's not true, it can't be. He's messing with me. I can do this, I can beat him. I can."

Matt grinned and glanced at Anthony. "He hasn't broken her yet. Look at her spirit."

"No, he hasn't," Anthony replied. "She's still fighting and not believing what Michael is telling her. She really is strong." He'd been told, but now he's seen it for himself. He was going over to Adam's later and had permission to tell him about the video lead they'd found. He'll be able to tell his brother, that he'd seen his fiancé fighting. Matt had printed off some images of Abi. Ones of her sleeping, looking restful and others with defiance in her eyes. Yes, she was bruised and injured, but Adam would be able to see how she was bearing up. No longer would they need to rely on what Michael sent them.

Anthony waited for Andrew to arrive and headed off the visit Adam. "Adam, I've something to tell you. There's been another breakthrough," Anthony said as he let himself into Adam's apartment.

Adam looked over at him, and noticed his brother was carrying a folder. He dreaded asking. "What's Michael done now?"

"Actually, it's a bit of good news. You know how Michael's sending us videos? Well, we've found his set up, where the feed has been going to. Matt's teams are watching it twenty-four-seven. We can see Abi. Adam, we can see and hear what's going on."

Adam didn't look any happier. "He still has Abi, watching it won't stop him. He can still hurt her."

"Adam, it means we may be able to trace it back to the camera he's using. Find her location. He hasn't made it easy, but Matt's trying."

Adam shook his head. "We all know I'm not getting her back. Michael knows what's he's doing. He'll make sure I never see her again. I know you're all trying, I'm grateful, really, I am. But I think we all know she's as good as dead. I can't keep believing anymore."

Anthony knew his brother was losing hope. It had been two months since Abi had been abducted, but they were making some progress at last. He pulled out a photo of Abi sleeping and placed it in Adam's hand. Adam just stared at it. "She's able to rest between visits, and he's giving her insignificant amounts of food and water. Adam, I've seen her fighting against him, even when he messes up her mind. Abi believes in you, you *must* do the same. Believe in her, she'll come back." He handed over another photo of Abi, one when she had defiance in her eyes. "Adam, look at her eyes, that's not the look of someone giving up."

Adam took the photo, and let his eyes focus. "Abi fight him, please. She's lost so much weight. Anthony, she can't keep it up. She'll be losing her strength." As he looked at Anthony. "I need to see her."

Anthony shook his head. "You know that's not possible, Frankie won't let you in there. But I promise to keep you fully informed. Matt's there all the time, he sleeps there. Matt's staying on site permanently, in case of any further breakthroughs. He has a team there with him, at least two other people at any time. Either Andrew or I am also with them. Someone is always watching her. She's not alone anymore."

"She doesn't know that, doesn't know you're there. As far as she's concerned she's still alone." Adam knew Anthony hadn't told him everything. "What else has he done? Anthony, what aren't you telling me?"

Damn, he had hoped not to tell him the rest. "He managed to get a sample of your voice and set up a little message for Abi." He pulled his phone and played it.

'I don't know if I still want her. If Michael's raped her, she's spoilt goods, broken. I won't be able to love her anymore. I've arranged to transfer back to New York. I'm not hanging around to pick up the pieces. Our engagements officially over. She's not my problem anymore. If I'd known about her past, I would have left her the hell alone. He's welcome to the bitch. It's obvious she spreads her legs for anyone.'

Adam's head snapped up. "What the hell, I'd never say that, never. Abi must know that. She knows what she means to me. Anthony, find her. You have to bloody well find her before he wears her down." The fight came back into his voice.

Anthony began the recording again, and Adam heard Abi's voice this time.

'No, he's not like that, he's waiting for me, I know he is.'

Anthony saw Adam smile. "Told you she was a fighter. Don't give up hope. She's not giving up, neither should you."

"Get me into that room. I *don't* care what Frankie says, just get me in there. She may not know I'm there, but I need to see her. *Please*, Anthony, I'm begging."

"I can't guarantee it, but I'll see what I can do. I need to get back over there. Adam, you *have* to keep on believing."

Anthony drove back over to the warehouse. He remembered what Adam had said. That Abi wasn't aware that she was no longer alone. Maybe they could change that. "Matt, is this video link one way, or can we change it," he asks when he entered.

"What are you thinking?" Andrew asked.

"I've told Adam what we are doing. How technically Abi is no longer alone, but he said she didn't know that. He's right. We need to let Abi know we're with her, getting closer."

Matt examined the video set up again. "It may be possible, but I'll need to turn it off for a bit. It'll need re-wiring and re-programming. I may not be able to get this link back, we could lose everything. I'll have to run it past the Captain." He went outside to make the call.

"How's Adam taking it?" Andrew asked

"Badly," replied Anthony. "I played the recording to him, and he smiled at Abi's response. I just hope it's enough to get his spirit back. Michael may not be breaking Abi, but he's breaking Adam. Andrew, he's giving up any hope of ever seeing her again."

Matt walked back in. "Captain's given permission. Let's see if we can do it."

Andrew left them to it. He had no idea on wires and computer programming, which was Anthony's area. He headed over to Jack's.

"Andrew," Jack said as he let him in.

"I'm just checking up on you. Have you heard the latest?"

"The video feed? Yes, Frankie told me. Said Abi's not coping too well."

"She's exhausted. Michael's barely giving her enough food to keep her going. She looks so weak. Personally, I think Nat's right, he wants this to continue. I think he's having too much fun. Damn it to hell. It's Abi that's suffering the most."

"He hasn't been in contact with me for a few days. I was beginning to think the worst."

"No, she's still going." He looked at Jack. "Your daughter has spirit, she's answering him back. It's not just physical abuse, but mental as well. She must be emotionally tired, but she's not showing it. She really is strong."

"That she is. All Michael will do is make her stronger if she can keep going. But the longer it is, the more I worry she can't."

"We must be getting closer. Hopefully, we'll have Abi back home soon."

"I hope so, I really do, but it won't be over. The recovery will be hard to. She'll push us away like before. Adam will need to be patient and wait for her. It'll be hard for him too."

Jack didn't tell him what he had said to Frankie, they would try to talk him out of it. But god help Michael if he ever got his hands on him. He would make sure his brother suffered a similar fate.

"If Adam knows Abi's safe, he'll wait as long as he needs to. You don't need to worry about that."

He didn't tell Jack about Anthony's plan. If they could make that video two way, they would be able to talk to her.

*****

Matt had re-programmed the camera. "I hope it works, or we've just lost everything." He switched it back on, and instantly the picture returned to Abi. "So far so good. Let's see if she can hear us." He turned to Anthony. "Do you want to try?"

Anthony nodded. "Hell yes." He turned the switch to open. "Abi, sweetie, can you hear me?" They watched the monitor, nothing changed. She was sitting with her head down, and they had no response. He tried again. 'Abi, we reset the camera. Can you hear us, baby?"

Abi lifted her head slightly. Anthony, she thought and looked around. She shook her head. Now she had started to imagine things.

"Abi, there's a camera in the corner. Michael's been filming you, but we now have control of the system. We can see and hear what's happening and hope you can hear us too. You don't imagine my voice. Please Abi, answer me. Let us know you can hear us."

Abi lifted her head and glanced into the corner, a puzzled look on her face. She removed her gag. "Anthony?"

Anthony grinned at Matt, they'd done it. "Abi, we may not be with you, but you're no longer alone. Someone is always watching the camera feed. We know what happened Abi, we're aware of how he abducted you. Nat's lead investigator and she's not letting this go. We'll have you safely back home as soon as we can.

Abi let a tear fall. "Adam?"

Anthony heard the heartbreak in her voice. "Abi, he's waiting for you. Ignore Michael, he's lying to you. Adam's not going anywhere.

106

You'll be back with him soon, I promise." He looked over at Matt and hoped he wasn't lying. They still had no idea where she was. "Abi, do you know where you are? We can't find out where he's keeping you. Any clues could help, no matter how small."

Abi shook her head. "I've only seen this room." She stopped and cocked her head.

Anthony noticed the look on her face. "Abi, what is it?"

She looked towards the door. "Michael's coming." She quickly replaced her gag.

They turned the sound back off, so they could only hear and not talk to Abi. They didn't want Michael to know they could.

Michael entered, and it was the same routine. He gave her food and sat back on his stool.

"How's it going Abi?" He pulled out a hunting knife. "My knife's sharp and ready to go, just say the word. It'll be quick."

Abi shook her head, she had more hope now. Knew that help might be closer.

"Oh Abi, I really hoped I wouldn't have to do this, but your beloved has abandoned you."

"What's he up to now?" Anthony asked. "Adam hasn't gone anywhere."

Abi ignored her uncle, Adam was waiting for her. Michael hadn't got that hold over her anymore.

"Your fiancé has gone back to New York. Handed in his notice and left. Guess you don't mean that much to him after all." He placed a photo in her hand. "Take a good look, Abi. That woman he's with? That's his latest hooker. Adam took her home."

"No!" Abi cried out. "That's not true."

"Oh Abi, it is. He spent last night with her. I spent the night in the next room and heard her screams. I must admit, he does sound good at it. I might ask him for pointers."

Anthony and Matt could only watch, as Abi began to cry. It became clear that she might be believing him. That photo must be damned good.

"Abi, no. Please no. "Anthony whispered as he looked back at her.

"Are you ready Abi, ready to let go." Michael walked up to her, pulled her to the floor and stamped hard on her stomach. She cried out. Her uncle laughed as he slammed her head into the ground. He kicked her several times in the chest, and she cried out once again. The pain was getting too much. She didn't believe him, Adam would wait, but the pain was too much. She'd had enough, couldn't live through it again. She whispered something, but Anthony couldn't hear what she said.

"Abi dear, speak up," Michael said.

"Kill me!" She screamed.

Chapter Thirteen

Michael pulled out his knife and held it above her heart. As he applied pressure, blood was drawn as he sunk it into her breast. "Good call Abi, I'll make it quick."

Anthony was straight on the phone to Frankie. "Abi's begging, he's killing her as we speak." The panic evident in his voice.

Frankie found Nat and forced her to a car. He sped off towards the warehouse.

"Frankie, what's going on?" Nat was worried.

"He's killing her," was all he said.

They rushed in, and Michael still held the knife over her heart. The point was digging in deeply. Abi was crying.

"What happened?" Frankie asked.

"He showed her a photo of Adam with another woman. Told her she was a hooker and that Adam had spent the night with her. Said he'd resigned and gone back to New York with her. Then stamped on her stomach, slammed her head against the floor and kicked her in the chest." Anthony couldn't take his eyes off the monitor. "He said he'd make it quick, but he's not. That knife must be at least an inch in."

Michael pulled the knife out and slamming it into her arm. "Not yet. I'll kill you quickly as I promised, but I need to make a call first" He left. This time he didn't bother to replace the gag.

Frankie made a call to Andrew. "Get Adam here," he ordered. Andrew heard the panic in Frankie's voice. Shit, he thought, something must have happened. He turned to Adam. "We need to go, now!"

They entered the warehouse, and the first thing Adam noticed was Abi. "Abi," he muttered as he rushed to the screen.

Andrew noticed everyone's faces. "What happened?"

Anthony told them. Adam turned sharply, the disbelief apparent in his eyes. "How could she believe him?"

"I'm not convinced, she did. It was during the beating that she begged. Adam, it was rough this time, even I felt it." Anthony put a hand on Adam's shoulder. "We managed to program the link, so we can talk to her. She needs to hear you now, needs to know it's all lies. It'll be hard if she's nearly been convinced that it's true."

Frankie cleared the room out, Adam needed to be left alone. Required time with Abi. Frankie just prayed she recovered enough to hear him.

"Abi," Adam called softly. She didn't respond, her eyes were dull. "Abi, sweetheart, it's Adam. I'm here. I haven't left you, haven't abandoned you. I'm waiting, trying to get you home." Still nothing, she looked like she had shut down. He knew the knife had gone approximately an inch into her breast and deeply into her arm. He knew she had to be hurting. Adam tried again. "Baby, he's lying, I love you too much to let you go. I don't care about your past, only the future we're going to have together. Please Abi, don't give up. Whatever he does, I'll wait for you. I'm not going anywhere, not without you. Abi, please stay with me. I'm begging you. Please fight him, you can do this, you're a survivor. Come on Abi, pull through this, *please*."

Come on Abi, he prayed. Don't let him win. He leaned his elbows on the table, sighed, and rubbed his face. He needed to get her attention, but how? "Abi, we have a wedding to plan, you're going wedding dress shopping with Michelle. Remember baby. Nat's already brought her outfit, you don't want her to have wasted her money. Hey, baby. You are so going to look stunning in your dress."

He sat back in the chair, still nothing, she's not even blinking. He stood up. Anthony and Andrew were standing at the back of the room. As he turned to them, he shook his head. "Abi's gone too far, she's shut down."

Andrew pointed at the screen. "Adam, look."

Adam turned back. Abi was trying to sit up, and he's back at the mike before he knew it. "Abi, baby."

Abi looked bewildered, she swore she had heard Adam, but no, he was in New York. She glanced down at the photo and picked it back up. Something wasn't right about it, but what? She flipped it over, then back again. What was niggling at her? She closed her eyes and sighed. Suddenly, she snapped her eyes open, focused once more on the photo, and shook her head to clear it. Adam's clothes, that's what was wrong. He wore those clothes when *she* went with him to the airport. When *they* flew to New York. Oh no, what had she done. Michael must have photoshopped someone else's head on. She lifted her head up, the determination was evident in her eyes. Abi didn't want to die. She had escaped once, surely, she can again. She glanced around her, tried to find that piece of glass that she used the last time. Put her hands in the water and felt around. Damn it, he must have taken it, or it broke. She lowered her head and felt defeated. She glanced back up, the rope she noticed. The rope was starting to fray. Joy swelled in her heart. She pulled at the rope with her teeth, nibbling at it, and hoped to break it. It took a few minutes, but she felt it give and pulled. It snapped, but she had done more damage to her wrists.

Adam was watching her, as he narrowed his eyes he called his brothers over. They watch as she managed to break free.
"Look at that determination in her eyes. She's nowhere near done yet." Andrew said excitedly, as he ran outside to alert Frankie and Nat.
Adam switched on the mike again. "Come on Abi, you can do this."
She stopped, raised her head, and looked towards the camera. "Adam?"
"Oh baby, yes. Get to the door. Try and find something so we can locate you."
Abi nodded and managed to stand. They watched her leave.

"I'll be damned," Frankie said. "Let's hope she recognizes where she is."

The minutes pass, and she hadn't returned. Then the door opened, and Abi fell through. Followed closely by Michael.

"Tut, tut Abi. Escaping once I'll allow, but twice? Did you forget it's time to die?"

"No!" Abi screamed at him. "You aren't killing me, not now, not ever."

"Not allowed to change your mind, once you beg it's done." He pushed her to the ground, raised the knife above her and plunged it deep into her abdomen. Abi screamed. Adam collapsed into a chair. They watched Michael as he twisted the blade and could do nothing as Abi passed out.

All of them were in shock. It's over. Abi was dead.

Chapter Fourteen

Frankie drove straight round to Jacks. As he arrived Jack's phone rang, and he put it on speaker.

"Brother dearest, how are you feeling? Has Frankie told you the brilliant news yet?" Michael knew Frankie had only just arrived. "Maybe not, so I'll do it. She begged Jack, screamed at me to kill her. The best thing is? Frankie has it all on tape." Michael hung up.

Jack stared at Frankie, his eyes begged for him to say it wasn't true, but the expression on Frankie's face was unmistakable. Jack couldn't speak. Abi, his baby girl, was dead.

"Jack," Frankie began. "He convinced Abi that Adam had left for New York with a hooker. After he'd attacked her, she wanted to die. Michael left her. We got Adam there, but it was too late, or so we thought. She managed to escape, but Michael came back. I'm so sorry Jack. He stabbed her in her abdomen, twisted the knife. She never stood a chance."

"You did everything you could. At least Adam was there. Got a chance to see her once more. Abi's not suffering anymore."

"Jack, I'm not giving up. I'm putting out a nationwide search for Michael. Every cop in the country will be gunning for the bastard. One way or another, I'm bloody well getting him." Anger dripped off Frankie's words.

*****

Adam staring at the screen. Abi looked so peaceful, no longer suffering. Anthony sat in the chair next to him. He didn't say anything, there was nothing he could say. It was over. All that mattered now was for Michael to return her body.

113

Nat went outside. Andrew joined her. Neither of them knew what to say or do. Two months, Abi held on for two months. Why couldn't she have held on a bit longer? Nat had called Julian and informed him of what had happened. She watched him pull up, and they both went inside.

Julian walked over to the monitor, studied Abi and something caught his eye. Surely not, he thought, as he moved closer to the screen. My God, she was. "Guys, you know she's breathing, don't you?"

Everyone snapped their heads up.

"What?" They all said together, then looked harder at Abi.

"She is," Nat said excitedly.

Adam grabbed the mike. "Abi, sweetheart, can you hear me? Baby?" Nothing, she didn't respond.

"Give her time, that stab wound could be serious." Julian glanced around. "Hopefully, it's not too serious. Matt, any luck on tracing that camera."

"No, Michael's too damned good. Sorry, but I'll keep trying." Matt looked at Abi. Surely, she couldn't come back from that, could she?

They stared at the screen, all prayed that she woke up. None of them planned on leaving, not until they knew how Abi was. Every so often Adam talked to her. It was nonsense, but he hoped she could hear his voice and knew that he was still there for her.

Over an hour later, Abi stirred slightly, then opened her eyes. They could see the pain in them, but she's still alive. She moved her one hand to her abdomen, lifted it, saw the blood and passed out again.

Nat turned to Julian. "What's the chance of her surviving with an injury like that?"

"Hard to say. It'll depend if Michael's hit anything major." He studied her again. "Doesn't look like she's bleeding out too much, but it could be all internal. If he's missed all the important organs, her chances may be decent. The sooner we find her the better."

Anthony joined in. "Problem is, we still don't know where she is."

114

Everyone stayed the rest of the night. All they did was to watch Abi. Nat had rung Frankie, and he'd come back with Jack. Jack had gone pale upon seeing Abi, but at least he could see that his daughter still lived.

The morning arrived quickly, Adam was watching the monitor, as Abi whimpers. Julian's instantly beside him. Her eyes opened, and her breathing increased. Adam grabbed the mike. "Abi?" He called softly.
She blinked. "Adam?" The pain in her voice was evident.
"Yes baby, I'm here. We all are. Abi, you escaped. Did you recognise anything? Can you tell me where you are?"
She shook her head and tried to sit up, but it hurt too much.
"Take it easier, Abi." Julian took over the mike. "We don't know what damage he's done." Nat went next. "Abi, we know you're in a warehouse, possibly one of the basements. Frankie's sent search teams out, they're checking all the warehouses in the area. We'll find you. Adam's staying here, you can talk to him whenever you want."

*****

The teams have been at it all night and so far, no luck. Frankie had pulled up all the maps he could of the area. Studied them and sent them out in groups of four. It was a lot of ground to cover and would take a few days. They could only hope Michael didn't return. If he found her alive, he would start again.

Unfortunately, their luck didn't hold. Michael returned a couple of days later. "Time to return your body," they heard him say as he entered. They see him stop, a smile appeared on his face. "Abi, my dear, you're alive. Guess I must be slipping. That wound must hurt a lot." He glanced at the camera. "Shall we see how bad it really is? He pulled out his knife. Abi had managed to pull herself into a sitting position against the wall. He grabbed her ankles and

115

dragged her back to the floor. Using the knife, he cut off her ripped shirt and pants, which left only her underwear.

They all gasped as they saw Abi's injuries. Bruises covered most of her body. There were deep cuts along her thighs, shoulder, arms, as well as that stab wound on her abdomen. No one said anything as Michael placed his hand on her stomach, above where he'd stabbed her. He put one of his fingers on the wound and pushed it inside. Abi whimpered then cried out, as he drove it in further. He pulled out, picked up the knife again, this time he cut off her underwear. The stab wound on her breast looked red and angry. Michael studied her. "Not enough, my artwork just isn't finished yet." He sneered back at the camera, then leaned over Abi. One of his hands ended up between her legs. Abi's eyes widened in panic. No, oh god, not like this, not while Adam watched. Please no. A finger slipped finger inside her, and when he removed it, he began to rub her sensitive spot. A tear escaped. No please, she kept repeating in her head. He stopped, stood, and evilly smiled back at the camera. "Just a taste of what's to come. Oh, Adam, she's so wet and ready to fuck. Tell me, whose name will she call when she climaxes? Yours or mine?" Michael whistled as he left.

Shock ripped through Adam. "Oh God no. We must get her out. Now!"

Nat dialed Frankie immediately, to update him on what's happened. They were running out of time. Frankie's dragged more officers in to help with the search. In fact, every available officer had volunteered.

Frankie returned to the warehouse a few hours later. They still hadn't found her. Anger burned through him as he saw Abi. The injuries worse than they'd imagined. "How's she doing?"

"Not well," Julian replied. "She's fully aware of his plans. Knows he'll rape her. With Adam watching, it's hard for her, but Adam won't leave. Just sits there staring at her. Any luck yet?"

"No, nothing. We still don't have a bloody clue. Every off-duty officer has come back in. I'm beginning to think it isn't an old warehouse, but somewhere else. I'm hoping he stays away, and gives us longer to search."

Adam opened the link, he wanted to speak to Abi. His fiancé needed to be aware that he wouldn't leave her. "Abi, sweetie, whatever he does, I'll still be waiting for you. I'll still be here for you. I'm not going anywhere. Baby, I'll always love you, and somehow, we'll find you. Just hold on, Abi, *please*. He won't break us up. I'm not letting him. We can work through this. I promise you, sweetie, we can." He turned the sound off, as his tears fell. Please God, he prayed. Please let Michael be quick, don't let her suffer.

Abi had heard every word but couldn't respond. She was fully aware of what Michael could do. By the end of it all, she would be in no state to be with anyone, ever again. "Goodbye Adam," she whispered, too quiet for them to hear.

They sat and watched. Frankie called the station for regular updates, but still nothing. Jack's phone rang. He answered and put it on speaker.

"Enjoying the show, Jack?" They all heard Michael. "I know how hard Frankie's looking, but will he be fast enough? I'll give him until midnight to find her. After that, well she's all mine. I know Adam's there, I promise to make her last time rememberable. Shame she won't live long enough to *really* enjoy the memory. I need to go, need to get myself all large and ready to thrust. Oh, and Adam, I can go on for hours. My cock takes a lot of fucking to sag. How many times can I fuck her, Adam? How many times will I climax and spill my hot seed in her? Make sure you count, you'll be impressed." They heard him laughing, as he hung up.

Adam went pale. Midnight. It was less than six hours.

Chapter Fifteen

Midnight approached. Anthony had tried his hardest to get Adam to leave, but he wouldn't. He'd stand by Abi, until her very last minutes. They watched as Michael returned. Watched as he removes his pants, and noticed him rub a hand up his hard cock. "Like it, Adam. Are you this big? Bet you aren't."

Abi lay there, she's aware of what's coming. Prayed Adam had left, she didn't want him to remember her like this.

Adam must remember the happy times. Nearly over she thought, I won't suffer much longer. One more thing to get through.

Michael positioned himself above Abi? As he bent over, he nibbled her nipples, then bit down hard on one. She bit the inside of her cheek, to prevent any sounds. She wouldn't give him the pleasure. He squeezed both nipples hard and twisted them, then kissed her hard on the mouth. His lips were hard and cold. One hand moved to between her legs, and he rubbed her clit. He stopped, and she could feel him at her entrance. He pushed himself slightly in, pulled out again, and then slammed into her hard. She cries out, couldn't help herself. The next thrust took him right up to the hilt. Oh, god it hurt, she let the tears fall. He kept slamming into her, harder and harder. Repeatedly. She could feel the bruising developing, felt herself tear. "Adam I'm so sorry," she whispered. His finger found her clit again, while he's still penetrating her. Her body trembled. No, she couldn't, not with him. The sensation built up, as he rubbed and slammed into her. The next time he bit her breasts hard, she cried out as she climaxed. He followed her, and his seed flowed inside her. Michael pulled out, and they noticed the blood on his cock, Abi's blood and saw it trickle out of her. But it wasn't over. Michael flipped her over on to her stomach and raped her again. He came and let his seed fill her yet again. They

118

watched as her eyes turned dull and lifeless, as her mind shattered, unable to take any more. But he kept going. Abi's rape continued. Michael took her from in front and behind.

They lost count how many times he took her, each time she lost more blood. Sometimes he stopped, kicked her a few times, as his cock sagged slightly, but after leaving the room for fifteen minutes or so he returned. Hard again. Eventually, his cock softened completely, and he stopped. He stood and sneered at the camera. "Adam, she really is still quite divine, I'm all spent. Were you counting, I was. Made it eleven times. Eleven times I fucked her, eleven times my seed went into her. Jack, enjoy the last memories of her, I'll return her very, very soon. I'll make her death quick. They watched as he dressed. The last thing they saw was Michael's face as he pulled down the camera.

Nausea overwhelmed Adam, he rushed outside and vomited. After he'd collapsed against the wall, he lets his tears out. His Abi raped that many times. The last thing she'd remember was that. He saw her eyes, she'd gone. She may still be breathing, but her mind had died.

Anthony followed him and gave him time, as he sat next to his brother. He didn't say anything, Adam wasn't ready to talk. Anthony sat and waited.

"She's gone," Adam eventually said. "Her eyes were lifeless. Abi may still be breathing, but she's gone. Why? Why did he have to be so rough? Wasn't once enough? Eleven times Anthony. Thank god, she shattered after the second. Thank god, she doesn't know how many times, and will never know."

Anthony put his arm around Adam and held him while his brother's tears fell. Michael had been rough, too rough. They'd all seen how hard he'd slammed into Abi, and saw the blood when he came out. Knew how much it would have hurt. But to keep going like he did? Totally unnecessary. Anthony didn't want to think about the internal damage. "Adam, she's in a better place now, she won't ever know what's happened. Her mind will block it out. However long he leaves her, before killing her, she won't be suffering."

Anthony knew it was no consolation to Adam. He would remember what happened for eternity. That type of thing never went away. "She was happy with you Adam, that kept her going. It may still do."

Adam lifted his head. "How? He won't keep her alive now. You heard him, he's spent. He's torn her apart, you saw the blood. She can't recover from that. No one could."

"There's hope as long as her body doesn't turn up. Without the video link now, we don't know what his plans are. Adam, I saw the look on his face. He was enjoying himself, climaxed every time. He may not be finished with her." Anthony voiced what everyone else thought. Michael succeeded in making Abi climax. The one thing they didn't think he'd manage. Anthony's gut feeling thought that it might not be over. Abi may still be found, but only God knew what state she'd be in.

Nat broke down. She stayed and watched for Abi's sake. With each rape case, she'd worked, Nat thought she'd seen it all, but Michael had been extremely rough, much more then he needed to be. Frankie walked over to her and rubbed her back. She turned and cried into his shoulder.

"Hush, Nat, it's over. That's the worst thing to watch, a friend having to go through that. He'll return her to us soon."

"Frankie what if he doesn't? You saw him, he was enjoying himself. Eleven times Frankie, eleven bloody times. Wasn't once enough?"

"He's done what he planned to do, broken Abi and Jack. Not to mention Adam. Then there's the rest of us. He's done so much more damage than he originally planned to. He can't make it any worse." He glanced over at Jack. Andrew kept him company, both distraught. "We have to live with that memory. All of us, but Abi won't. That's the main thing here. Abi. She shattered after the second time. Her mind wouldn't have registered the rest. She's in a better place now, he can't hurt her anymore."

Nat knew what Frankie meant. Abi was the main thing here. She might be bruised, battered, and now repeatedly raped, but she would never know it. The damage he'd done, Nat knew he would have broken her a long time ago, but Abi, she'd held on right to the end.

*****

Michael sat on his stool and waited. The moment she'd shattered, would never be forgotten. The moment her eyes went lifeless, he knew he would continue. Good, he thought. He sat there for a couple of hours, watched her, waited. Wondered if Abi would recover. He hoped she did. She'd proved she could fight, but could she remain strong? Eventually, it paid off. Abi began to move. Her eyes focused. She started to hyperventilate, as she remembered. Her mind screamed rape. She felt the bruising and the violation. She thought back to when she was fifteen, he'd assaulted her then. Done similar things to her, and she'd fought to stay alive. Her mind began to recover. No, she won't give up, couldn't. Adam, he'll still want her, he loved her. She'd heard him say he'd wait. She turned her head and spotted Michael.

He smiled at her. "Abi, you're as good as I remember. We had a lovely audience, including Adam. You turned off after the second time, missed the other nine. Eleven times Abi, eleven times I fucked you. You've become a screamer. Tell me, was the orgasm as good for you? I was going to kill you, but..." he trailed off as he stood. Knelt over her and placed a hand on her stomach. "I've kept a date of your periods over the last couple of months. I chose last night for a reason, it was the best time for you to ovulate. Jack's first grandchild could be mine. "

Abi paled, pregnant by him. No, please god, no. She remembered her test results. The chances of her becoming pregnant were highly unlikely. She couldn't help but laugh.

"What's so funny, Abi?"

She stared back at him. "I can't get pregnant, you made sure of that when I was fifteen."

"But Abi, does Jack and Adam know that? You've seen how good I am at fake photos."

121

She went even whiter. No, she'd told Nat and Julian. They would tell her father and Adam, but this meant he didn't plan on killing her, not yet. She could play along and stay alive. Give Frankie a longer to find her. "Maybe not, they don't know I got tested."

"Have to go, sweetheart. I've got plans to make. You can't have a baby in a damp old basement."

Abi stared at the ceiling. Eventually, she got herself back into a sitting position. The stab wound still hurt. She placed her hand on her stomach and prayed she wasn't pregnant. She closed her eyes, eleven times. She probably was.

*****

It's been two weeks since Abi's rape, and Frankie couldn't understand why her body hadn't turned up. With no more contact from Michael, they'd no idea what he was doing. The camera feed no longer existed either. It had hit the station hard. Abi was well liked, and her rape would upset everyone. Most officers, regardless of rank, continued to search, but they were running out of places to look.

Nat walked in. "Adam's back on duty today."

Frankie thought it had been too soon, but Adam said he couldn't stay at home. Needed something to get his mind off Abi. The rape had hit him the hardest, so he'd gone back to New York for a week. Adam's family supported him. His father, Samuel, tried to help the best he could. He'd rung Frankie, asked to be kept informed. Frankie agreed, but Abi seemed to be lost forever. Samuel informed Frankie that Adam might transfer back to New York, as he'd spoken to his old captain. He'd been surprised to see him return. Adam had merely said he needed to be close to Abi, wasn't ready to give her up. Told Frankie that he wouldn't give up on Abi, not until her body turned up. Andrew and Anthony had gone back to New York too. The whole business had hit the family hard. Jack only just managed to keep it together. Without Abi's body, everyone wondered what Michael was up to. He'd planned to rape and then kill her. He'd promised to return her body and yet, still nothing. Frankie turned to Nat. "What's he doing? Why hasn't her body turned up? He promised to return her."

Nat wondered that too. "No idea, but I don't like it. Michael's too quiet, not gloating. Why?"

"He's planning something, has to be. Damn it, doesn't he think he's done enough damage. What else could he do?"

"Whatever it is, it won't be good. I've asked the watch commander to put Adam on desk duties for the week. Break him back in slowly. I'm surprised he's staying in LA."

"So am I, thought he'd stay in New York. Guess he's not ready to let her go, but that rape hit him hard. I wish we'd forced him out of the room."

"It's not easy, especially when it's your own fiancé, but I think he needed to see it. Needed to be there for Abi." Nat shook her head. "He was so rough, the amount of blood she lost. He didn't even use a condom. I just hope her death was quick."

"She wouldn't have known. You saw her eyes, Nat. They were lifeless, he'd broken her spirit. Did what he said he'd always do. I've started a nationwide search, but so far no one's seen anything. Even the FBI have taken the case. I don't like how quiet he's being."

"Frankie, what if she's still alive?" Nat voiced her deepest fear.

Frankie had already had the same thought and hoped it wasn't a reality. "Nat, she shattered. You saw her eyes, Abi had gone. If by any chance he hasn't killed her, she'd be an empty shell. Michael couldn't do anything else to her. No, she's dead, we all know it. I wish he'd send her home. And soon, for all our sakes."

Chapter Sixteen

Abi managed to pull herself back up into a sitting position. She was sore all over, but her mind had recovered. She glanced at the stab wound to her abdomen. It wasn't bleeding, and with her being so coherent, chances were it wasn't serious.

It wasn't the first time he'd raped her, even if he was rougher, but she'd recovered once and vowed to do it again. She would play along with his little games; hopefully, the worse was now over, but she knew he was capable of a lot worse, so it probably wasn't. If Michael wanted a baby, then he must treat her better. Look after her. She'd bide her time because at some point he would make a mistake. She smiled, she's thinking like a cop again. She could do this. Adam, I'll see you again, we'll be back together, I promise. Her wrists were still wired together, but no rope and no gag. She managed to stand, walk around, even though she was weak, then tried the door. It was locked. No problems, she could wait.

She didn't need to wait long, Michael returned.

"Abi, how bright you're looking, and I've got you a new place to stay. It's all sorted, and we fly out tonight." He pulled out a syringe. "Sorry, I need you asleep, but don't worry it won't harm our baby." He injected her in her arm, and she's soon fast asleep. He picked her up, realised how much weight she'd lost and carried her out to a car. An old Ford Mustang he'd nicked. He's managed to book a medical flight to New York. The sedative will keep her out for 24 hours. By the time she woke up, she would be settled in her new home.

*****

Abi woke confused and lay on a bed. She rolled onto her side and sat up. The room contained a bed, toilet, and sink. She's still naked, but her wrists are no longer wired. Instead, she wore handcuffs that were attached to a long chain. Which in turn was hooked to the wall. She looked back down at her wrists. The wire had dug in profoundly and had left deep wounds, which were painful, and rubbed against the handcuffs, but they gave her more movement. Still trapped, she thought, but bearable. She smiled, she could do this. A key turned in the lock, and Michael entered.

"You're awake, brilliant. Do you like the new place?" He sat next to her and took her wrists. Abi winced in pain. "Sorry about that Abi, I've started you on antibiotics to stop any infection and sutured that wound on your abdomen. It wasn't serious enough to kill you. I need the potential mother of my baby to be healthy now, don't I? The worst is over, I'll take care of the both of you, but there is a condition."

Abi lifted her head and sighed. "What?"

"Well, it's like this. In a couple of weeks, we'll do a pregnancy test. I'll leave you alone until then. I'll supply you with food, you must keep your strength up. If, however, the test is negative, I except full services until you do get pregnant. That means full consent Abi, it won't be rape anymore. Once the baby is born, you'll give me full guardianship. After that, I'll let you go."

"I told you, I can't have children."

"We aren't in LA anymore, I've moved us far away. No one's looking for you as I've convinced them I was going to kill you. If you fail to conceive, then I'll just keep going. I'll also keep the other deal. You have enough and beg me to kill you, I will. It's a win, win situation for you. Give me a baby, I let you go. Die, I let you go."

"What if I don't agree?"

"It'll be rape, and it'll be rough. Agree, and I'll be gentle. I'm getting that baby Abi, the choice in how it happens is down to you. I'll let you have a couple of hours to consider my offer. Either way, your old life is over."

Michael left. Abi felt persecuted. She couldn't give herself to him, but if she didn't the alternative was unbearable. Continued rape would happen anyway, whether she agreed or not. Maybe she could let him touch her, let him do it willingly. If she could make him trust her, she might be able to escape. She's got no choice, she must give consent. Oh God, it's going to be so hard, but with it being her only chance to get home, she needed to agree. She would have two weeks to prepare herself. Two weeks of freedom. She lay back down and decided to rest before he returned.

Abi woke as Michael came back. He sat down on the bed, next to Abi and gently rubbed her leg. "Well Abi, what's it to be?"

"You've given me no choice." She felt fifteen again, he'd given her the same deal then. Rape or consent.

Michael grinned. "You made the right decision." He stroked her face, bent down and kissed her hard on the mouth. His lips were cold and dry. "You made the right choice, it won't be so bad."

He repeated and left her again. She continued to lie there. What had she done?

*****

The two weeks passed, and Michael kept his promise not to touch her. They sat on the bed and watched the pregnancy test, she'd just done. Her hopes fell, as it turned negative.

"Prepare yourselves Abi, we start tonight," Michael said, as he left.

Abi trembled, part of her hoped it would be positive. She lay down and tried to meditate. She lost track of time, but as it began to go dark Michael returned. He's naked and already hard. He climbed over Abi and positioned himself at her entrance. As he pushes forward, she tensed and began to fight him.

"Abi, you gave full consent. Relax, you'll enjoy it more."

She stopped fighting and went limp. He entered her fully and thrusts gently. In, out, in again and soon her body matched his movements. She feels an orgasm build, and she screamed out as she climaxed. He followed her, and she felt the warmth of his seed inside her. He rolled them over, pulled her into a tight embrace and nibbled her ear. His cock was still within her. "Wasn't so bad now, was it? See how gentle I can be? Probably better than Adam."

Abi tensed at Adam's name and wondered how he's doing. I'll see you soon, she thought. I'm still alive, still breathing, I promise I'll

126

return home. God knows what state I'll be in, but I need to feel you hold me again. Tell me I'm safe. She sensed Michael as he fell to sleep, then relaxed and drifted off herself.

Abi woke as dawn rose, and felt Michael's cock harden inside of her. He began to thrust. They climaxed together. Abi lost count of many times they did it. Day in, day out, and several times every day. Before she realised it, another two weeks were gone, and they're staring at another pregnancy test. Negative again.

*****

Abi's lost track of time. They'd done several tests, and all were negative. Michael was still gentle with her, which made it bearable. She's always handcuffed, and he only fed her a minimal amount of food. Michael returned, and she looked up.

"Abi, pregnancy test time again. I've been keeping an eye on you. Do you know that you've missed your last two periods? It might be good news this time."

She did the test, and they waited. Negative. Michael glanced at her. "Never mind, I've still got plenty of stamina. I can go another round. I'll let you rest, but I'll be back later, as hard as ever."

Abi didn't know how much more she could stand. Michael might still be gentle, but Abi could tell he wanted to lose control. Wished he could be rougher with her. Once or twice he'd slipped and been rougher. Her breasts were hurting from the bruising and bite marks. As she couldn't loosen the chain, Abi knew there was little chance of escape. He'd really thought it through again. She lay down and thought of Adam. She now knew she would never see him again. No baby, no freedom. That was the deal. Maybe death would be better. No, not yet. She could take another round. She knew her periods had stopped. Knew it was more than likely down to stress and the weight had dropped off her. The meals he gave her were small, but enough so she could survive. He'd told her she would get bigger meals when she was pregnant, but she knew that would never happen. It was slim to start with, but with the condition she

127

was in now, it'll be impossible. She heard Michael's approach and readied herself.

Chapter Seventeen

One-year post car explosion

Jack headed over to see Adam. It's been a year since Abi was abducted and her body still hadn't turned up. Nor had they heard from Michael. Jack couldn't help but wonder what his brother was up too. He arrived at Adam's apartment, with something to tell him. "Adam, you know it's been a year since Michael took Abi."

Adam nodded, he knew the date well.

"He's not going to return her body, he would have done it by now."

"Why?" Adam interrupted. "Why hasn't he? What's he got to gain by it? It doesn't make any sense."

"God knows Adam. I'm arranging a remembrance for her next Saturday. We all need the closure, to put her to rest. It's the only way that we'll be able to carry on. I know it's hard Adam, especially for you, but she wouldn't want you to keep suffering. She'd want you to continue living."

"I know, but it's difficult. Knowing what Michael did to her, what her last few moments were. Part of me glad she's gone, that he killed her. I'm not convinced she'd ever recover from it."

"Come to the remembrance, Adam. She'll want you to." Jack got ready to leave. "Please come."

*****

Jack's booked a function room for the remembrance. As he glanced around, he realized how decent the turnout was, and he moved to the front of the room.

"I'll like to welcome everyone here today. We all know why we are gathered. Abi was taken from us a year ago. She may no longer be among us, but I know her spirit lives on. Today is a celebration of her life. I want you all to remember the first time you saw her, the first time her light arrived in your life. The happy memories, not her last." He paused, looked around and spotted Adam at the back. He smiled, glad he'd come. "Abi was a happy child, didn't let anything faze her and enjoyed life. Some of you know how much time she spent at the station. Helping, even if it was only filing records. I was a proud man the moment she put on the police uniform. The moment she followed in my footsteps. I always knew she would. It was obvious from how many questions she asked. Always jumping on officers, asking what they were doing. Curious was her middle name." He raised his glass. "A toast to Abi. May she now be at peace."

A round of cheers went up. "To Abi," everyone shouted.

Adam walked up next. Knew he had to say a speech, say his goodbyes to his beloved fiancé. "I have no idea why I decided to transfer to LA. I put it down to boredom and needed a change. My family thought I was mad." He heard his brothers laugh. They were both here, along with his parents. "But the day I walked into the station, I saw the reason why. Abi. Even better I got partnered with her. We hit it off at once, and I knew she was the girl for me. I never expected her to agree to a date, let alone to marry me. I felt like the luckiest man alive, even if she did make me think she was going to say no."

That brought another round of laughter. Everyone knew about that photo, courtesy of his brothers.

"I only knew her for a short length of time, but she was the light of my world, and I still love her with all of my heart." He walked away, unable to contain his tears.

Nat pulled him into a hug. "Well done. Abi would be so proud to hear that."

Jack watched as many more people made speeches, all of them saying how much Abi meant to them. Officers left, and others arrived as shifts changed. He'd hired the hall until the evening, giving everyone chance to come. A large photo of Abi, from when she graduated from the academy, was at the front. Her smile contagious, when everyone looked at it. Her smile, the one thing he wanted to see again. Hear her laugh, hold her when she cried. No longer would that possible, but he'll have the memories. Michael couldn't take them away, no matter how hard he tried. The memories everyone would share today, were permanent. His brother couldn't make them forget those. Never.

Jack didn't see a man enter and stay at the back.

Michael smiled. So many happy people, all remembering Abi and sharing their happy memories. She still wasn't pregnant, and he knew she would become depressed soon. It wouldn't be long before she begged to die, knew he didn't have much longer with her, but he still had time to cause trouble. He'd dyed his hair and was wearing coloured contact lenses. Certain no one would recognise him, he headed to the front. He stood in front of the large photo and pulled out a small picture of Abi, and placed it behind. That was his happy memory of Abi. A photo of her pregnant, how he loved photoshop, he'd even left a message on the back. He smiled as he went, and knew it would be found when they tidied up. Michael grinned as he thought of the distress it would cause.

*****

Anthony and Andrew had volunteered to clear everything away.

"Decent turnout," Anthony said.

"Yes," replied Andrew. "So many lovely memories, Abi would be proud. I bet she's smiling down on us, probably laughing too."

"Oh, I just bet she is. It's the type of thing she'd enjoy." Anthony sighed. "I wish we hadn't needed a remembrance in the first place. Why the hell didn't he return her body? I just can't get my head around it."

"Me neither, it doesn't make any sense. Michael has managed to destroy everyone, he knew we were watching. He hasn't even been in touch, part of me wishes he would. At least we could try and get some answers. I'm surprised he's not gloating."

They finished stacking the chairs, and Anthony headed towards the front. The photo of Abi was going to the station for a while, with the remembrance book, allowing people to still enter their memories. Jack had agreed for Adam to have the book when he was ready. As he picked up the photo, he noticed something fall from behind it. When he picked it up, his eyes widened in shock. "Shit," he couldn't believe what he saw.

Andrew glanced over at him and noticed how Anthony had gone pale. "Anthony?" He asked, as a chill trickling down his spine. He didn't like the way his brother looked and dreaded the answer.

"The bastard was here. The bloody bastard was here." He hesitated. "Andrew, she's alive."

"What?" Andrew walked over to his brother, saw the photo, and went faint himself. They both couldn't help but stare at the picture. It apparently was Abi, naked, lying on a bed and handcuffed to the wall. Her eyes open, precisely focused and directed straight at the camera.

"Her eyes," Andrew said. "Look at her eyes, how bright they are. He hasn't broken her, she's still in there."

"Andrew, there's something else," Anthony said quietly.

Andrew studied the photo. "Bloody hell. Tell me I'm seeing things." He'd noticed her stomach, no longer flat, but round. Round as in heavily pregnant. "Shit," Andrew continued. "This will kill Adam. The bastards kept her alive. Wants to breed from her." He turned the photo over. There were strands of blonde hair taped to the back and the time stamp was only a few days ago. They read the message.

'Hope you enjoy my memory of Abi, I just couldn't miss today. Jack's first grandchild is due any day.
Tell Adam, she's really enjoying her exercise. Screams my name every single time, even has multiple orgasms.
Can't wait until the baby's dropped and I can start all over again.'

They both dashed out to the car and sped directly to the station. Frankie noticed them and called them into his office. "What's wrong?"

Andrew threw the photo onto the desk. "Michael was there."

Frankie glanced down, then collapsed into his chair. "No, it can't be." His eyes widened as the shock ripped through him. "Pregnant. Oh, hell."

He rang Nat. "Get over here, now!" he ordered before he hung up.

Nat picked up her phone when it rang and heard Frankie's message. What the hell? She drove over to the station and entered his office. The expression on Anthony's and Andrew's faces filled her with concern. "What's wrong? What's happened?" Why did she get the feeling, she didn't want to know?

Frankie pointed to the photo. "The boys found this when tiding up. The bastard was there."

Nat picked up the photo. "Abi. She's alive," she breathed. Then suddenly. "My god, no! She looked up at them and remembered what Abi had told her. "It's not true, she isn't pregnant."

Frankie raised his eyebrows. "Really, because it looks pretty damning if you ask me."

Nat shook her head. "I spoke to her, remember, the night I sent her home early. She told me that she had concerns about conceiving. She'd seen Julian the week before, and he'd given her the test results the afternoon of the explosion. She had serious scarring around her uterus and ovaries, from Michael's previous attack. The stab wounds were deep. Julian told her straight that the chances of conceiving were slim, and she had an even less chance of carrying full term. I'll get Matt to check this, we know Michael's good at faking photos." She took the photo and headed downstairs.

Matt saw her approach. "Back in the lowly levels, are you?" His jaw tensed when he spotted her expression. "Nat, what's happened?"

She showed him the photo.

"Abi? How?"

133

"Michael left it at the remembrance, and we need to know if it's real. Can you keep it quiet? We'd rather Adam and Jack didn't hear about this development, not until we know for certain. Can you also pass the hair strands to Josie? Ask her to test it against Abi's DNA, if she can."

"No problems. I'll let you know asap."

Nat went back upstairs, she's scared for Abi. Michael's had her for so long, even if the photo turned out to be fake. She re-entered the office. "Matt's working on it. He'll get Josie to do a DNA match if she can."

Frankie nodded. "Let's call it a night. I doubt any of us will sleep, but we need to try. Meet back up here tomorrow at 10am."

They all went their separate ways. All they can do now is wait.

Chapter Eighteen

The following morning the two brothers met their parents for breakfast. Samuel noticed both his sons were quiet and distracted. Probably from yesterday's remembrance, but he's not entirely sure. He waited until Martha left. "What's up with the two of you?"

They quickly glanced at each other. "Nothing," Andrew answered.

"Out with it, something's going on between you two."

Anthony inhaled deeply. "Michael was there yesterday, he's left us a message. Abi might be alive."

The shock of his sons' sentence hit him. "What type of message?"

"A photo. We're waiting for forensics before anything is announced. The last we want to do is to upset Adam if it's not true."

Samuel shook his head. "The lad's been through enough. Why's Michael still doing this?"

None of them could answer, and the brothers got ready to leave. "Dad, we'll keep you informed. We're meeting the Captain this morning to discuss our next move." Anthony said as they went.

The brothers went straight into the office and waited with Frankie and Nat. Matt walked in, and they all looked at him. Everyone prayed that photo wasn't real. Their thoughts on what Abi would be going through if it was.

"The photo itself is real. It is Abi lying on a bed, but he's photoshopped another body onto her. Done a damned decent job too. Josie's rushing the DNA through. She may have it later."

They all signed in relief. Abi wasn't pregnant.

"Are you saying she's alive?" Frankie asked.

Matt confirmed it. "The date stamp is real. So, she was when it was taken a few days ago, but Josie should be able to confirm it."

"Thanks, Matt," Frankie dismissed him as Josie walked in.

"I can confirm what Matt's told you. It is Abi's hair, and when the hair was plucked she was alive."

"How old's the sample?" Nat asked.

"I'll say it was taken a couple of days ago."

"Alive," Nat said. "He's kept her alive. After all this time, why tell us now? We have to tell Adam, we have no choice."

Frankie agreed. "Let's get this over with."

Frankie got straight to the point when Jack answered. "Jack are you meeting Adam later?"

"Yes, for lunch, he's coming around midday."

"Keep him there. I'm sending Nat over to speak to you both." He hung up. "Nat take it easy with them, especially Adam. I've spoken to Julian, and he confirms what you send. She's highly unlikely to become pregnant. Her injuries were too serious."

Nat left, she's got a bit of time to kill before midday. Informing Adam and Jack of this development wouldn't be easy, and she wasn't looking forward to telling them.

*****

Nat reached Jack's place shortly before Adam. They waited patiently until Adam arrived. Jack let him in, and Adam's surprised to see Nat. She told them both to sit down. This would hit both hard, and she took a deep breath before beginning. "I need to tell you something, but it's not exactly good news." She paused and glanced at the two of them. "Oh, to hell with it. Abi's alive, or she was a few days ago." Nat saw the moment her words sunk in, as the shock passed over their faces.

"Alive?" Adam responded first. "How?"

"Michael must have been at the remembrance. Anthony found a photo when tidying up. Michael must have left it, there's no other explanation. I need to show you, but please remember how good he is at faking photos. Matt's pulled it apart. It is Abi, there's no

136

doubt on that, but the rest is fake. I beg you to remember that." She pulled out a copy, they'd left the message off the back on purpose. What was the use of upsetting them more than necessary? She handed it over and waited.

Both men studied it, and Adam noticed it first. "My god, no. Please, it can't be."

Jack then saw it, and he closed his eyes briefly as nausea passed through him.

Nat took the photo back. "She's not pregnant, as I said, Matt's pulled it apart and proved it. Adam, Abi was concerned she couldn't have children after her last encounter with Michael. She had Julian run tests, and he confirmed it was highly unlikely she would ever conceive. Michael's causing trouble again."

Jack stared at her. "Where is she?"

"We don't know, but he's moved her. We still don't have any leads, none what so ever. But while there's a chance she's alive, we may find her."

They took it better then Nat thought they would. Hope had flared again, but with no idea where she was, it wouldn't last long. "We're notifying all the national police forces and the FBI. If he's out there, we'll find him. Michael has to make a mistake." She left them and headed back to the station. Adam's brothers were flying back to New York tonight. She hoped they have better luck.

Chapter Nineteen

Andrew's back in New York and things haven't been going too well. His captain allowed him to continue with the investigation, but nothing's come up. Michael sent that photo, Abi's alive, but where? He's on his way to Anthony who's at his firm's offices and hoped he's fared better.

Andrew went straight in on arrival. "Anthony, please give me some good news. I'll take anything at the moment."

"Wish I could and believe me I've called in every favour. Michael's disappeared into thin air, yet again. I'd love to know how he's doing it."

"Wouldn't everyone. Abi must be going stir crazy. I wonder if she knows his latest trick."

"Andrew, that photo, what if that's what's he's really trying to do. God help her if that's his plan. The number of times he must have raped her over the last year..." Anthony didn't want to think about it himself.

"Trying not to think about it. Abi's never going to trust any man again, let alone be intimate with one. Adam will have his work cut out for him. Hell, they'll probably never get back together."

"Christ, that'll kill him. I can't stop thinking about Abi's eyes. How bright they were." He sat up suddenly. "Shit, that's it, her eyes."

"What?"

"They were bright, shiny."

"Lost me."

"If you'd repeatedly been raped by some bastard who wants you pregnant, your eyes wouldn't be bright. You'll be depressed, almost suicidal. But Abi, she doesn't look it. In fact, I'd say the opposite. She's fighting him; still fucking fighting him."

"Yeah, but you saw the chain, she can't go anywhere."

138

"No, but if she's a good girl, behaves herself, maybe he lets her out."

Andrew thought about it. "It's asking a lot, she'd have to be willing. Is Abi capable of lying there and simply taking it? Is she that strong?"

"Question is, can she play him at his own game and win? I'd say she's trying, but where's he keeping her? We need something to break and soon."

*****

Andrew and Anthony had no idea, they'd hit the nail on the head. Abi tried her hardest to behave and still fought to return home. She never truly relaxed, couldn't with Michael. Oh, he kept it gentle most of the time and made her climax, but she only survived by letting her mind go blank.

They're sat on the bed and staring at yet another negative test. Michael left while Abi collapsed back onto the bed. Another two weeks of him touching her. She couldn't do it anymore, she's tired. Tonight, she thought, it must be tonight. Michael had started to let her out after every test. Gave her a perfectly cooked meal. Yeah, he kept the cuffs on, but she could move around the house. She's used the time carefully. Used the main bathroom, been in the kitchen. In fact, she'd found a reason to investigate most of the rooms. Knew where all the doors and windows were found. It used to be a derelict house, she knew that, but Michael decided he needed more light. He'd fitted a back door and removed a few boards from the rear windows. The front still seemed derelict. She smiled, tonight she's damn well getting out.

Abi waited patiently for Michael to return and didn't have to wait long. She kept quiet as he removed the chain and she followed him to the table. She would give him credit he could cook, and she did enjoy these meals. After all, she only got bread and water during the two weeks of sex. She finished her meal and smiled seductively at him. "Can I use the bath?"

Michael grinned at her. "Certainly, my dear. Go and get yourself cleaned up. I want you sparkling for my grand entrance later."

She walked off towards the bathroom, but once out of sight changed direction to the back door. She's already discovered where the key was kept. She stayed quiet and winced at the slight squeak the door made when it opened. She smelt the fresh air, felt the rain on her skin and couldn't help but smile. So far so good. She took a few more steps, the ground dug into her bare feet, and she took time to make a quick glance around. Trees surrounded the house. Damn it, she thought, no neighbors. Abi walked as fast as she could, wincing every so often as she stepped on stones and pebbles. As she reached the trees, her heart began to soar. All she needed to do was to find somewhere to hide for a bit.

Abi didn't hear someone approach her from behind. Not until she felt his arms around her. She screamed and kicked at him.

"Bitch. Think I didn't know your little plan. Keep me happy, behave yourself and run for freedom. I've enjoyed our little banging sessions, but feel they're ending. I'm fed up with being gentle."

Michael dragged her back to the house and threw her on to the bed. She's surprised when he removed the handcuffs, but not for long. He picked up a small roll of barbed wire and wrapped her wrists tightly. He wrapped them in a figure of eight, so wire dug into both sides of her wrists. Abi bit the inside of her cheek as she tried not to cry out. Panic set in and she knew tonight she would be killed. Tonight, one way or the other, it'll be over. She'd be free. The thought began to calm her.

Michael noticed the calmness settle and put his face directly in front of hers. "Think I'm going to kill you. Oh Abi, you'll wish I would. By the time I'm finished what I did before will be nothing." He stroked her breasts. "These beauties will be battered." He moved his hand between her legs. "This will be shredded to bits. You won't ever be able to have another man inside of you." He pulled her to the floor and picked up a baseball bat. She screamed out in pain, with every hit and kick she received. Abi knew instantly when some of her ribs broke because her breathing became painful. Michael pulled her up by the hair and slammed her head against the wall;

140

then he bent her over the bed face down. She heard him remove his pants.

"Ready Abi? I've made myself extra-large for you this evening. You'll scream, but definitely not in pleasure." He put one hand on the back of her neck, and Abi felt him when he positioned himself. Her breathing increased, and she started to panic. He slammed into her hard and quick, and she screamed as she felt the tearing. Michael began to thrust, and the pain got unbearable for Abi. He lifted her hips and slammed in again, this time right up to the hilt. Abi couldn't contain her tears any longer and repeatedly screamed with every thrust. She sensed when he was close to climaxing, and as he pounded into her one last time, he pushed her head into the bed. She couldn't breathe, her head went light, and she knew it's time to let go. As the darkness began to descend, Michael turned her over. "Oh no Abi, not yet. You don't get to die just yet."

When Abi opened her eyes, she spotted the blood on his cock immediately. Her blood. Michael dragged her into a kneeling position and put himself in her mouth. He thrust so profoundly that she gaged. He kept going until he came again and forced Abi to swallow. When he moved away, she fell to the ground. He kicked her several more times. Stamped on her arms and legs. He left, and when he returned she heard him place something on the sink. He pulled her back onto the bed face down. He didn't stop. Abi felt him pounding into her intensely. Every time he climaxed, he pushed her head into the bed. Finally, his weight moved off her, and he turned her over. Once more she saw the blood on him. His cock was covered in it.

Michael noticed her look. "Large isn't it. I bet Adam's small and doesn't fill you up. Well, he won't get the chance now, will he? You're still bleeding." He placed his hand between her legs and moved it in front of her eyes. Her blood dropped off his hand onto her skin which made her feel sick. She closed her eyes, with a bit of luck she would bleed out. "I'm experienced at causing pain, guess you know that, now don't you? However, I'm not finished."

Her uncle grabbed her wrists and pulled them sharply apart with a twist. She screamed once more as blood ran down her arms from where the wire lacerated her skin. Michael left the room. Abi's eyes widened in pure fear when he re-entered. The whip he held frightened her, but it was the tips that terrified her. It was leather with five strands, and each strand had a metal barb. Her heart pounded as he flipped her onto her stomach.

"I think we'll start with fifty lashes." He said quite calmly.

Abi was anything but calm, she screamed as every single lash shredded her. Her back bled from every strike. The pain vibrated through her. Finally, he stopped and raped her once more. With each thrust, he pressed on her freshly, damaged back. She cried out when he turned her onto her back.

"I've gone all soft, so another fifty I think." He flipped her back onto her stomach and picked up the whip.

Abi continued to scream. Please let it be over soon, she prayed. She took every lash and dreaded the damage it would cause. Eventually, she realised he's stopped. He turned her over onto her back. Abi hoped he'd finished, but he hadn't. He bent over her and bit down hard on each nipple which made them bleed. Then several move bites, around her breasts and neck. She couldn't do anything when he picked up the bat, he hit her hard over her chest and rammed it into her stomach. She felt her legs getting separated and could do nothing as he plunged the bat into her. She let out a blood-curdling scream as it went full force up to her cervix. When he pulled it out, he plunges it in again, but this time he twisted it. Abi knew she was severely ripped, as she felt the blood pour out. Michael stopped and studied her, but he's not quite finished.

Abi watched him move towards her head. This is it, she thought, now I finally die. But it wasn't to be.

Michael placed the bat end down against her throat. He lifted it and slammed it down fast. Abi couldn't scream, her throat felt crushed. Breathing became hard and extremely painful.

Michael threw the bat on the floor and slammed his fist into her face several times. Finally, she felt him stop.

"Oh Abi, it wasn't so good for you this time, but I've had so many orgasms I'm knackered. Sorry love, but your internal injuries are still bleeding, quite severely." He sneered at her as he lays a knife by her side. "I'll give you twenty-four hours to use that knife. Then I'll be back, and we'll do it all over again. I might even be bigger, and I will be fucking that beautiful, little ass of yours."

Abi heard him leave. Her throat sore, breathing painful and every inch of her hurt. She managed to roll onto her side, into a ball. The tears all spent, she let the darkness take her.

Chapter Twenty

Anthony and Andrew still weren't having any luck. Both have been working hard over the past few days, contacting all their informers, yet again. They'd even managed to put out a reward for any useful information, but zilch. They were back in Anthony's office, both felt deflated. They've exhausted every angle. They just sat there in silence, their thoughts on Abi. They didn't even acknowledge Steve when he walked in. Didn't notice the expression on his face.

"Guys, I think I may have something."

They both glanced at him when he continued, their faces full of lost hope.

"You know I did that surveillance work, at a small airport out of town a few months ago."

"Yeah," Anthony answered. "You were waiting for a plane coming in with a load of drugs. Good bust if I remember right."

"I've looked back over the photos. Don't ask me why something didn't feel right at the time. I've checked all the flights for the week I was there. Not just the ones the client wanted. There was one that caught my eye. A small medical plane. Apparently, it was on a private hire. The pilot was asked to fly from LA to New York. The client asked specifically for an overnight flight. I've spoken to the pilot, he told me it was a man with a woman. She was out cold. I've shown him a picture of Abi."

Both brothers held their breath and sat up straight. Hope shone on their faces.

"He's confirmed it was Abi. Michael flew her to New York."

Anthony reacted first. "Bloody hell, she's been right under noses, but he could have her anywhere."

"Nope," Steve continued. "The pilot remembers the flight, as he remembers how severely injured the woman was. Said her robe

144

came open and he saw how badly bruised she was. Had some nasty cuts and a serious looking wound on her stomach. There was a private transport vehicle waiting for them, and he remembers the company. I've spoken to them. They remember the call, thought it was odd. They didn't go to a hospital, but to a derelict house. The man told them that the women was severely depressed and had to be kept sedated during transit. Told me that the house was being turned into a rehabilitation centre, but due to the nature of the women's mental state, they needed her in before they were officially open." He placed a note on the table, with an address wrote on it.

The brothers' smiles grew. Things were looking a hell of a lot better.

"Steve, I'm giving you a pay rise and promoting you," Anthony said excitedly. "It's the bloody breakthrough we needed."

Andrew jumped out of his chair. "You two coming?"

All three headed to Steve's car. He'd already been to the address and knew where it was.

*****

Abi woke up as dusk fell. The pain still ripped through her, and she spied the knife when she opened her eyes. When she picked it up, the movement in her wrists caused the barbed wire to dig in deeper. She didn't care, a bit more pain wouldn't make any difference. She rolled on to her back. Another night, she couldn't do another night like that. Her body couldn't cope with it. No one's looking for her. If she didn't know where she was, how the hell could anyone else find her? She'd held on for so long, but these injuries she knew she would never recover from. She held the knife over her stomach. "Adam, please forgive me," she whispered as she plunged it into her. Once more, pain tore through her, and she let out one final scream.

*****

Andrew's out the car first. Both brothers drew their guns. Steve stood back. This was their turn, he'd follow them in later. Andrew broke the door down. They searched each room together, but only a few rooms looked like they'd been used. Eventually, they went into a spare bedroom. They noticed untouched bed, but they spotted the baseball bat and whip.

"Shit, I'm hoping that's not Abi's blood," Anthony said, but deep down he knew it would be. A chill trickled down his spine. There was an awful lot of blood, and he'd noticed the metal barbs on the whip. "That whip will have ripped her skin to bits."

Andrew searched around, and after he'd picked up a small bucket, he called over to Anthony. "Think that idea we had could have been right."

Anthony joined him and closed his eyes after he'd seen the contents. "Pregnancy tests. They all seem negative. Bloody hell, she's not had it easy. Come on, we'll get forensics in here later, I think there's only one more room left." They went back out onto the landing, both heard the scream at the same and rushed towards the last room.

Anthony pushed the door. "Abi, no!" He yelled when he spotted the knife and saw her hands push it in further. Her eyes were closed, but he noticed the smile on her face.

Abi heard Anthony's shout. She smiled as she pushed the knife in further. If she heard Anthony's voice, she must be close to death. She felt someone remove her hand from the knife and the bed sunk as they sat next to her. "You're too late Michael. She managed to whisper. "I can hear Anthony. I'm too close to death for you to hurt anymore." She smiled again, it's nearly over. She would soon be free.

Andrew moved and sat on the other side of the bed. The horror clear on his face, as the brothers stared at Abi. There wasn't a bit of her that wasn't injured. Both noticed the pool of blood between her legs and her breathing's unsteady. Steve's went out and called for an ambulance.

146

"My god," Andrew broke the silence. "What the hell has he done to her? She stabbed herself. If she'd held on a few more minutes, she would have been found."

Anthony turned to face his brother, he'd thought the same. He sat on the other side of the bed, placed a hand gently on her shoulder and tried not to cause Abi any more pain. "Abi, sweetie, can you hear me? It's Anthony, Andrew's here too. Come on baby, you're safe, we have you now. There's an ambulance on the way."

Abi didn't respond.

"Abi, we need you to answer, let us know you can hear us. Please Abi, come back to us. I'm so sorry we didn't find you, but we have you now." He turned to Andrew. "She's giving up. Damn it, we were so close. So bloody close."

Andrew stared down at Abi, as an idea formed. He saw the lost hope on his brother's face. "Let me try something." He can't believe he's going to do this and placed his hand on Abi's other shoulder. "Officer Lawton. It's an offence to ignore a senior officer." He ordered.

Anthony stared at him in disbelief, and he's about to have a go at him for being insensitive when Abi snapped her eyes open.

"Andrew?" She managed to whisper, as her voice broke. "That was low even for you."

The brothers couldn't help but to laugh. Only Abi could make a remark like that when she still had a knife in her.

"I am dreaming? Is it over? Am I dead?" She asked hoarsely due to her damaged throat.

Anthony stroked her shoulder. "No baby, we have you. You're safe. The ambulance will be here soon. We'll get you in and then arrange to fly Adam up."

"Please no, not Adam." Her eyelids felt heavy, so she closed them. "He'll never forgive me for what I've done. I let him do this, I let him rape me, consented. I shouldn't have tried to escape. All he wanted was a baby. Why couldn't I have given him a baby?" Her breathing settled, as she drifted off.

Anthony got Steve back in. They needed photos of the scene. Steve paled when he saw Abi but got the photos. Andrew came

147

back with a blanket and covered her bottom half. They waited until the ambulance arrived and she's taken straight in.

*****

When they arrived, they found Crystal on duty, and she smiled when Andrew entered. "Didn't know you were working tonight?"

"Unofficially," he answered, but Crystal heard the sorrow in his voice.

She spotted Anthony and Steve behind him with the paramedics. Anthony held the person's hand who lay on the stretcher. She recognized the woman and gasped in shock. "Abi! You found her."

Andrew answered. "It's bad Crystal, she'll need a lot of care. She may never recover."

Crystal understood what her partner said. "I'll stay with her. Does Adam know?"

"Not yet, I'll ring Nat. Let her tell him in person, once we know how serious her injuries are."

Crystal followed Abi into the emergency room.

Steve left, he's not needed and wanted to get the photos developed. The police would require the evidence. Andrew had called his captain, and he'd sent a team over to the house.

They took Abi into the operating room. Anthony rang his parents, and they came straight over. All four of them waited for news. Four and a half hours later the doctor, Garth Reeves came and spoke to them.

"Are you here next of kin?" Garth asked.

Anthony spoke for them. "We're her fiancés family. Abi's only family in New York. You can keep us informed until Adam, and her father arrive."

"Her injuries are serious. The stab wound in her abdomen sliced through part of her small intestine, but we've been able to repair it. She has an appalling amount of internal bruising, including her kidneys. Her blood results show that they aren't working at their best. I'm hoping with time the normal function will return once the bruises have subsided. She has eight fractured ribs, but luckily

148

none are displaced. The skin on her back has, to be blunt, been ripped to shreds. It'll heal, but she's going to scar horrendously. Her wrists are also severely injured from the barbed wire used. Her throat is damaged, but she can breathe unaided, and her face will be badly bruised. He hesitated, this would be the hard bit. "She's also been severely raped, and he was rough. She's been severely torn internally, and we've had to repair it. She'll be in pain, in that region, for quite a while. I'll speak directly to her fiancé when he arrives."

"Will she recover?" Anthony needed to know. "I need all the facts when I contact the detective in charge of the case."

"Physical yes, but as I said she'll have numerous scars. Emotionally, I can't say. I'll be honest, those injuries are the worst I have ever seen, and I've seen plenty of severe abuse cases before. I'll be surprised if she recovers enough to resume a normal life. Due to her being abused by a man, I've asked Crystal to be her personal nurse. She's agreed and will stay with her. I'll be her doctor, but I'll ask a female doctor to examine her, when necessary. I doubt she'll let a male touch her for an exceptionally long time."

"Can we see her?" Martha inquired.

The doctor arranged for all four of them to sit with Abi. He's informed them, that they would be keeping her sedated for twenty-four hours.

Samuel held his wife as she cried out when she spotting Abi first. "Find him. Find the bastard who did this. Find him and make him pay. And don't let him have a quick death, make sure he suffers." Samuel ordered his sons. Abi's state shocked him. Only a sadistic bastard could do this. One who had no remorse. None what so ever. "Anthony, when are you calling Nat?"

Anthony checked the time., It's 3am. LA was roughly three hours behind. "It's midnight there, let them have the night. They won't get much sleep for the foreseeable future."

"Here you go, get this into you. I know none of you will leave." Crystal said as she came back and handed them all coffees. She went over to Andrew, who wrapped his arm around her. It would be a long night.

149

They took it in turns to hold Abi's hands. She may be sedated, ·
but they wanted her to know she would be cared for now. Andrew
waited until 10am to ring Nat. It's 7am in LA, and the chances were
Nat's awake.

Nat answered her phone, as she walked into the station. She
couldn't sleep, so decided she'd go and catch up on some
paperwork.
"Andrew, how's it going over in New York?"
"Nat, we have Abi." Andrew got straight to the point.
Nat stopped dead when she entered her office and closed the
door. "Andrew, it's early, but I swear I just heard you say that you
have Abi."
"We do, we found her last night. Nat, she's alive."
"Alive? How?" Surely, she couldn't have heard right.
Andrew took a deep breath. Abi's injuries would hurt Nat too.
"I've got photos of the scene, I've emailed them to you. Nat, it's not
pretty, she's taken one hell of a beating. Michael's raped her worse
than before. Her injuries are horrendous. I'll be truthful, I don't think
she'll recover. Not this time." He hesitated, knew he needed to tell
her everything. "We found her, Nat, just as she stabbed herself."
Nat gasped. No not Abi, she'd been so tough, and held on for so
long. "Thank god you got there in time."
"The doctor says her physical injuries will heal but will scar. It's
her emotional state, that won't. Can you tell Adam? Nat, she
doesn't want to see him, but I know he'll come anyway. Get Jack up
here too. She'll need her dad."
They ended the call. Abi alive? Nat opened her email; the photos
had arrived. Oh God no. She saw Abi's battered body, the blood
between her legs and the knife. Oh Abi, how are you going to
survive this? Andrew was right, she may be breathing, but her life
might be over. She put her head in her hands and cried. Abi, her

friend, a woman who knew how to fight to stay alive, might never let her fiancé, friends, or family back in.

Frankie walked past Nat's office and froze when he saw her crying. Only one thing would upset her this much. Abi. After he'd knocked, he entered. Nat lifted her head.

"What's happened?" Concern laced his voice.

She turned the monitor around, Frankie noticed the photo that Nat had been staring at earlier. "They found her in New York." She said quietly.

"Bloody hell," he collapsed into a chair. Abi, my god what did he do to you? Her last moments must have been awful. Frankie turned back to Nat. "I'll arrange for her body to be flown home." He eventually said.

"That won't be needed."

"It's our case, *we'll* do the investigating. I want to get the bastard myself."

Nat looked at him sadly. "Alive," she managed to say.

"Nat, you're deceiving yourself. Her injuries, loss of blood. For god's sake, she has a knife stuck in her abdomen. It's Michael's way of showing us how he killed her. I'm sorry Nat. I know you two were close, but she's at peace now. Michael can't hurt her anymore."

She shook her head. "Frankie, Michael didn't send them. Andrew did. The boys found her last night. I'm not explaining it well am I?" She began at the beginning, how they had a theory about her consenting. How Steve had figured out where she may be. "They arrived just had she'd stabbed herself."

Frankie stayed quiet and listened, as Nat told him everything. Abi had been in surgery for nearly five hours but remained alive. Andrew sent them a full list of injuries. He shook his head, as the horror crossed his face. "Michael went all out, didn't he? She'll need the support to get through this. Adam will have to be strong for her."

"She doesn't want to see him. Thinks he won't forgive for consenting to it."

151

"Forced consent is still rape, and it won't stop him going. I take it he doesn't know yet?"

"No, nor Jack. Let them have a bit of a lie in, they won't get much rest over the next few days. Adam's on the middle shift. I've left Jack a message to come in at the beginning. Frankie, how do I tell them?"

Frankie moved and sat on the arm of Nat's chair. He held her as she let the tears fall again. He could barely keep them in his self.

*****

Adam entered the station, ready to begin his next shift. He saw Nat in Frankie's office, Jack's there too, and Nat's eyes were red.

Frankie opened the door. "Adam, can we have a word?"

Adam's stomach knotted. Abi, he knew it concerned Abi. Frankie asked him to take a seat. Memories of last year replayed in his mind when he was called in after the car explosion. He turned to Nat. "She's dead, isn't she?" Finally, Abi's at peace.

Nat glanced at Frankie, she couldn't do this. He understood and nodded towards her. "Adam your brothers found Abi last night."

Adam looked at him confused. What? His brothers were here in LA.

At his confused expression, Frankie continued. "Michael moved her to New York, he's held her there for several months. Steve figured it out from some old surveillance photos, he took a couple of months ago. I'll keep it short." He paused when Adam hung his head, convinced Abi's dead. "Adam," Frankie said softly. "She's alive. Abi's alive."

Adam whipped his head up sharply, the disbelief in his eyes. "Alive?"

"Yes, but it's not pretty. Michael gave Abi a damn good beating. Fractured ribs, cuts, bruising." He hesitated and took a deep breath. "Adam, he raped her several times, the last night he was extremely rough. She's severely injured and not just externally. He gave her a choice and left her with a knife. Told her he'd do it all again the next evening unless she killed herself. Your brothers arrived just as she stabbed herself in the abdomen."

Adam's heart pounded, and he let out his tears. Abi, oh god, his Abi forced to kill herself. "Where is she?"

"In the hospital. We are flying up there this evening. All of us." He couldn't bring himself to tell Adam, that she wouldn't see him. He'd heard enough for now. Let him deal with that first.

Chapter Twenty-one

They went straight over to the hospital. Adam spent the night crying at Abi's side. She looked so fragile and pale. Her face battered. The doctor had told them what her injuries were, and he'd felt sick. She'd been torn her apart, literally. He'd been told that the internal scaring would make sexual intercourse painful, if not impossible. They doubted she'd ever recover emotionally, but Adam couldn't give up. While his fiancé breathed, he'd do everything he could to help her. To bring her back to him.

Nat saw the love in Adam's eyes and hoped Abi would change her mind when she woke. She knew Adam would stand by Abi, but would Abi let him. She'd seen the list of her injuries and had spent the night at the hotel crying. No women should have to suffer that. She doubted Abi would ever let a man touch her again. Adam would be devastated, and she hoped Abi would eventually let him back in. They all prayed for her in their own way.

Abi began to stir and slowly opened her eyes. The light hurt them, and she blinked several times. Jack's stood with his back to her and stared out of the window.

"Dad," she managed to say, her throat dry and still sore.

Jack turned and sat on the edge of the bed. He took his daughter's hand. "Thank god you're awake." It had been four days since they'd found her, and he'd been worried when she hadn't woken. The doctor mentioned it would take a while, but Jack needed someone to stay with her. Someone always sat with her. They didn't want her to wake up alone.

"I can't see him. Please, dad, keep him away from me."

"Abi, Adam's not left your side except for when I kick him out, and then he doesn't go far."

"Please dad, I can't. He'll never forgive me." Her eyes closed as she drifted back off, too exhausted to stay awake.

Jack knew Adam's in the corridor and went out to him. "She woke up briefly, let's get some air."

They found a quiet bench. This was going to strike Adam hard, Jack thought. "Adam, she's asked not to see you. She's convinced you won't forgive her."

Jack's sentence left Adam confused. "I'm not leaving her. Michael forced her into it, she had no choice. I'm not allowing him to break us up."

"She's scared, Adam. Hurt and scared." He stopped and remembered her previous recovery. "The last time Michael took Abi, it took her a long time to recover. He had her for three months and raped her several times. And it was just as serious. She was a happy teenager, had that nervous streak, but hardly anything fazed her. But when I got her home, she became withdrawn and wouldn't go out. Abi didn't leave her bedroom for weeks. Her eyes became dull, and she barely ate anything. One day she eventually came downstairs, and I saw a slight spark in her eyes. That's when I knew she'd be okay. Six months later she went back to school, repeated the last year. I made sure she was taken and brought back every day. Several of us took turns, and the school knew who exactly who was coming and when. I kept her so wrapped up, that she told me she was getting suffocated and eventually I started to let my guard down. She started to walk to school and not long after she really started to be happy again. She had nightmares for over a year. Adam, guess what I'm trying to say is, give her time. She'll come around. You've seen how much of a fighter she is. Just give her the time she needs."

Adam glanced over towards the hospital. Abi's in there, and he couldn't see her. It would hurt, hurt a lot, but he knew what Jack was saying. Abi had fought against Michael for over a year. Struggled to stay alive and when found, worried about how he would react. He smiled sadly. Abi considering someone else's feelings, even when she lay close to death. He could wait for her to recover. He looks back at Jack. "Can you give her a message? Can you tell her I'll wait? I'll give her as long as she needs, but when she's ready, I'll be there."

Jack thanked him and went back inside. Adam needed time to digest this. God knows it would take a strong man to cope with it.

*****

Two weeks later Abi's fit enough to leave the hospital. She didn't need any other surgery, but she hadn't spoken since that first time she'd woke up. All she did was stare with dull, listless eyes. After a couple more days, Jack flew her back to LA. She did the same as before. Barely ate and stayed hidden in her room. He spent time with her, sometimes just watched her sleep, but held her through the nightmares. Nat visited every few days, and she'd agreed to counsel her, but Abi didn't respond. Adam rang every day, but all Jack could say was not yet.

*****

Three weeks went by, and nothing changed. Julian kept an eye on her health, the physical wounds were healing, but her wrists and back were severely scarred. Emotionally, she didn't show any signs of recovery. She flinched and tensed when anyone accidentally touched her. No words were spoken, and she shed no tears. She merely stared, her eyes barely focused and didn't eat enough. The weight dropped off her as if she hadn't already suffered enough.

Julian wasn't happy and mentioned it to Jack. "Jack, Abi's not recovering as well as I'd like. She can't afford to lose any more weight. I know you won't want to, but I think she needs to be back in the hospital."

"No," Jack said adamantly. "She won't let us hold her or even comfort her. Even in her nightmares, she pushes me away as soon as she's awake. Strangers will make it worse."

"She's fading away. Jack, I'll give her as long as I can, but if there's no change soon, I'll do it anyway. You won't stop me. Get her to eat and soon."

Jack agreed but wondered how on earth he'd manage it.

156

*****

One month later Abi's lay in her room and heard voices downstairs. Most of her physical injuries were healed, but some pain persisted. She sat up and listened. Her dad's talked to Julian and someone else. She opened her bedroom door slightly more and sat back down. She heard her the conversation more clearly now. The third person spoke. She gasped, Adam. It's Adam, here. Why? There's no way he would want her now, not after what Michael had done to her. She's broken and no good for anything. He must know what Michael did to her, and no one could love a person who gave permission to be continually raped. If only she'd been better with that knife, managed to hit something vital. Then he could move on. She heard Adam's voice raise slightly.

"Damn it. Jack, she needs to understand that there's nothing for me to forgive. She did what she did to stay alive, he gave her no choice but to consent. It was her only chance. Part of me is glad she did, otherwise he would have killed her a long time ago. At least this way I have a chance of getting her back. Even if it's only a slim chance, it's there. I love her too much to let her go. She's a cop, deep down she must know that forced consent is still rape. She did nothing wrong. Julian, what are her chances of recovery. The truth, please."

Julian glanced briefly at Jack, then back to Adam. "The truth? At the moment she won't. She's barely eating, totally withdrawn, losing weight too quickly and fading fast. I've arranged for her to be hospitalised on Monday. It's Friday today, so Jack, I'm giving you the weekend. If there's no change I'll have no choice. She needs to accept what's happened and admit it to herself. Until she does, she'll never bounce back. What Michael did was extremely hard on her. Serious enough for her to try and kill herself. To be honest, I'm surprised she hasn't tried again."

Abi's heard every word and couldn't believe what Adam said. He still wanted her. Still loved her. How? Julian was right, she'd buried

157

what had happened, hid it away at the back of her mind. Didn't want to remember, but Julian was dead on, she needed to. Abi sat back against the headboard, wrapped her arms around her legs and rested her head on top. She tried to keep her breathing steady. She could do this, had to. Adam still loved her, and he was the reason she'd worked so hard to stay alive. If she didn't do this, she'd die. Michael would have won. No, she wouldn't allow it. She would show Michael, show him how tough she could be. She closed her eyes, took a deep breath, and let the memories return.

Her heart began to pound, and her breathing increased, as everything came back. The blood hurt and pain, of how he violated her. The first rape that everyone witnessed, the last time and all the times in between. That final beating. Oh god, how had she survived? She didn't hear Adam and Julian leave as she visibly shook, the tears fell fast.

Jack closed the door and knew he had very little chance of Abi not being hospitalised. He walked back into the lounge, then rushed upstairs as he heard Abi cry out in pain. As he raced into her room, Jack froze as he saw her, thought it was another nightmare. Then he realised she's awake. He took a chance to comfort her, hoped his daughter wouldn't push him away. He sat beside his daughter and wrapped his arms around her. The surprise went through him as she leaned into him and he held her tight as she continued to cry. It was apparent the memories were hitting her hard, but he's also aware that she might now recover. Knew she must have heard them talking and knew how strong she must be to attempt this. "Let it out," he said. "You're safe now, protected. No one's harming you ever again."

"I'm sorry," Abi kept repeating.

"You've nothing to be sorry about, nothing at all." He held her until she fell asleep, thrilled that his daughter would now try to recover. He lay her down and covered her with a blanket. Then sat and watched her. She looked so much more peaceful. Tomorrow, she'll start to recover. Tomorrow, he got his daughter back, and god help anyone who tried to take her away again.

158

Abi slept well that night, didn't have a single nightmare. She woke up, showered, got dressed and felt refreshed. Today was the day she recovered. The day she showed Michael he would never win. She reached into a drawer and pulled out her small gun, checked it was loaded and secured it into her ankle strap. She didn't feel secure enough to not carry it, even if she did stay inside. She went downstairs and knew her dad was already up.

Jack had heard her movement and had coffee already waiting. She sat next to him and drank it in silence. When finished she curled up next to him, and he held her close. Her head on his shoulder. He kissed the top of her head and waited for her to make the first move.

"Dad, I'm sorry. I was letting him win. I thought I'd lost Adam and had nothing worth living for."

Jack smiled, he had an idea that may have been the problem. "Abi, he understands and will wait until you're ready. He told me that straight."

Abi took a deep breath, she had to ask. "Adam saw it didn't he." She left it as a statement.

"We all did. Abi, it hit us all hard, but Adam the hardest. We tried to get him out, but he refused. Needed to see it. Damn it Abi, what he did..." He trailed off.

"He told me. I blanked out after the second time. Dad, was it really eleven times?"

"Yes, over a few hours. Frankie's put out a shoot to kill order. I can tell you that every officer in that station, has a bullet with his name on. Every single one of them, won't hesitate to use it. Personally, I think he needs to suffer, and I know that Adam has plans to do exactly that, given a chance."

Abi smiled. "He would too. Dad, I heard what he said and what Julian said. I don't want to be hospitalised, stop him please."

"I can't, but you can. Start eating Abi, you need to get some weight back on. I know Michael didn't feed you a lot, know you probably aren't hungry. Julian said your body would adapt, learn to not need so much to food, so we can take it slow. Small meals, let's get you built up." He paused. "Abi, Adam really wants to see you."

He felt Abi tense. She wanted to but not like this. "Not yet, I'm not ready. Please let me start to heal first. Maybe in a few weeks."

"I understand, but I'll tell him how you are doing, keep him updated. He's worried about you. We all are." Her dad sensed her breathing settle as she nodded off and noting how much more relaxed she was. His baby knew how to fight. Twice she'd be attacked brutally and twice she would recover. And if Jack knew Adam's family and Frankie's officers, Michael wouldn't get a third try.

Abi slept for a couple of hours. Jack settled her down on the couch and covered her with a blanket. He sat opposite and watched her. Prayed for her recovery, now it had started, went smoothly. She woke and stretched.

"Are you hungry?" Jack asked. "Sandwich?"

She sat up and agreed. Jack returned with sandwiches and coffee. He watched as she picked at her sandwich. She noticed her father's face, Abi wasn't hungry but knew she must try. She picked up the sandwich and took a bite. She chewed and swallowed, didn't enjoy it, but forced the rest of it down. Followed quickly by the coffee.

Jack smiled back at her. "Well done. I know it probably tastes horrible, Julian also mentioned that you taste buds may not be the same. But they should return to normal once you start eating properly. Give it time." He noticed the tears in her eyes again. He sat back next to her and held her, once more, as she lost control.

"I can't do this." Abi cried. "I'm not strong enough."

"Abi, you can. You're made a start, but it will take time. You don't need to rush it. You've proven how strong you are. Don't try and do it all by yourself, let us help. Come on, you're tired. Let's get you back to bed."

Her dad supported her as they headed upstairs and waited until she fell to sleep. When he went back downstairs, he rang Julian.

"Julian, she's let it out and is totally heartbroken. It's knocked her hard. Can you come over later and speak to her? I'm fairly sure she has questions but is too scared to ask."

"Sure, I expected as much. Let me guess, she'd thought she'd lost Adam and didn't want to accept it?"

"Got it in one. She heard us talking, and that's what did it." They sorted a time for him to go around.

*****

Julian arrived later in the afternoon, and he went straight upstairs. He entered her bedroom when Abi called back. She sat on her bed and glanced up as he sat next to her. Julian hugged her, happy when he noticed that she didn't flinch.

"You scared us this time Abi."

"Sorry," she answered and hung her head. She still felt unsure of herself.

Julian started to rub one of her wrists, remembering that it used to relax her. He smiled as he realised it still did. "Abi, how many times do we have to tell you not to be?"

"It hurt so much to remember. Julian, he used a whip. How bad is my back?"

Julian knew precisely what Michael had used. After seeing the damage that whip had done, he hoped to get a chance at Michael himself. Only a sadistic bastard would be capable of doing that to another person. "Abi, haven't you looked?"

She shook her head. "I wanted too, but I'm too scared. It hurt so much."

"Abi, you need to." Julian waited, Abi needed to make the decision herself. He didn't have to wait long as he watched her remove her top. He let her walk over to the mirror and moved next to her. She stood with her back to the mirror and slowly glanced over her shoulder. Her breath froze in her throat. My God, she thought. Her back had been shredded to bits. There wasn't an inch without a mark on it. The wounds were highly visible. The shock caused he legs to buckle beneath her. Julian caught Abi and carried her back to the bed. He held her as she started trembling. To his surprise, no tears fell, and she pulled away from him.

"How bad is the rest?" She whispered after she'd pulled her top back on.

Julian knew she wanted to know about her internal injuries. "Abi, it not as bad as before, but there was severe tearing. They operated to repair the damage, that first night when they found you. There's scarring again. You probably still have some pain."

Abi did. "Can I?" She stopped and tried again. "Will I be able to?" She couldn't finish, but Julian understood.

"Abi, the scarring will make you tight again. But a sexual relationship should be possible if you feel up to it in the future. I've already spoken to Adam, he's aware it will be painful for you for the first few times, while you stretch to accommodate him. You may tear slightly and bleed, but nothing too serious. If you do start to think about it, talk to me first. There are things you can do to make it easier."

"I want Adam back, but I'm scared that I won't be able to feel anything. That Michael's ruined it for us. That I won't be able to keep Adam happy."

"Adam's not going to rush you, he'll wait until you are ready. Abi, you're worrying about nothing, that man is going nowhere. Believe me, all he's doing is annoying Jack all the time. He really does wants to see you."

Abi smiled sadly. That would be like Adam, but she's not ready. "I need more time."

Julian noticed the way she studied her wrists as they spoke. "Abi, we can't do a lot about your back, but your wrists are different. I've already spoken to a plastic surgeon who's happy to have a look." He wondered if he could risk the next sentence. "Abi, I know you heard what I said about hospitalizing you on Monday. I don't want to, but would you be willing to go in for a few hours. To talk to a dietician, come up with a plan to help you put weight back on. I can re-run your blood tests too, and Marcus can look at your wrists. Just a few hours, Abi. That's all."

Abi didn't want to. It would mean going outside. Could she do that, actually go out? She didn't feel safe in her own home. "Michael," She eventually said.

162

"He won't get near you. Your dad will be with you all the of time, and I'll alert the hospital security."

Abi thought about it. "Okay, I will." She said nervously.

"That's our girl." Julian thought she would flat out refuse. Her strength was shining through once more. It was a good sign. He noticed her eyes droop and left her to sleep.

Julian told Jack about her decision, and Jack agreed it's a good idea. She needed to get out, get some fresh air and if her wrist scars can be reduced, even better.

*****

Abi's nervous, it was time to go to the hospital. Why did she agree? *He's* still out there, he could grab her en-route to the hospital. She would be at his mercy again. She couldn't do this, it wasn't safe. She'd wasn't fully healed yet, and he would tear her apart again. Destroy her. The panic crossed her face, and she ran back upstairs.

Jack noticed and rang Nat, asking her to come over. She didn't know about Abi's improvement.

"Jack, what's up?" Nat asked when she arrived

"Abi, she needs to go to the hospital today, but she's scared of going outside. Terrified Michael's going to abduct her again. I wondered if you could tag along, keep her company. It'll make her feel safer with the two of us."

"Yeah." Nat knew that Julian might need to hospitalize her friend today. Adam had filled her in. She felt downhearted. Hoped Abi would come around, but it had only been six weeks, and it took four months last time. "Guess she's no better."

"You'll see," Jack tried to keep a straight face.

Abi told herself to calm down. Her dad would make sure that Michael wouldn't get to her. She went back downstairs. "Nat," she said when she spotted her friend.

Nat swung round. "Abi?" She said with surprise. "What?" She was totally confused. She noted Abi's eyes, their brightness and a slow smile appeared on her face. Frikin' heck, things have changed, Abi seemed brighter. More like her old self. But Abi surprised her again when she walked over to her and pulled Nat into a hug. "Thanks, Nat. Thanks for not giving up."

Nat pulled away, and the smile on her face spread right to her eyes. "Abi, you're back. Oh, thank god. What's this about the hospital?"

"I'm just going in for routine tests, and to see about getting my weight back on. Nat, I'm sorry for making you all worry, but I plan on getting better. I really do, but I guess I need a bit of help."

"Good for you and you are going to get lots of help. All you have to do is ask." Nat knew how hard that sentence would have been for Abi to say, but it was the first step in the right direction. Nat couldn't be more thrilled.

Jack indicated that they needed to go and soon they arrived at the hospital. The dietician, Helen, spoke to Abi first. She explained that Abi wouldn't be hungry due to Michael starving her and that her tastes may have changed. But as time went on, she'd start to feel like she could manage more, and her taste should return to normal. Helen advised Abi not to try and gain weight too fast, to let her body re-adjust to regular meals again. She admitted Abi was way underweight and was surprised she's so stable. Julian had warned her about what Abi had been through. Knew she'd only been given enough food to barely sustain her and now barely ate. She'd expected Abi to be a lot weaker. Helen gave them a diet plan of meals to try and arranged to visit Abi at home in a couple of weeks. Julian then took a blood sample.

Marcus arrived nearly three hours later. "Abi, I'm Marcus Carlo, the plastic surgeon that Julian mentioned. Do you mind if I see your wrists?"

Abi held them out and let him examine them. Jack and Nat noticed how nervous she was. They weren't surprised, Marcus was unknown to her, a stranger, but she seemed to relax slightly.

"Abi, I'll be truthful. I can't eradicate the scars but believe I can reduce them. They'll need to be bandaged for a couple of weeks while they heal, and you won't be able to do anything strenuous. If you want to go ahead, I can fit you in this afternoon. You'll need to stay overnight, but be able to go home tomorrow. Julian can do the post-op care."

Abi began to panic. Overnight? Unprotected? "Dad, I can't." She managed to stammer, her eyes full of fear.

Nat got in first. "Yes, you can. I'll get you a police guard for overnight, and I'll stay in the room with you. You'll be perfectly safe." Nat knew just the officer for the job.

"Adam, I want Adam as the guard, but he stays outside. I'm not ready to see him yet, but I'll feel happier knowing it's him." Abi answered. It would sort out part of the problem and allow Adam to see her. Even if it would be through a window.

She must be able to read minds, Nat thought. "I'll contact Frankie now and get it arranged. Abi, he'll be glad to be near you."

"Abi, I'll go and get you booked in. I'll arrange for a private room. The nurse will collect you when it's ready." Julian had warned Marcus about Abi's condition, and he was amazed she was so brave. He'd arranged to do her wrists privately and would cover the costs himself. He only wished her back wasn't so bad, but there was too much damage and reducing those scars would be difficult. However, he could suggest some creams she could try. Maybe something to hydrate her back, keep the area moist until her skin becomes subtler. Her back must be sore and tight.

Two hours later, Abi's settled in. Her operation was scheduled for 5pm. Adam would arrive around 8pm and Nat would sleep in the room with her. Jack would stay until his daughter returned to her room.

Adam came shortly after Abi's out of surgery and after Jack had left. He spotted Nat outside the room. "Nat, what's going on? Frankie said you wanted me on guard duty overnight."

"Actually, you were asked for personally by the patient. Feels happier with you on duty, but to stay outside. However, she's still under the anaesthetic, so we've agreed you can have ten minutes with her. But make sure she doesn't find out."

He followed Nat into the room. "Abi," he whispered. He remembered what Nat said and noted her bandaged wrists. Dread filled him which sent a cold chill down his spine. He knew she hadn't been doing well, but surely, she hadn't harmed herself. "Nat, what happened? Please tell me she's okay. That those wrists aren't by her own hand."

"Nothing to worry about, she's not done anything stupid. In fact, I'm fairly sure she won't, not now. Plastics have reduced the scars on her wrists, that's all. Julian suggested it, hoping to make her feel more confident, but she panicked at the thought of being here overnight."

"That's why the guard duty." Adam understood. He looked back over a Nat. "You said she asked for me. Nat, what's going on?"

"I'll let you have some time with her, but if she stirs, get out and fast. She'll kill me if she sees you."

Adam watched Nat leave, then sat on the edge of the bed. Abi looked so thin. Apparently, she'd lost more weight. "Oh Abi, what are we to do with you." He muttered as he took her hand. He sat and stared at her, feeling helpless that she wouldn't let him in. Wouldn't let him help her. He stood and kissed her forehead. "Abi, please let me in." He said before he went back outside to Nat.

"Talk to me, Nat," Adam said as soon as he saw her.

"She heard what you said, the other day."

"Hell, she wasn't supposed to. Is that why she's here? Julian said he'd hospitalize her if she didn't improve."

"Actually, you'd be surprised. Adam, she blocked out the memories of what happened, but that wasn't the problem. You were. Adam, she's aware that you know what Michael did that night. That you saw it all and she couldn't get over it. She'd convinced herself that she'd lost you, that you could no longer love her."

Adam shook his head. "But that's just daft. She should know that."

166

"But with the emotional stress she'd also been under, she probably didn't." Nat paused. "Hearing what you said changed that, she knew you were still waiting. Adam, you should see her now. It's only been six weeks, but she's bright-eyed and willing to live. It was you that kept her going, and it's you that's brought her back. She wants to live, because of you."

"So why the bloody hell won't she see me?" He ran his hand through his hair, baffled by his fiancé's attitude.

"Guess there's a still a small amount of doubt. Give her time. Anyway, go and get us some coffee. It'll be a long night, especially for you."

Adam did as Nat said, returned with the coffees, and stood outside the room. It's hard as he knew Abi's in there, and he couldn't speak to her. He only wanted to let her know, that he still cared and would wait. Michael might have attacked Abi, but it had affected everyone involved, yet Abi only refused to see him. Why? The frustration spread through him. He knew she needed time and would wait, but he was getting tired. Maybe he needed a break. He would speak to Frankie to arrange a couple of weeks off and go back to New York. See the family. Perhaps when he came back, Abi will be more willing to see him. He could only hope.

*****

The night went quietly, and Jack arrived bright and early. "How's it been?" He asked.

"Quiet," Adam answered.

"Seen Abi?"

"Nat let me in briefly while she slept."

Jack could see he was downhearted and swore to speak to Abi. She must let him back in and soon. "I'll try and speak to her, persuade her to at least phone you. But to be honest, it's still going to take a while for her to fully bounce back." Jack knew Abi's concerns now revolved around her scars and how Adam would respond. Emotional, Abi might be fine, but Adam seeing those scars would still be a big step for his daughter.

167

Jack sat by Abi's side. "Hey, sleepy." He said as she opened her eyes.

"Dad, morning already?"

He got straight to the point. "Abi, you need to speak to Adam. He's hurting too."

She shook her head and went pale with fear.

"Abi, please. He looks so downhearted out there."

"Dad, please not yet. I'm not ready."

"You're fighting a losing battle there, Jack," Nat said. "I've tried most of the night. Adam's thinking of having a couple of weeks back in New York."

Abi gasped out loud. Leaving, Adam's leaving? Tears sparkled in her eyes. No, he can't. He'd said he would wait. Didn't he love her anymore?

Nat noticed her reaction which must be a good sign, Nat thought to herself. Abi must still love him. "Abi, only for a couple of weeks, he'll be back. But you do need to stop pushing him away."

They both watched her fall back to sleep, and Adam left shortly afterwards. Nat told him about her reaction. "Adam, she still loves you, it's obvious. She'll come around. Just wait and see."

Julian turned up late morning and informed Abi that her blood tests are all back to normal. That her kidneys have recovered and are now working fine. He also confirmed that Michael hadn't transmitted anything to her, with all the unprotected sex they'd had. Abi sighed in relief. Shortly afterwards she's back in her own bed.

*****

The next month went quickly. Abi got stronger every day, and as she ate better, her weight improved. Everyone commented on how much better she seemed. Marcus gave her some cream to try and help keep the skin on her back healthy and subtler. Nat applied it when she visited every other day and counselled her, which made her emotional state improve too. Abi still slept quite a bit but became more active. She wasn't brave enough to venture outside yet but managed to sit in the garden for an hour or so, with her visitors. Even Michelle spent a fair amount of time there. Basically, they never left her alone, and she always carried her ankle strap. She couldn't get over the fear of Michael trying again. There'd been no sign of him, he'd disappeared again, but she knew he'd be watching. Waiting for another chance and the next time she knew she wouldn't be so lucky.

This brought her to one of the reasons why she ignored Adam. It'll be him that got hurt, the moment Michael grabbed her the next time, and she couldn't bear the thought. He'd been so good with her, waited patiently for her to make the first move and didn't force the issue. She felt persecuted. Let him in, and she'd be happy but only until Michael tried again. Or push him away permanently. Then they'd both be unhappy, but Michael would have no reason to come back. Why would he? He wanted her unhappy and miserable, but then he would have won.

Add to that her scars. How could Adam possible love her, the way her body looked now. Yes, the bruises had gone, but the scars were a permanent reminder of what she'd endured. Every time Adam noticed them, he'd be reminded, and it would be unfair to him. The surgery on her wrists had reduced them a fair bit, but the others were still highly visible. It could take years for them to fade, but they would always be visible, even then. Adam hadn't seen them yet. Oh, she was aware he knew about them, knew she'd been poorly treated, but to actually see them and touch them? Would he feel the same about her then? Was it possible for him to get past what she'd been through? To still see the real her inside? Deep down Abi was scared that he wouldn't be able to, so she kept him far away.

Then they intimacy could be a problem. She'd been torn apart by Michael's rape. The scaring would make it painful. But she'd gotten over that once, she could do it again. But would she still feel anything for Adam? If they tried sex, would she be able to overcome her memories of Michael and be able to enjoy it? Or would she be genuinely ruined and broken to the degree she would feel nothing? Be an empty shell. Again, it would be unfair to Adam. He deserved someone who could enjoy his touch, not just spread her legs, and hope it would be over soon. She cursed Michael. Her one chance at happiness and he'd succeeded in taking it away, and she bet he knew it.

She knew she should just try, see him, and take it from there, but the thought alone scared her. Letting him back in would be the easy bit, watching him walk away would ultimately break her. No, it would be easier not to even go there. In time, he'll forget her, find someone else. It would be the best option, so why did her heart break, all over again.

*****

It's been over four months, and Adam couldn't take much more. Abi wouldn't see him. She's seen everyone else, let them back into her life, but not him. He had to admit it, she wasn't his anymore. He flipped through the album from their engagement for the umpteenth time. She'd been so happy, so full of joy, but now it was over. Why? Why would she push him away? He knew she'd been hurting, but by all the reports she'd improved. In fact, Nat had told him she was nearly back to her old self. He knew there were days when Abi felt depressed, but there were many good days too. He'd watched the house from a distance, hoped to catch a glimpse of her, but zilch. She never ventured outside, not since the hospital. He'd made a hard decision. He couldn't stay in LA and not be near Abi. His heart overflowed with the love he felt for her, but he needed to get away. He'd begun a transfer back to New York. He would go over to visit Jack this evening once Abi had gone to bed. He had to tell a Jack his decision in person.

Jack let Adam in and gave him a cup of coffee. Adam had rung and said he needed to see him urgently and looking at his face it wouldn't be something he wanted to hear. Jack waited and allowed Adam to start.

"Jack, you know how much I love Abi, but I can't take much more. I know she's letting everyone else back into her life but still refuses to see me. I understand why. Really, I do. Everything

170

Michael's put her through, she must have doubts about us, but she's not even giving us a chance." Adam stopped and took a drink of his coffee. "Jack I've thought hard about this, and it hurts to say it, but I've asked for a transfer back to New York to start in two months. It'll be six months than since Abi was found. I can't sit around here and wait. If she comes around then all she has to do is call, and I'll come running, but I can't stay in LA and not have her in my life. Frankie's agreed to keep a position here for me in case things do change, but I'm not holding out any hope. Not now. Nat's told me she's recovering well, putting her weight back on and basically back to her old self, to a degree and I'm glad to hear it."

Jack wondered how long it would take. Abi knew she'd been pushing Adam away, and Jack knew Adam could only stand it for so long. Both Nat and himself brought up Adam's name in most of their conversations with Abi, but she'd never responded to his name. It was obvious what she was doing.

"Adam, I understand. Maybe a break for both of you would be a beneficial idea, but personally, I don't think it is. I've tried Adam, both Nat and me, but whenever we mention your name, she blanks us out. Julian thinks it's a mixture of things. Michael still being out there and her injuries, her scars."

"Jack, I know what her uncle did to her and I know he's left her badly scarred, but I don't care. Hell, I don't even care if our relationship is limited, but I think we both know it's over." He handed Jack the photo album. "Give her this for me. She deserves to know that at some point she knew how to be happy. I hope in time she'll let someone else into her life. She's way too lovely a person to stay single. I know she still has a lot of love in her, it's a shame it won't be me." He finished his coffee and stood to leave. "Two months, Jack and I'll be out of her life for good."

*****

Unbeknown to both men Abi sat on the landing. She'd heard every word. Adam would be leaving. Abi wanted that, him to find someone else, so why was she crying? Why did she want to run downstairs and tell him not to be so bloody stupid? She went back to her room and waited for her dad to go to bed. Once she was sure he was asleep, she went quietly downstairs. Whatever Adam brought and left for her must have been significant, and she needed to know what it could be. She closed the lounge door and switched the light on. When she picked up the album, she opened it, and her heart stopped. Their wedding proposal photos stared back at her. She flicked through them, tears burnt in her eyes. She'd been so happy, he'd been perfect for her. Adam helped her to heal from her previous abduction, gave her hope and she'd pushed him away. He wasn't the stupid one, she was. She was the one causing the hurt now, not Michael, but could she repair things? Could she find it in her heart to trust him? She didn't know, but she needed to find out before he left. Once he'd gone, it'll be too late, she needed to do it now. If she tried and it didn't work out, then she could let him go, and neither of them would feel guilty. She lay down on the couch, hugged the albumin her chest and fell asleep. And that's how Jack found her the following morning.

Jack checked on Abi when he woke the following morning, surprised to see she wasn't in bed. When he entered the lounge, he found her asleep on the couch. He couldn't help but smile while he prepared the coffees. Abi's awake when he returned and stunned him with her first sentence.

"Dad, I've been thinking, I want to go back to work. I'm feeling suffocated, staying here all day with nothing to do."

Jack sat next to her. "Abi, it's not been five months yet."

"I'm fully aware of the time, but I'm bored."

"Ok, I'll speak to Frankie, but he has the final say."

The station, she would see Adam at the station. They could take it slowly, speak to each other at work. See if they could still be together. Perfect.

Chapter Twenty-Two

Jack couldn't help but to be proud and amazed. Five months since she'd been found, since she'd escaped Michael's abuse and his daughter wore her uniform. He'd asked Frankie after Abi mentioned she been bored and he'd agreed to desk duty only. Break her in slowly, but if she wasn't ready he'd have her back on sick leave. Desk duty and for a couple of days a week.

"Abi are you sure?" He couldn't help but ask for the hundredth time.

"Dad stop worrying, I'm fine and ready to go back. Need to go back."

"I'm your dad, I think I'm allowed to worry. Well, if you're sure, let's go."

Not long afterwards, they've parked in the station's car park. Jack noticed how nervous Abi looked. "Abi it'll be fine." He knew she's worried about Adam. She hadn't seen him since refusing to at the hospital, five months ago.

Jack turned to her and lifted her head. "Abi, he's not just the man who loves you, the one who will do anything for you, he's also a cop. Adam understands how hard it's been for you, how you were hurting and still are. He's waited for you to make a move, he'll wait a hell of a lot longer if he must. He won't be angry with you. Trust him Abi, just trust him. Let him be there for you. Let him back in. Let him help you finish recovering."

They headed towards the entrance, and Jack opened the door for her. She entered and smiled at seeing the officers milling around, getting along with their business. Suddenly, they began to notice her. Smiles started appearing, they never expected her. Several of them came over to hug her. Abi began to relax and searched around for one particular person. Where was he? She'd seen the duty roster and knew he would be in the station this

173

morning. Nat walked over to her and pulled her into a hug. "Welcome back Abi. He's around here somewhere."

Adam strolled back from the records office. When he entered the foyer, he glanced around. There were smiles on everyone's face. Why? He's never seen so many officers being so cheerful. He shook his head and decided to stay away from the coffee. Everyone's gone crazy. Suddenly, he glimpsed a flash of gold. No, he thought, it couldn't be. He closed his eyes. Jack told him she was recovering, but she wasn't ready to see him. He still waited. But five months of not seeing her took its toll. He needed to see her, hold her, make sure she was okay. But he'd had enough and was going back to New York next month. It was all arranged. He opened his eyes has a gap appeared in the crowd. "Abi," he whispered. In uniform? She couldn't be ready? Their eyes caught each other's gaze. Before he knew it, he'd moved halfway across the room and pulled her into his embrace. "Abi. Oh, baby. Thank god you're okay." He blinked back his tears. Knew his sweetheart was back where she belonged.

Abi flinched at first but then snuggled into his neck. "Take me home." She whispered against his neck. Something Adam thought he'd never feel again. His fiancé's breath across his skin.

Frankie gave up trying to get any work out of either of them. Told them to leave. In fact, he'd given them the rest of the week off. Adam gladly took his advice and smiled all the way. Abi came back which gave them a chance. His day grew brighter.

*****

Later that evening Adam sat on the couch. Happy Abi was home with him, where she belonged. She walked over and snuggled up next to him, but he'd noticed she couldn't entirely relax. Give it time, he thought. It had been so long since he'd held her, but it was a feeling that he was happy to get the chance to do again. Tonight, he would sleep on the couch, Abi could have the bed. He wouldn't pressure her. He knew how badly Michael had damaged her, especially internally. Julian had warned him she may never be able to have sex again. That she'd been torn badly. Yes, she would heal, but the scars could be painful for quite a while. Adam didn't care. He would have waited forever to have her back in his arms, back where she belonged. Even if he'd gone back to New York, he would still be waiting. And she'd come back. Abi yawned.

"Abi, bedtime sweetie." He saw her tense, as the panic flared in her eyes. "Baby go to bed, I'm sleeping out here. No one's going to hurt you." He watched her move into the bedroom. His heart broke as he heard her sobs.

Abi's spent all night crying. She couldn't do this, couldn't let Adam back into her life. She thought she could. Her heart soared when she'd seen him at the station. The way he'd rushed to her. She'd seen the happiness glint in his eyes, thought she'd made the right decision, but now Abi knew she hasn't. She needed to let him go. She would no longer be a good fiancé, knew she would never let a man touch her again. Adam needed a stronger woman, someone he could love. She started to stand and left the bedroom, her heart completely broken.

Adam cooked breakfast, he'd barely slept last night. He'd heard Abi's whimpers and knew she hadn't either. She was home, come back to him, but she still had a war to win. One he'd damn well make sure she would. He turned when he heard her enter the lounge and his smile died has he spotted her face. He led her to the couch and held her has she cried.

"Hush, baby, it's fine. Let the pain out."

She pushed away from him. "Adam, I'll never be the person I used to be. I can't do this anymore. I think it's for the best if we split up. I'll move back home, you can have the apartment." She rushed back into the bedroom.

Adam's heart froze. No, not going to happen. Damn it, he'd thought they were getting somewhere. Nat, he thought. He needed to speak to Nat.

175

Abi lay on the bed and cried her heart out. It's the right decision, she knew that, but her heart hurt so much. She heard the front door close and knew Adam's left.

*****

Adam found Nat in her office and sat opposite her.

Nat became instantly alert, Adam looked upset. "Adam, what's wrong? Is it Abi? Is she okay?"

Adam filled her in. "She told me she wants up to split up. Says it's over between us. Nat, I don't know what to do."

Nat decided it's time. He hadn't seen the files yet, the photos of Abi when she was found. He knew she'd stabbed herself, knew Michael had been extremely rough, but not how rough. She pulled the file from her drawer. It contained everything. The photos, forensics, statements. She placed it on the desk. "Adam, you need to see the file. It'll be hard, but it'll help you understand what she's been through. Give me your keys, and I'll go and see her. Adam, she may still need time, may have come back to early." She left him to it.

Adam didn't want to open the file, didn't want to see those pictures of Abi. He remembered his fiancé in the hospital. How pale she'd been, how fragile. How she'd refused to see him. He lowered his head into his hands. If he opened that file, it wouldn't change a damned thing. Abi could be stubborn. Even hurting she'd turn him away. He thought of New York, it seemed as if he might be going back.

After rubbing his hand over his eyes and through his hair, he realised how exhausted he felt. Abi must be feeling worse. He needed to stop feeling sorry for himself. Abi required him to be strong, and he'd stand by her, no matter what she decided. That meant opening the damned file.

The first thing he saw were the photos Steve took from the crime scene. He gasped has his skin went cold. Oh God, she's covered in bruises, cuts, and the blood. There's so much blood, especially between her legs. Bite marks on her breasts and neck. There wasn't a part of her that wasn't injured. He saw the photos of the bat and whip Michael had used. Holy hell, the whip scared the hell out of him. How many lashes did Michael do? He knew Abi's back was shredded, but the skin would have been ripped from her.

The knife he knew she'd stabbed herself with. No wonder she's in turmoil. Adam forced himself to continue reading. He picked up one of the reports. They'd found several pregnancy tests, all negative. The bloody bastard, he'd really put Abi through it. He knew she'd been raped a horrendous amount of times, but to see the proof made his blood boil. He read the forensic reports that detailed her full injuries. The tears streamed down his face. His Abi. She'd been through so much, but he wasn't giving up on her. Michael wouldn't win, not if he could do anything about it. He noticed how late it's got, he'd been here all day.

As he stood he made a vow. Abi agreed to marry him, and he wouldn't let her change her mind. There would be a wedding. He would show Michael that Abi belonged to him and no sick bastard would ever hurt her again.

*****

Nat let herself into the apartment, headed to the bedroom and found Abi lying curled up on the bed. Abi's in her robe. "Oh Abi," She said as she sat by her side. "Abi, what's going on in that head of yours?" Nat knew she needed to take it easy. Abi's obviously still hurting more than she let on." She waited as Abi sat up, wanted her to make the first move. Nat could tell she's all cried out. "Abi?"

"I'm sorry Nat, Adam deserves someone who can let him love her. Someone who isn't scared to be touched, one who can sleep with him. Someone stronger than me. I have to let him go, just have to. I thought I could do this, give us a chance, but I can't."

Nat rubbed her back and noticed Abi tense. "Abi, he's not rushing you, is he?"

"No, it's me, I want to. I want things how they used to be. I tried Nat, I really did. We snuggled on the couch. I couldn't quite fully

177

relax with him, and when he said it was bedtime, I panicked. He'd already decided that I could have the bed and he'd sleep on the couch. It's not fair on him. Why should he suffer because of me? Maybe, I should have done a better job of stabbing myself, then he wouldn't be suffering too."

Nat's shocked, she had no idea Abi felt like this. She seemed to be recovering, but this? These feelings? She couldn't be healing. "Abi, he's only suffering because he wants to help you and doesn't know how to. It's hurting him, not knowing how you're feeling. Adam's spent the last five months going out of his head. He's never even asked to see your file, doesn't know exactly how badly Michael hurt you. I've left him at the station reading it. Forced him to. He needs to know so that he knows how to help you and he can Abi if you let him in. Please Abi, don't do this."

"It's pointless, he won't want me at all, not once he sees the scars. There isn't a bit of me that isn't marked. I'm not the perfect fiancé he asked to marry. I'll never be. Can't be. I must let him go. Nat, I have too."

Nat knew she must change Abi's mind. Make her see that Adam would be the one to bring her home. "Show him. Show him the scars, show him the injuries. Show him what Michael did. Let him decide if he wants to go, don't do it for him. Don't push him away. If he wants to walk, then you were right, and he's not the man I thought he was. He's completely heartbroken, doesn't know how to help you. Give him a chance." And I'll kill him myself, if he leaves you, she thought.

"I can't."

"Abi, you can. You have been so strong, held on to the very end, but now it's time to let someone else take over. To let someone else take the pain. To let someone help you. Let Adam be that person. Abi, you don't need to do it on your own, not anymore."

"I'm not strong enough. Never was, otherwise I wouldn't have let Michael..." Abi gave up as her voice broke.

"Oh Abi, you are. A weaker person would have been broken within a few days. You didn't." She paused, she must say it out loud, must make Abi see sense. "Abi, that first rape we all saw it, including Adam. He stayed and watched, even though we tried to kick him out. Even though it nearly killed him. He stayed, so he knew what Michael did to you, knew how rough he was, how you reacted. Abi, I don't know any other man who would stay that strong to help save his girl. Abi, you need to let him make his own decisions. He's had plenty of time to walk and so far, he hasn't. That must tell you something."

"But he is, I know he's arranged to go back to New York."

"Only because you've forced him into it. He loves you too much to stay and see you like this. Abi, his heart is breaking. He needs to be near his family, while you decide what to do. He needs the support. It's not just you that Michael's trying to destroy and he's succeeding. Don't let him win. You know you can do this."

Deep down Abi knew Nat's right. She did need to let Adam see the damage, but It would be so hard. Abi nodded, it's all she could do.

Nat pulled her close when she noted the difference in her friend. "Abi, you can do this. Believe in yourself," she repeated.

Nat stayed while Abi grabbed a shower. She made them sandwiches and became amazed when Abi came out. She's back in her robe but seemed refreshed and determined. They ate in silence, but Abi broke it. "It won't be enough to see, I have to let him touch me. I'll try Nat, I promise I will. I just need time."

"Give him a chance, don't keep running. Adam will wait. He won't go anywhere, not while you're back with him." Nat waited, there's something else. Abi's not told her everything.

Tears threatened to fall when Abi lifted her head back up. "What if he comes back."

Nat noticed how exhausted Abi sounded and tucked some of Abi's hair behind her ear. "Abi, we know he's out there, and we are doing everything we can to locate him and to put it bluntly, kill him. Adam knows about him now, so he'll protect you. He's not going to let you out of his sight, not while there's still a threat. I know you're still scared. Hell, you have every right to be, but you need to live. Do the one thing Michael doesn't want you to do. Live and be happy. Show him how strong you really are. Twice he's had you, twice he's lost. Come on, even you know it has to say something about you."

Abi knew Nat's right, she must live. She's fought to stay alive but, something niggled the back of her mind. There's something else she knows but couldn't quite pluck it out of her mind and figure it out. Abi shook her head slightly to clear away the thoughts. "Nat, I have a bad feeling he's done something else to me, but I can't remember what. Something bad that'll split us up permanently."

"And if he has we'll sort it out. Together, all of us. Just give Adam a chance, promise me that."

Abi agreed because she knew Nat's right. She must try and promised she will.

Nat hugged her again as she left. Then texted Adam to meet her.

Nat handed his keys back over. "Adam, give her a chance and don't rush her. Just be there when needed. She concerned it's not over and to put it bluntly, she's probably right."

He nodded briefly at Nat before he headed back in. He stopped as he spied Abi sitting on the couch. Her head hung low, and Adam noticed how exhausted she looked. When he sat down beside her, he rubbed her shoulder. "Abi, I've seen the file, seen the photos and the forensics. I know how much he hurt you. Please don't do this, don't leave me. Don't let him win. If you really want me to go, I'll go through with the transfer back to New York, and when you're ready, I'll come running back. You've been so strong, so brave, through all of this. You kept your mind, found ways to escape, won against him again and I have no idea where you got that strength from. But you don't need to anymore. Let me be strong for you. You don't need to do this on your own, not anymore. Abi, let me back in please, I'm begging. Let me help."

"I'm not the perfect fiancé I used to be. He's made sure you won't want me anymore. Made sure we can't be together."

Adam knew she's exhausted and needed to sleep. Her voice too weak and quiet. "Abi, you're tired, go to bed. I'll be out here all the time. Go and sleep, you'll feel better for it. We'll talk tomorrow. Okay?"

"Promise me you'll still be here when I wake. I can't do this on my own. I'm sorry for trying to push you away again, please say you'll be here."

Adam knew how hard Abi would have found that to say and he's proud that she could. "I'll be here. I'm not going anywhere, not without you. Not ever."

She went to bed but became restless. She tossed and turned before her body ached so much, that she climbed into the darkness.

Adam heard her restlessness. He found it hard to stay away but eventually heard her go quiet and fell asleep on the couch.

*****

Adam woke suddenly but couldn't figure out why. It was still dark. He sat up and turned on the table lamp, then heard Abi cry out. He moved quickly to the bedroom and found her tossing and crying out. "No, please no. Oh god, no. Michael please no more. Kill me. Oh god, please just kill me." She let out a scream.

Adam went instantly to his fiancé's side. "Abi, baby wake up. It's just a dream, a bad dream. Come on baby."

She pushed him away but didn't wake up. "No, please oh god, I can't take any more." "Abi, baby, come back to me."

She scratched him, tried to roll away, but still didn't wake up. Adam knew he needed to get her wake up. "Abi," he said sternly. "Michaels not here and never will be. Come back, baby."

She struggled against him. "Michael no," she let out a blood-chilling scream deep in her dream. The cry went right through Adam, and he tried again to hold her.

Abi's eyes snapped open, but they were unfocused. She screamed once more and fought against him.

"Abi, it's Adam. You're safe, he can't get you anymore." Jack had mentioned the nightmares, but he hadn't known they were this bad. "Abi, baby, listen to me. You know who I am. I'm not going to hurt you."

181

Abi froze. "Adam?" She shook her head and tried to clear away the bad memories. Michael's not here, it's not him. Adam felt her when she began to relax. "That's it, baby, you're safe."

Abi leaned into him, and Adam supported her while she recovered. "Adam, I'm sorry."

"None of it's your fault. There's nothing to be sorry about. Not now, not ever. Whatever happens, remember that. You'll have all the support you need."

"Hold me, hold me while I sleep. Help me keep the nightmares away."

They lay down, and Abi snuggled up against him. He rested his head on top of hers and listened while he heard her breathing settle. While she stills blamed herself, she would never heal. He needed to speak to Julian, come up with a plan. Get her through this. Make her feel special like she used too.

Adam cooked breakfast, while Abi showered. Today's the day he started to help Abi to recover. She'll never forget what happened, but he could make the memories less painful. Make sure he gave her new ones. Hell, he would start right back at the beginning. Take her out on dates, picnics, like he used to.

"Abi, I need to pop out later." He noticed the panic in her eyes. "I won't be gone long. Your dads coming over, so you won't be alone."

Jack arrived, and Adam spoke to him quickly. "Abi had another nightmare last night. She's still blaming herself. I need to speak to Julian to try and figure out how to help her."

When he arrived at Julian's, Adam got straight to the point. "Abi's still having nightmares. It was bad last night, and it took too long to get her out of it. She's still blaming herself." He hesitated. "Julian, she told Nat that she should have done a better job of killing herself."

"Adam, I know you've seen the file now. You must understand what he did to her."

"Believe me, I do. I'll kill the bastard on sight if I ever set eyes on Michael. But I'm still worried about her. What if she tries again? Decides she can't carry on."

Julian used to have the same worries, but Abi hadn't made any other attempt. "I used to think the same, worried she couldn't carry on living. Wouldn't want too. That's why we made sure someone was with her always, made sure she was never alone. It took her so long to respond to us, she'd withdrawn so deeply. Adam, you know how it works. They shut down completely. The fact she's back with you, letting you hold her, shows how strong she is. She hasn't attempted anything yet, and I don't think she will. Bear with her, it's going to be a long haul."

"I've decided to start again. Try and give Abi a new beginning. Take her out on dates and take it slowly."

Julian agreed. "Best thing for her. Just don't push her hard, let her make the first move. Abi will come around, just watch her." He smiled at Adam. "You'll get her back."

Adam headed home but made one more stop at her favourite Italian restaurant. He ordered a takeaway for later that evening.

Abi's resting when he arrived back. "How's she been?" He asked Jack.

"Quiet. She's resting now. Adam, she's withdrawing again. I feel like I'm losing her. I'm concerned she doesn't want to live and beginning to think she may need hospitalizing again."

Adam shook his head. "No, that'll be the wrong move. Leaving her with strangers could make her worse. Make her feel unwanted. I've got a plan and want to try it. If it doesn't work, then I'll agree with your idea. Let's give her a chance first. I know she wants to live but doesn't know how to. I'm hoping to change that."

"Adam, I'll give you a week. If she gets worse, I'll go over your head. I'm not letting Michael win."

"I wouldn't expect anything else."

Adam checked on Abi, who's still asleep. He set the table up for the evening. A beautiful romantic meal to remind her what she meant to him. The meal arrived, and he put it in the oven to keep warm. He would let her sleep.

183

Abi woke, yawned, and stretched. She knew she's getting worse, knew she's getting depressed, but couldn't get rid of the dark thoughts. Adam was trying his best, but she couldn't shake the feeling that he'd be better off without her. That there was something else going on with her. Maybe everyone would be better off if she hadn't survived. If she were dead, they'd be able to grieve then carry on. With her alive they suffered. She tried to shake the feeling away, but the darkness got worse. I must fight this, I must, but she couldn't make herself believe it. She rolled back up on the bed and cried.

Adam heard her move and then whimper. His heart broke, maybe Jack's right. No, he'll give her tonight. Eventually, she came out. He could see how red and puffy her eyes were, as well as how dull they were, but he waited. She looked over at him, then spotted the table and gasped. Adam saw how her eyes lit up. He held the chair out for her and dished up. Adam observed her, noted the dark spots under her eyes, how tired she seemed, but also that she cleared her plate.

"Thank you," she said as they walked towards the couch, Adam placed an arm around her shoulder. "Adam, I'm sorry."

"Abi," Adam interrupted.

"No, let me finish. I'm letting Michael win. I can't help but think everyone would be better off if I hadn't survived. I'll admit that I've thought about suicide, about ending it all. I want to live, really, I do, but everything's so dark, and I can't get past it. I don't know how to, or even if I can." She stopped and glanced at him, took a deep breath, and continued. "Help me, Adam, help me make the memories less painful. I know I'll never forget but help me overcome what he did."

Adam knew how hard that had been for Abi to say. Admitting it was the first step. "Abi, I'll do anything to help you, you just need to ask. I'm not going anywhere, no one is. We're all going to help you get through this."

Abi yawned.

"Come on sleepy head, let's get you back to bed."

"Hold me again." Adam picked her up and carried her back to bed. He held her again and let her sleep.

*****

The next few days went the same way. Adam allowed Abi to make all the moves. He cooked every night for her and made her feel special.

One morning she showered and got dressed, and Adam felt elated. She gained weight and looked healthier. He contacted Frankie and asked for extended leave for the both of them.

Frankie had agreed, he'd been shocked when he'd heard she'd thought of suicide and knew admitting it must have been hard. He told Adam to let him know if they needed anything and to take as long as they needed.

Today Adam would suggest a picnic. He arranged it with Nat and found a quiet spot in the woods. Abi always enjoyed walking and listening to the birds. It would be his next step.

"Abi, how do you feel about going out?"

A flash of panic flashed through her eyes. "Scared, but I'll try." She went to get ready and remembered her ankle strap.

Adam drove them out to the woods and placed his arm around Abi and heard her surprise when she spotted the picnic. There, he thought, as her gaze met his. The sparkle returned to her eyes, she hugged him and sat. Adam felt how relaxed his fiancé became when he sat next to her. She stayed relaxed the whole time.

Time passed, and he picked up on how tired she felt. "Time to get you home." He knew Nat would come back later to tidy up. Abi smiled, genuinely smiled. He could see it in her eyes. His heart soared as he realised she's returning to him. That they had hope.

The following day, Adam took Abi to visit her dad. Adam wanted him to see her, see how far she'd come. Jack still worried that they were losing her, but Adam had informed him they weren't. He father extended the deadline until the end of the month, which approached fast. Julian would meet them there.

Adam went into the kitchen with Julian, he wanted to give Abi some time alone with her dad. Julian broke the silence. "Abi's looking better, how's she doing?"

Adam thought about his answer. "She still has bad days, fewer nightmares and any she does have are shorter. I'm letting her make all the first moves. She's more relaxed, putting on weight. I'll admit to being less worried."

"That backward step was a bit unexpected. She asked to go back to work, wanted to see you, but I just can't understand why she deteriorated like she did."

"I think it's Michael, he's still out there. Julian, she won't cope again, I know she won't. Until Michael's found, she'll never completely recover. That's the key to all this. She thinks he's done something else to her but can't remember what."

"I can't think what else he could have done, that didn't leave her marked in any way. Mentally and emotionally yes, but again, there's nothing obvious."

"Guess we just wait and hope she's imagining it."

The problem was Michael, Abi couldn't get him out of her mind. She kept remembering how he'd had sex with her, how she'd liked it. How she missed it. How he'd make her climax every time. Well, except that last time, but she'd asked for that. After all, she did try to escape, but couldn't remember why. He'd been the perfect partner.

They returned to the lounge with the drinks, and Abi forgot what went around her mind. She curled up on the couch, and Adam sat next to her. Jack and Julian both noticed that she didn't flinch, as Adam pulled her to him. Both smile, as they realized that she trusted Adam.

.

Jack studied his daughter. She did trust Adam, something a part of him thought he'd never see again. It would only a matter of time before she took the next step. Adam knew what Abi required of him. Time. But Jack knew he'd been concerned too. She'd considered suicide, but now as Jack studied the pair of them, he

186

knew that Adam wouldn't let her go. Abi had found herself a wonderful man and Jack was happy for them. His thoughts returned to Michael. He might still out there, Abi wasn't safe yet.

Julian gave Abi another medical, and he couldn't be happier. Her scars were still highly visible, but he could tell she wasn't quite so bothered by them. He'd warned her again, to take things slowly. Asked if she was still using the cream on her back. She'd said no, as it was Nat that used to apply it. She let him rub some in, he noticed her skin was getting tight and reminded her to use it every couple of days. He also warned her clearly, the first time would hurt and that he'd already spoken to Adam about it, and her fiancé said he wouldn't rush, but Julian knew Abi was worried that she wouldn't be able to feel anything with Adam. That all she'd remember would be Michael and that she didn't know if she would ever be able to be intimate with Adam, ever again.

Julian spoke to her at length, told her the first step was to let Adam see her, let him look at the scars, but she'd panicked at just the idea. Gently he reminded her, of what he'd already said.

They stayed until early evening, then Jack noticed how tired Abi seemed. "Adam, think it's time to take someone home."

Adam glanced over at Abi. "Come on sweetie, time to go."

Abi slept most of the way and seeing how tired she felt, Adam carried her up to the apartment and placed her on the bed. Today must have been too much for her. He left her there and went back to the couch.

*****

Abi pretended to sleep, so he'd leave her. She needed to think. She sat up and changed into her robe. When she sat back down on the bed, Abi knew she needed to show Adam her scars and knew it must be soon. She sighed and then whispered. "I have to show him. Have to give him the chance to walk away." Adam slept on the couch, so she headed out towards him.

187

Adam woke up on when he heard the bedroom door open. "Can't sleep, sweetheart?"

She shook her head. Come on Abi, you can do this. She told herself. "It's lonely, can you join me?"

Adam returned to the bedroom, sat next to her, and stayed quiet as she untied her robe and let it slip off her shoulders. His breath caught in his throat at the sight of her back. He'd known that Michael had used a metal-tipped whip on her, knew she'd be marked by it, but her back was shredded. He leant over and kissed Abi on her shoulder and slowly worked his way down. He covered her whole back with peppered kisses and noticed she flinched with ever one. He needed to see the rest of her and knelt in front of her. Anger flashed through him when he saw the state of her skin. The bloody bastard. He swore Michael would die at his hands. No one else would get a chance. He noticed her eyes were closed and spotted a tear running down her face. He sat back down next to her and gently wiped away the tears. Then he took her hands and softly called her name.

Abi knew she's about to lose him. No one could possibly love her looking like this, except for Michael, he could. Maybe she'll hunt him down once Adam walked. Where had that thought come from? She would never go back to Michael. She heard Adam call her name. She ignored him, hoped to have a little more time before he left.

Adam knew Abi could hear him and could guess why she ignored him. She'd trusted him enough to show him her body, now it's time for her to believe in him. "Abi, please look at me. Don't push me away again, it won't work." He waited while she opened her eyes and slowly lifted her head.

Adam tried to get Abi to relax. She tensed, and he saw the fear in her eyes. "Abi, I didn't fall in love with you because of how your body looked." paused long enough to place his hand on her chest. "I fell in love with the person in here. The woman who lives her life to the full. The one who makes me laugh and the one who is so strong, she fights for what she wants. Abi, these scars only show

how hard you fought to stay alive and how strong you really are. I'm not going anywhere. How many times do I have to tell you? Stop fearing the worst."

Abi heard every word he said and knew he meant them. She knew then that she must recover. Needed to trust him fully. "Kiss me." That would be the next step.

Adam smiled back at her; finally, she'd figured it out. He picked her up and laid her on the bed. Lying next to her, he kissed her on the mouth, gently. Amazed when she let him in. She nibbled on his lip which made him groan. He deepened the kiss, and she met him. Eventually, they came up for air. Abi turned and faced him, then snuggled into his chest. Adam pulled her into his arms, and both fell happily to sleep.

Chapter Twenty-three

Abi woke first. She felt so relaxed and so much happier. She's been insecure for a long time, but now that she knew Adam's would stick by her, she could get her life back on track. She made a significant decision. Michael might still be out there, but she would try her hardest to forget what he did. Adam's already given her lots of new memories, but now she needs to let him know exactly what he meant to her. She needed to make the next step and let Adam know she's ready to move on.

She moved slightly and sensed Adam wake. Now she thought before she changed her mind. She nibbled on one of his nipples and ran a hand between his legs. Abi felt him instantly harder, the moment she rubbed him.

"Abi," he warned. "Don't start what you can't finish."

She smiled seductively at him. "Adam, give me happy memories, take his away. Make me forget what he did."

Adam grinned back at her. He kissed her on the mouth and happiness filled him as she responded. Mine he thought, I'll make her all mine. He kissed both of her breasts, then trailed peppered kisses down her abdomen and paid attention to every scar as he went. When he placed his hand between her legs, he began to rub her sensitive area. He heard her groan and felt tremors ripple through her body. Adam sensed Abi coming close and paused long enough to lower his head. He licked and suckled her pussy, while still casting small circles with his finger. When he felt Abi start to tremble, he sucked harder and increased his finger rhythm. Abi buckled as it hit her, and she cried out his name in delight.

Adam lay back next to her, lightly kneading her breast.

"Thank you," she said as she fell back to sleep, with a big smile on her face.

Abi woke first again. Adam might have made her come but didn't pleasure himself. She could still feel his hardness. She moved and licked his cock. When she took him in her mouth, he woke and gasped. She continued to lick and suck him. She knew when he's about to come, sucked harder and let her teeth lightly scrape along him. Adam cried out her name as he fell into bliss, and she sucked him dry.

Adam could n't believe what she's just done, and he's still as hard as ever. Abi looked up at him seductively. "Adam, take me. Take me all the way."

Adam stared down at her. The vixen he'd grew to love stared back at him but was she sure about what she wanted.

"Adam, please, I need you inside me." She begged.

"Abi, I want it to but not yet. You aren't ready yet."

Abi's eyes turned dark. "Fuck me Adam. Now!" The dark intent became apparent in her voice. "Get that damned cock in my ass."

Shock vibrated through Adam. "Abi? What did you just say?"

"Didn't you hear me? Fuck me. Slam right up my ass. Make me bleed from the pain."

Adam narrowed his eyes. He knew damn well Abi never talked like that, something's wrong. His cop instincts kicked in. Abi said she felt as if Michael must have done something else to her and now she's talking like this. Why? More to the point her eyes seemed slightly off too. "Abi, I'll make love to you when you ask more nicely."

She turned away from him and winced as the scars on her back pulled tight. Adam noticed and tried to talk to her again. "Abi, is your back sore?" He knew it must be, those scars would have made her skin tight.

"Yes, it's the scars. I'm supposed to have cream put on every other day, but Nat hasn't been coming as often."

"Oh Abi, why didn't you tell me? Where is it?"

"Bathroom."

Adam wandered over and came back with a jar. "This one?"

Abi nodded and rolled on to her stomach. Adam sat beside her and began applying the cream. Massaged it in slowly. He noticed her tense and knew he'd upset her, but this would be their first time again, and he wanted it to be unique. On top of that, he'd noticed how dry she'd become and needed to buy some lube. It would be painful enough as it was, he wouldn't make it worse. He smiled, the weekend. He would take her out for a meal, make a night of it. He finished with the cream and spied the tears in her eyes as she sat back up. Hell, upsetting her was the last thing he wanted to do. "Abi, please don't cry."

"You don't want me anymore, do you? Deep down I knew you wouldn't. How could you love this?" She ran a hand down her body and hung her head down when she'd finished her statement. She couldn't remember what she'd said. "And I did ask nicely for you to make love to me."

"Abi, what exactly did you say?" The warning bells rang in his head.

"To take me and that I needed you inside me."

"Nothing else?"

"No. Adam I remember everything I said."

Adam became overly concerned. He remembered precisely what Abi said, and she apparently didn't. Her eyes seemed normal again too. It wasn't over, she must be correct. Damn it, Michael still had the advantage.

"Adam, you only need tell me if you want to leave. I'll understand. My body is disgusting now."

What had he got to do, to get her thoughts away from this? "Abi, I still love you, I really do, but I want it to be special. Not rushed."

"I'm sorry," she whispered.

"Abi, promise me something. Don't ever use those words again in relation to this. Michael's the one that'll be sorry when I find out where he's bloody hiding."

Abi heard the anger laced in his words. She had no doubts her fiancé would protect her and smiled at him. "Thank you, but please let me watch."

They both laughed and lay back down. Sleep hit them both.

Adam woke first, texted Nat and asked her to pop round.

"Adam, what's up?" She asked when he let her in.

"Abi still blames herself."

"To hell with it, haven't we sorted that out yet."

"We had, but I sent her backwards last night."

Nat studied him. "What did you do?"

"Nothing."

"Adam." She warned.

"That was the problem. Abi asked me to make love to her, and I refused. Nat, she only wants to do it to see if she can, and I told her I wouldn't. It needs to be special. I'm not going to have a quick fling."

"I'd kill you if you did. Adam, what else haven't you told me?"

"She's right, Michael has done something else. But I just figure out what."

"What's he done?" Her voice went cold. Adam's tone of worried her.

"It's what she said when I refused. Her eyes went dark, and she ordered me to fuck her up the ass. To make her bleed from the pain."

"What the hell? Adam, she'll never say that. Never." Nat knew damn well that Abi would never ask for that. "Did you question her?"

"Yeah, that's the strange thing. She didn't remember."

"Shit."

"My thoughts exactly. Nat, I'll keep an eye on her and see whether it's a one-off. Hopefully, it is. Can you stay? I need to pop out and arrange something for the weekend."

"Sure, it's my day off, nothing better to do. Adam, make sure it's something she'll remember, you need to wipe him from her mind. It'll be him she remembers, not you." But Nat wasn't happy, not happy at all. Adam was right. Something else must have been done, but what?

"Don't worry; I plan on it." Adam left, and Nat checked on Abi. She's still asleep but seemed less fragile. Adam must be doing something right, helping Abi relax. Nat left her friend to sleep, completely worried and unable to relax. Why the hell would Abi say such a thing?

*****

A couple of hours later Nat heard Abi whimper. She checked back in at her, as Abi began to have a nightmare.

"Oh god Michael, please just kill me. I can't go on." Abi cried.

Nat moved instantly at her side. "Abi, you need to wake up." She didn't respond but screamed. Nat didn't hear Adam return, but he rushed in. "Damn it, not another one." He tried to hold her, but she fought him. "No, please God, not again. I can't take anymore."

Her cries went straight through Adam. He sat on the bed and rubbed her arm vigorously. "Abi, time to wake up sweetie."

Nat watched, it didn't seem like Abi would wake up anytime soon. She fought Adam, scratched, and punched him.

Adam turned to Nat. "She's too deep, I can't wake her. Call Julian."

Nat did and explained the problem. "He's coming straight over. Adam, are they always this bad?"

"No, usually I can wake her. Julian may need to sedate her? Christ, I'd thought we'd gotten through the worst."

Abi managed to push Adam away and reached under the pillow. Both stared in disbelief as she pulled out her small gun, while still rooted in her nightmare. Adam dived for it first, tried to wrestle it away as Abi took off the safety. Nat followed closely behind.

"Abi no!" Adam shouted. "Baby wake up."

Abi tried to put the gun to her head. Adam and Nat tried their damned hardest to stop her. Adam wrestled it away as Abi prepared to fire. Nat took it off him and put the safety back on as he attempted again to wake her, with no luck. Abi wrestled with him and screamed loudly.

Nat heard the bell and let Julian in. "Julian do something, she's just tried to kill herself," Nat ordered him, the panic evident in her voice.

Julian administered a sedative, while Adam continued to hold her as she relaxed. "What happened?" Julian asked.

Nat filled him in, and Julian's shocked. "Let me get this right. Abi tried to shoot herself while still asleep?"

Adam nodded. "Yes. The nightmares were getting less. When they did happen, it was getting easier to wake her, but this one...Julian, if she'd been alone." He didn't need to continue. If Abi had been alone, that gun would have fired. She'd be dead.

"Do you know what may have set it off?" Julian asked.

Adam told him about last night. Abi wanting to make love and what she said when he'd refused. Julian had a bad feeling, that shouldn't have set Abi off. He needed to speak to someone urgently as that gut feeling got worse. God, he hoped his idea was wrong, but Abi might have been right. Michael had done something else to her? Something Julian would never have thought off. Something that wouldn't leave a physical mark.

"She'll sleep for a few hours. Hopefully, she'll be fine now, but I'll leave you a couple of doses in case." He showed Adam what to do if it happened again. "Whatever happens, do not leave her alone. Ever. Next time we may not be so lucky."

"Any side effects to that sedative?" Adam asked.

"No, she's had it before, and there were no problems then. Just keep an eye on her. Any problems let me know."

After Julian had left, Nat glanced over at Abi. "Adam, that was too close."

"Damn right it was. Why the hell would that happen? Why would she try to kill herself? She told me straight she wanted to live. It doesn't make any sense."

"Let's just hope it was a one-off. Keep that gun away from her. I'll go and inform Jack. Keep me informed if she does or says anything else.

Adam let Nat out and sat back next to Abi. Things could have been so different. He nearly became a widow.

*****

195

Adam lay next to Abi when she began to stir. Her head hurt, but she couldn't understand why. As she sat up the room started to spin, and she stumbled when she tried to stand. Adam heard her woke up himself and moved instantly to her side.

"Abi, sit down." He noticed her eyes seemed slightly unfocused. "Are you okay?"

"Headache." Nausea washed over her, and she managed to reach to the bathroom in time. Adam supported her and took her back to bed.

"Adam, what's wrong with me? I feel awful."

He told her about her nightmare.

"What!" Abi tried to sit back up, but the room spun again. "Why would I try and kill myself?"

"Take it easy, I'll get you some water." Adam's now very worried. Abi went dead white and felt sick every time she moved. He couldn't understand why, she'd been fine last night. What had changed? Julian told him that he was going to check something and hoped that Julian could figure it out and soon. He went back to Abi helped her to sit up, and she closed her eyes while the nausea passed again. He held the water to her mouth, and she took a few small sips.

"Thanks. Adam, is this from the sedative?"

Adam wasn't convinced about that but didn't want to worry her. "Possibly. Hopefully, it'll pass. Lie down and get some rest."

"Adam, I'm scared. Stay with me please."

Adam lay next to her and snuggled up to her while she fell asleep. After a while, he got up and grabbed a sandwich. Abi came out of the bedroom shortly afterwards. "Feeling better, baby?" He asked but got no response. "Abi?" He called again, as he followed her into the kitchen. She walked around the counter, and Adam noticed that her eyes weren't focused again. "Shit," he muttered, as he rushed over to her.

Abi picked up a knife and turned it towards her. Adam couldn't get there in time, couldn't do a damned thing but watch, as she plunged it into her stomach. Adam screamed her name and caught her as she fell. He grabbed a towel and applied pressure to the wound while dialing for an ambulance.

"Stay with me, baby. Please stay with me." Blood poured through the towel. Where the hell was that ambulance?

Chapter Twenty-Four

Adam waited at the hospital as Julian, Jack, Frankie and Nat arrived.

"What happened?" Julian asked.

Adam told them. "I couldn't get there in time. Didn't realise till it was too late. Julian, what the hell's going on? She was fine, happier. This doesn't make sense. They're operating now."

Julian spent the afternoon talking to an old friend. Explained what his theory. Asked her if it might be possible and she'd confirmed that it may be. She agreed to see Abi and explained what might have happened, but now it may be too late.

"I had a theory but wanted to run it past Susie. Hoped I was wrong, but she confirms it may be a possibility. Adam, how did Abi feel when she woke?"

"Rough. A headache and vomiting. Why?"

"That wasn't the sedative, it may be a hangover from what else Michael may have done to her."

"Like what. What else could Michael have possibly done?" Jack asked, the anger evident in his voice.

"Then she was right," Adam said.

"What the hell are you on about? Someone going to explain?" Jack asked confused.

Nat took over. "Jack, she told me that she'd thought Michael had done something else to her but couldn't figure what. None of us could. But now she's trying to kill herself, or worse." Nat turned to Adam.

"She asked me to sleep with her. I refused, saying she wasn't ready." He paused, still unable to believe what she'd said. "She told me to get my cock up her arse and to make her bleed from the pain."

Frankie and Jack gasped in shock. Abi would never ask for that.

198

"There could be a reason for it. Susie can confirm it, she's agreed to see Abi. Providing we aren't already too late. But you won't like it. There's a possibility that Michael may have placed a hypnotic thought. Adam, you said this started after Abi had made it clear that she wanted to sleep with you. Michael may have hypnotized her so that if that happened, she'd kill herself."

"What!" All of them said at the same time.

Frankie quietened them. "Julian, is that possible?"

"Everyone is different. Some people are easier to hypnotize than others. Abi was under a lot of stress already, hypnosis could have been easy. All he'd have to do is bury the thought until conditions were right. I wouldn't expect Abi to even be considering a physical relationship yet, so I also suspect that thought was also placed. As I said, it's a crazy idea, but with what's happened it kind of makes sense. Abi was healing, there's no other explanation I can think of."

"So basically, you're saying, she'll keep going until she succeeds. Bloody great, Michael's really done her over. How on earth are we supposed to stop this one." Adam's got angrier by the minute. "Every time we think we are getting somewhere, the bastards one more step ahead."

Nat placed a hand on his shoulder. "Adam, we'll figure it out. Julian, can we keep her sedated until we can?"

"I'd prefer not to. I'd prefer it if we told her, keep her informed."

"Right, I'm placing her under police guard. Two officers always. Adam, I know you won't leave her side, so one of us will also stay with you. She's going to be here for a while recovering, and it leaves her back in the open. Julian, can it be reversed?" This would be the last time Michael ruined her life. Frankie would make bloody sure of it. Abi deserved to be happy, and Michael being killed would ensure that.

"We won't know until Susie tests her. If she can't, she may be able to change the thought, but it depends on exactly what he's done."

They noticed a doctor walk towards them. "Abigail's in recovery. The damage was limited, so she should make a full recovery. She was fortunate. If the knife was angled slightly more upwards, things could have been vastly different."

They thanked him and waited for a nurse to fetch them.

Abi regained consciousness the following day and became totally confused. She managed to glance around and realised that she's attached to a drip and her stomach hurt. She whimpered from the pain and Adam heard her.

"Abi, take it easy," Adam took her hand.

Abi then noticed her dad and the concern on both of their faces. "Where am I?"

Jack let Adam take the lead. "Abi what do you remember?"

"Feeling sick after the nightmare. Adam, what's going on?"

"How do you feel now?"

"Painful. Adam, talk to me. Why I am in the hospital?"

Adam looked at Jack who nodded at him. He turned back to Abi. "Abi, you stabbed yourself. I'm so sorry, I didn't get there in time."

Fear crept through her. Stabbed myself? What's he on about. "Why would I do that?" She managed to stammer.

Adam saw the fear creep into her eyes and told her what Julian thought. He didn't believe Abi could go any paler, but she did. "Baby, now we know we can keep a closer eye on you. Stop you if it happens again."

"He's determined to win, isn't he? Adam, I can't fight this. Can't do anything to prevent it. This time he's won."

"No, Abi, he hasn't."

"Hypnosis. Adam, I can't change that." Abi couldn't believe it, everything was going to plan. She'd improved and thought she was finally getting somewhere, but this was something she couldn't control.

"Julian knows someone, she's going to come and speak to you. Susie knows about this and may be able to help. If we're lucky she can remove the thought."

"And if she can't?"

"She may be able to change it. Abi, don't give up yet. While you're still breathing, there's a chance. You won't be alone. I'm staying put, and you have guards outside."

It didn't calm Abi. She couldn't win this one. "Adam," she whispered as she drifted off. "Next time don't stop me."

Shock ripped through Adam. Her words were clear enough and a chill spread through him. "No. No bloody way. Not after everything she's been through."

"Adam, we may not be able to stop her. Not if he's buried that thought deep enough. If he's re-trained her mind, then he's won. Let's wait until Susie's tested her, see exactly what he's done." Jack admitted to himself that he'd realised the same sick thought. Michael wanted him to suffer, and he was managing it in the worst possible way. Destroying several lives in the process.

*****

Abi felt depressed again. So far, her stay in hospital had been without any problems, but for how long. It's been a week, they wanted her in for another week. Then how long before she's back, or worst, in a morgue? By her own hand? She turned her attention over to Adam, asleep in the chair. Nat left to get some coffees. She sighed and sat up. She had a horrible feeling that Adam would soon be out of her life, for good. She felt her head start to hurt, panic hit her, and she tried to wake Adam up. But soon her eyes became unfocused, and her mind turned to his gun. She knew he's armed, she just needed to get to it. She stood quietly and tiptoed over to him. He's wearing a shoulder strap under his jacket. She reached slowly under and began to slide the gun out. Adam didn't move. Abi managed to remove it and slowly took off the safety. She took one last look at him as she raised the gun to her head.

Nat re-entered and dropped the coffees. "Abi," she yelled. Adam jolted up and grabbed her hand, this time Abi didn't struggle, and he managed to remove the gun. He caught her as she fell unconscious.

"Damn it, I was too tired, didn't feel what she was doing. Thank god you came back, Nat." Adam couldn't believe it's happened again.

"I'm contacting Julian, he can get his friend here. Get this sorted. Adam, she's going to succeed very soon."

Adam fully agreed. He stayed with Abi while Nat went out.

She returned shortly. "Julian's going to fetch Susie. Hopefully, they'll be here soon." Both watched Abi and waited. It was all they could do.

Julian arrived with Susie a few hours later. Abi still hadn't come around, and Julian examined her. "Susie, if she keeps trying and failing, what else could he have planted?" Julian asked.

"I'm not sure. From what you've told me, Michael wants to destroy her happiness, but that doesn't seem to be the case anymore to me. It seems to me that he wants all of you to suffer. Doesn't want Abi and Adam to be together. Julian, you told me, that he didn't like to share. As far as Michael's concerned, Abi belongs to him. Therefore, Adam sleeping with her is a definite no go, and he won't stop at anything to prevent them getting back together. Is she usually out this long, after an episode?"

"No. This is the third time, the most has been about an hour." Adam answered.

"And how is she when she wakes up?"

"Headaches, vomiting. Generally feeling rough. Worse the second time."

"Okay. So, it takes longer for Abi to wake up and the sickness is worse. If I hazard a guess, I'd say, at some point, she won't wake. Possibly go into a deep coma. It'll be as good as dead. No way to wake her up. I'll need to test her as soon as she wakes." She turned her attention towards Adam. "Adam if I can do anything I will, but please understand that it may not be a perfect outcome."

"Just make sure she stays alive."

They waited, it's late when she finally stirred. She vomited immediately and collapsed against Adam, too weak to support herself.

"It happened again didn't it?"

Adam told her, and she closed her eyes to try and hide the tears but failed. "I can't do this. Please, Adam, don't stop me next time."

Julian took over. "Abi, if he doesn't, I'll kill Adam myself. I need to introduce you to Susie McDonald. She's a hypnotist and may be able to help you, but she needs to test you now. We can't wait any longer."

Abi nodded her head, in agreement.

Susie spoke directly to Abi. "Abi, I'm going to put you under. Don't be scared, but I need to know exactly want he's planted. The chances are it's deep, and you won't want to remember. It could also be painful. But without knowing I can't help you. Are you ready?"

Abi looks at Adam, fear filled her heart.

"You can do this." He told her. "All of us will stay with you." Frankie and Jack had joined them.

"Alright," she said to Susie and took a deep breath.

Susie managed to put her under. "Abi, I'm going to ask you to remember what happened to you. I'm looking for a time you felt sleepy when Michael was with you, but not from a sedative."

"Every time we had sex we both fell asleep," Abi answered.

"Alright, any other time?"

Abi's quiet for a bit, while she thought about it. Suddenly, she cried out in pain.

"Abi, try again, but this time you'll feel calm."

Abi tried but cried in pain again, tears flowed down her face.

"Abi. There's no pain. You won't feel any panic or fear. You'll remain calm, collect and be able to tell us."

Abi concentrated. This time the memory came readily. "We had sex, he fell asleep still hard and in me. When he woke he retook me. Then we did another pregnancy test. He wasn't happy, it was negative again. Told me I was a useless whore. That I didn't spread my legs enough for him. He tied my legs so far out it hurt and raped me again. I felt his seed in me, then he left. I was still tied up, and when he came back, he was still hard. He told me I was getting

203

tired and to rest. That I'd remember what he'd do to me physically, but not what he said." Abi stopped.

"You're doing fantastic Abi. Now can you tell us what he did physically to you?"

"He had something in his hand, I couldn't see what it was. I felt him place it in me and he pushed it in deep. It was hard and cold, and as it penetrated, I knew it wasn't good. He pushed it right up to my cervix. He then raped me again, and I screamed. Even time he thrust, whatever he'd placed in me, dug deeper into me and it hurt, like a thousand needles sticking into me. I screamed. Every time he thrust he pushed the thing deeper in. He climaxed, and I noticed blood on his cock. Lots of blood, my blood. He removed the item and showed me. It was metal and full of spikes and covered in my blood. But it wasn't Michael that was raping me. It was Adam."

Everyone felt sick. Abi hadn't given a statement yet, so they only knew what had happened from her injuries. But that had been unbearable to listen to.

Adam was fuming. "What the hell did Michael do to her? Why the hell would she think I'd raped her?"

"Susie will get to that," Julian said. "Let them finish."

"Abi, you're doing well. Now can you remember what he said? Remember, you are feeling calm, and nothing can hurt you."

Abi concentrated, and as she was about to tell them, she screamed out in pain. Tears streamed down her face.

"Abi, nothing will hurt you. You are calm and collected and able to speak without feeling any pain. Remember that."

Abi tried again. "He told me before he raped me that he was Adam. That I'd remember that Adam had raped me and hurt me. He said that I wouldn't make it out alive. Even if I were found, he'd still kill me. He said that if I ever went back to Adam, ever let him fuck me again, I'll remember the pain of what he'd just done and would be determined to kill myself. I could fuck anyone else, just not Adam. Unless he stuck his cock up my ass, then I'd be fine. Said that would be the only way we could fuck, without me wanting to kill myself. That I'd enjoy it and keep asking him to do it, till he ripped me apart."

204

They looked at Adam. He'd gone pure white. "No way," he said. "No bloody way."

"Okay. Abi, did he say what would happen if you failed. If you tried and failed to kill yourself?"

"Yes. He said I had four attempts, then I'd fuck Adam and die while we did it. While he was still in me."

"What if Adam didn't let you have sex?"

"Wouldn't be able to stop me. I'd wait till Adam was asleep then spike myself on him. It would only take a few seconds."

"Abi, is there any way to prevent this happening?"

"No. The only way is for Adam to die by his own hand. Michael said that would prove his love to me. Killing himself to save me. Then I'd be fine."

"What if Adam moved away?"

"I would find a way to let Michael know and go back to him. Let him fuck me. Any way he wanted to. That I'd remember how good we were together, and I'd enjoyed his lovemaking. We'd be happy with Adam out of the way. Be a family." Abi smiled at the thought. "I'd be happy. Spread my legs anytime he wanted me to."

"Bloody hell," Frankie said. "Even I can't see a way out of this one."

"Abi, you've done fantastically. I'll wake you up now, and you'll remember what you've told us."

Abi returned, was violently sick and curled up next to Adam. She remembered everything and couldn't stop the tears.

Adam held her close, his eyes blazed with anger. He glared at Susie. "Can you change it, do anything?"

"I don't know. The wording is specific. I'll certainly try. It could be painful, and I can't prevent the pain. It's the pain that allowed him to place it in the first place. Add in the starvation, torture, and lack of sleep. It would have lowered Abi's defenses. Suicidal thoughts aren't easy to place, you normally need to have some sort of suicidal tendency to start with. But with Abi's mental and emotional state, Michael could have done it easily. Deep down, Abi may have wanted to die. I'm concerned I may need to do something just as

205

painful to overthrow it. Her defenses are better now she's more healed, and those suicidal thoughts are deeply placed."

"Can you do it tonight?" Abi whispered.

"No. I'd rather do some research first. I suggest that Julian sedates you tonight and we try tomorrow."

Julian agreed, and Susie left, but the rest stay.

"Christ," Jack finally said. "He's really thought this through, hasn't he? Covered every damned angle."

Nat stayed quiet, and Frankie glanced over at her. "Nat you're very quiet."

"You do know that if Susie tries and succeeds, or thinks she succeeds, there's only one way to test it. Adam will have to sleep with her."

The one thing they wanted to do, and it could kill Abi. Adam shook his head. "Is it worth it? The risk. I'd rather know Abi's alive."

Abi looked at him. "But I may not stay that way."

"I'll take a chance at moving away. If she's tried four times and failed, then it should be safe."

"No, I'm not losing you again. I can't go back to Michael. Let Susie try. Please." Abi yawned.

"Right, let's get Abi sedated and let her sleep. Tomorrow's going to be hard on her." Julian said.

"Nat go home, I'll stay tonight with Adam," Frankie told her.

They went their separate ways. All dreaded the following day.

*****

The morning came around quickly, and they re-gathered. Abi's still asleep. Susie would be in after lunch. Jack told Adam to go and take a break. Abi would need him to be wide awake, and he'd been offered a staff room.

Julian waited until Adam left. "Today's going to be hard for them both. This either works or doesn't. There's a high chance Susie will need to cause her a hell of a lot of pain, to get her defenses low enough to overthrow Michael's hypnosis. Adam may not cope with it."

206

"I'll get him out if necessary," Frankie said. "Abi's the important one here. She must come first, at all costs."

Jack sat on the edge of his daughter's bed. "She's been through so much pain already, and now we're going to do it on purpose. It's just not fair." He held her hand as she began to stir.

She spotted all of them as she opened her eyes. "Where's Adam?" She realised he's not there.

"Getting some sleep, he'll be back soon." Her dad answered.

Julian sat on the other side of her. "Abi, are you sure about today?"

"I have to try, I love him too much."

"Okay, Susie's in after lunch, rest until then."

She settled back down, but shortly afterwards her head started to hurt. She bolted up, and they look at her.

Nat saw it first. "Her eyes, she's unfocused again, and it's the fourth time."

Abi searched around, all of them carried guns, she should be able to get to one of them. She looked at Frankie, no he'd overpower her too quickly. Abi waited, one of them would approach her. She knew they all carried shoulder straps, she could grab one when one of them got close enough.

"Julian, you're the only one unarmed. We can't approach her, not when she's like this," Frankie told him.

Julian's fully aware of this. "Everyone out, now!"

They emptied the room out, and Julian saw Abi's eyes dart around the room. She searched for another way. Her eyes flew to the window. Shit, Julian thought. The third floor. If she jumped from here, it would surely kill her. He slowly moved to her side and snapped the handcuffs onto her, that Frankie gave him. She snarled at him, realised that she'd been trapped and thrashed against them. "Bastard. Guess I'll have to fuck Adam then."

Julian dialed Susie, knew this time she wouldn't come out of it. Told her they're out of time and needed to act now.

Abi acted feral and tugged at the handcuffs, which made her wrists bleed. Julian turned as Adam entered. Abi noticed and smiled at him. "Adam, baby. I'm all wet and ready for you. Come and fuck me. Now! I need your nice, hard cock in my tight ass." She started to remove her pants with her free hand, the best she could.

"Adam get out now! He must have put in another command, that we don't know about. She won't stop until you take her. Susie's on her way in."

Jack pushed him out but stayed himself. "Julian I'm unarmed. Why didn't she tell us this?"

"She may not have known," Susie said when she entered. "Luckily, I was on the way in. This command may have been buried beneath one of the others. I have to act quick in case there are others."

"Adam!" Abi screamed. "What's up? Aren't you up to it? Aren't you as good as Michael? My ass is all ready for your grand entrance."

Susie sat on the bed and grabbed Abi by the chin. Abi pushed her away with her free hand. Jack pinned her down, and Susie grabbed her chin again, pulled her head around sharply and she put her under. Abi slumped and went quiet.

"Okay," Susie said. "Let's try. Abi, you need to forget what Michael has told you."

"No!"

"Yes. You love Adam and want to live a full, happy life with him. Decades of each other. You don't want to die, living is your new command."

"No! I want to fuck him, now!"

"Abi, you're in pain, so much pain. It hurts, and you're screaming."

"Fuck off bitch. Give me Adam."

"Abi, you don't want to fuck Adam. You don't love him, hate the feel of him touching you. You feel sick at the thought."

Abi stopped and concentrated on Susie. Then smiled sweetly. "Adam's the love of my life. He's hard all the time, and he really wants to fuck me. You will not stop us. No one can. I will fuck him, and he'll have to watch me die and live with that for the rest of his life. Or he can return me to Michael. It's his choice."

Susie glanced towards Julian. "It's not working. We have to go with the pain."

Susie turned towards Julian. "We have to go with the pain."

They'd already discussed this privately, and Julian had a syringe that would make Abi feel like she burned alive. He moved towards her, and she snarled at him. Susie grabbed her arm, and Julian injected her.

It doesn't take long. Abi began to scream loudly, the pain excruciating.

Susie tried again. "Abi, you want to live, so badly. Your love for Adam is genuine, and nothing will break that unless you stop loving each other. You won't die if you sleep together. You don't want to die, you want to live. Abi, everything Michael's told you will be forgotten, and you will go back to how it was before he abducted you. Remember what you felt, Abi you must forget Michael's commands."

They watched as she screamed one last time and collapsed slumped on the bed, with laboured breathing and gleaming in sweat.

"Abi, you'll sleep now, and when you wake, you will not remember any of Michael's commands."

Abi drifted off, and everyone re-entered the room. Adam went right by her side and stroked her head. "What the hell did you give her?" He yelled at Julian.

Susie answered. "I couldn't get past Michael's commands, we had to get her defenses lowered. Adam, it's my fault, I suggested it. It was the only way. She would have stayed like that until she'd got to you and she would have. This Michael guy is damned good."

Adam looked at Abi, who'd gone pure white. "Will she remember the pain?"

"Yes, unfortunately, she will. I'll leave you to it. Julian let me know what happens." Susie left, and Frankie passed Adam and Jack their weapons back.

It took a few hours, but Abi regained consciousness. They force Adam to the door in case things went wrong. Julian sat next to her, with a sedative to hand.

"Adam," she whimpered. Nat pushed him out of the room. "Where's Adam?" She muttered as sleep re-took her.

Abi slept right through to the following morning and woke confused. Julian sat by her "How'd you feel?"

"Sick. Extremely sick and my head hurts."

"We expected that. Abi, Michael's commands were deep, we had to use pain to stop them. I'm so sorry."

"Adam?"

"He's outside with everyone else. I'll get them."

Adam's went right to her side. He pulled her close and kissed her forehead. She snuggled into him as sleep reclaimed her. Everyone relaxed. It may be over at last.

*****

They kept Abi in the hospital for another five days. It took a few days for the nausea to pass and to make sure that Michael's commands were really gone. She didn't try anything else. Adam drove her home, and she went straight to bed. She said she was tired, but Abi needed time alone. She removed her top and winced, her back tight again. She pulled her robe on and wanted to call Adam, but she's scared. She lay down and flinched again. She's wide awake when Adam came in. He held her and realised her back hurt. He disappeared to the bathroom and returned with the cream. She rolled onto her stomach, and he slid her robe down. When he applied the cream, he continued down to her lower back. She turned over, and he moved in for a kiss. Abi responds, and Adam deepens the kiss.

"Adam, take me please," she whispered.

Adam gazed into his fiancé's eyes. "Abi, I want to, really I do, but give it a few more days. I want to make sure." Concerned filled him about any potential lingering thoughts. He waited, remembered what happened the last time.

"I understand," Abi replied and nestled back up to him. Adam couldn't help but smile at her response. He'd try again, the

210

weekend. Take her out for a romantic meal, and then he'd make sure she forgot Michael. For a while, anyway.

*****

Saturday arrived, and Abi seemed to be okay. In fact, Adam thought she'd looked a lot happier, the depression gone. Julian visited her yesterday and was delighted with her. Adam mentioned that she wanted to make love, but he'd held off and her response. He explained his plan for the weekend and Julian agreed to it. He handed Adam a tube of lube and told him to use it. Make it easier on Abi. Reminded him, that the first time would hurt.

Abi didn't have a clue about his plan. He smiled. This evening he'd get the love of his life back. Tonight, their life together began again. He couldn't be more thrilled.

Abi finally appeared out of the bedroom and joined him on the couch. She curled up against him and rested her head on his shoulder. Adam turned and kissed the top of her head.

"Abi, I forgot to mention that we're going out tonight. Celebrate getting you back. You alright with it? Just a quick meal. We don't need to stay long."

"Sure, why not. Bit fed up of being cooped up, anyway."

Adam couldn't be more delighted. She'd been inside since she'd gotten out of the hospital and he'd been worried when she didn't seem bothered it. Hoped she wasn't withdrawing again, but he'd been worrying over nothing.

Her dad had rung daily to check on how his daughter and Adam informed him of his plan to take her out. Jack warned him not to push her but agreed she needed to get out. They spent the day lounging around. Abi slept against him, she still tired easily. Eventually, he woke her up.

"Come on sleepy, time to get ready. Wear something beautiful for me."

Abi stretched and gave him a quick peck on the mouth. Beautiful? She would show him. Remind him exactly what a vixen she could be. She showered, and Adam sorted out her back. He then jumped in the shower, and Abi got dressed. She waited in the lounge, ready to go, when Adam came out dressed in a black suit. He stopped dead at seeing Abi. Christ, she'd taken his words literally. He'd forgotten how stunning she could be. She'd dug out her little black dress. Slim, straight and showed off all her curves. Stopping short above her knees and short sleeves, just off the shoulder. She'd topped it off with her black heels, which made her legs look long and black shawl. She'd curled her hair, and the tight curls bounced, every time she moved. Adam would be the envy of every bloke there. He pulled her into a tight embrace and kissed her with hunger he hadn't felt for a long time.

She pulled away. "Adam, we'll be late."

Damn it, all he only wanted to do one thing. Carry her straight to bed and forget about the meal. He hoped no one would spot how hard he'd gone. The next few hours were going to go, way too slow.

Their cab arrived, and soon they are at Abi's favourite Italian. A waiter showed them to a table, and shortly afterwards, Adam spotted the manager as he headed towards them.

"Miss Lawton, it's good to see you back. Mr. Leroy, this is on the house. Enjoy your evening." The manager poured them a glass of champagne each and left the chilled bottle. He couldn't have been happier when Adam booked the table. Glad to see Abi back on his arm.

They keep the conversation light as they ate, and Adam kept a close eye on Abi. He wanted to make sure she didn't overtire herself and became amazed when she cleared off her plate and ordered dessert. Not long later they head home.

Abi jumped on him the moment they got in the door. She pulled him into a deep kiss, while she tugged at his jacket. He lifted her and carried her to the bedroom. Neither of them could get their clothes off quick enough. Abi lay down and pulled Adam with her.

"Adam, tonight, please. Make tonight perfect for me. You've been hard all night." Her voice went husky.

He looked at her in surprise.

"Think I wouldn't notice?" The mischief danced in her eyes.

Adam laughed. "If I'd known, I'd have dragged you back a long ago. Been damned painful, having to wait."

Abi moved down and licked the top of his cock, making Adam moan. She really was going to be the death of him. She sucked, and his cock twitched in response as she licked off a drop of moisture. She glanced at him before she continued to lick and suck and massaged his balls with a hand. When she felt him stiffen and groan, ready to release, she sucked him harder and swallowed every drop of him as Adam cried out.

Adam wasn't letting her get away with that. He pulled her up. "Minx." He said and followed it with a fierce kiss. He trailed kisses down her neck and sucked on both nipples. It's Abi's turn to moan. He continued trailing kisses down her stomach, and it wasn't long before he's between her legs. He licked her clit. Abi gasped get louder as he continued to lick and nip at her, while he pushed a finger inside her. Abi screamed out as she flew over the edge of bliss. Any doubts she might have about not feeling anything vanished.

"Adam, please," she managed to stammer out.

He knew exactly what she wanted. "Are you sure?"

"Oh god Adam, please. Take me all the way. I need you too."

Adam knew the damage Michael did would make her dry. She wouldn't be able to lubricate herself. He reached over for a tube, and she watches as he squeezed a squirt on his fingers then rubbed it inside of her. She gasped and clenched around him. "Adam, please." She begged again as she felt the heat inside her burn for him. He removed his hand and plastered the rest of the lube onto himself. After positioning himself, he eased slightly in and felt her tightness as she tensed.

Adam stopped. "Abi, we don't have to. I can stop, wait until you're readier. It's going to hurt. I'll have to stretch you; the scarring has made you tight."

"Please," she whimpered. "Please, I need to forget. Help me forget what he did."

Adam moved slowly, and as he sunk inwards, he took her mouth in his. Kissed her hard as he penetrated her deeply. He swallowed her cry as he felt her stretch and tear slightly. After he'd paused to reposition himself and to let her get used to him, he slowly began to thrust. She matched his movement, thrust for thrust and they took it slowly. He gazed lovingly into her eyes and smiled, as he lowered his head to capture a nipple between his teeth. She moaned out in pleasure, her excitement built with the thrill of Adam within her. A scorching heat spread throughout her, and she felt ready to explode, as she buckled and screamed his name. Clenching around him, she milked out every single drop. Didn't want to waste a single bit of it. Adam collapsed to her side, both panting hard, sweat gleamed on their skin. Abi could feel his seed deep inside her, and she couldn't be more delighted.

Adam leaned upon his arm and stroked her face. "Baby, are you okay?" He'd felt her tear and noticed the blood.

"Bit sore, but I'll be fine. Adam, you haven't lost your touch." She smiled back at him.

He disappeared into the bathroom and returned with a damp cloth. "Let's get you cleaned up." Wiping her gently, he removed the lube and cleaned away the blood. Abi whimpered slightly when he cleaned around where she'd torn. He then quickly wiped himself clean. Next, he crawled back onto the bed and pulled Abi close, as he briefly kissed her nose and pulled up the duvet. Hopefully, the next time wouldn't be so painful for her.

*****

This time Adam that woke first. He couldn't believe how ready and how brave Abi could be. It might have been a risk, but they needed to do it, and now Abi could go back to where she belonged. His, all his, and he'll never let her go again. He quietly got up, so not to wake her. Pulled on his robe and headed into the lounge to ring Anthony.

"Anthony, I need another one of your favours. I want to do something special for Abi."

"Abi?" Anthony said confused. As far as he knew, Abi still ignored Adam.

"Yep, Abi. She's come back, weeks ago. It's been tough. She thought about killing herself, but she fought back and won."

Anthony's head cleared. "Suicide? Adam, please tell me Abi hasn't done anything stupid."

"No, she came close, but she talked about it. God Anthony, I really thought she would. She tried to go back to work, wanted to see me, but took a hell of a step backwards. It's been a long haul, but she's back in my arms." He told Anthony about the hypnosis.

"Bloody hell. She alright now?"

"After last night, I can definitely say she is."

Anthony's over the moon. "Brilliant news, Adam. What can I do for you?"

"Can you get the whole family down here, the last Saturday of next month? I want to arrange a special evening for Abi. A meal she'll remember."

"Sure, I'll sort it. Adam, I'm happy for the both of you. I know how hard it's been. The family will be chuffed."

Adam heard Abi, get into the shower. "Need to go, I'll text you the details. Keep it quiet, I want it to be a surprise." He hung up. Breakfast he thought. After last night, she would need to replace her energy.

*****

Abi's been pottering around in the apartment, while Adam had popped out. Boredom set in. Adam hadn't been happy to leave her alone, but she'd insisted she would be okay. He made sure she locked and chained the door after he'd gone. She discovered her uniform and phoned Frankie. Asked him to come over.

Abi let him in, and he hugged her.

"You've put your weight back on Abi, and you look so much better. Everything alright?" In fact, he would say she glowed.

215

"Yes. Frankie, I'll get straight to the point. I want to go back to work."

Frankie knew this would be coming. Jack had warned him about her recovery. "Are sure? Abi, you tried it before."

Abi knew he would bring it up. "I know, it was too soon. Too early. This time I'm ready. Frankie, I'm getting bored, and I know Adam won't go back till I'm ready. It's unfair to him, to be stuck babysitting me."

"Abi, he doesn't mind."

"I know, but I really am getting bored. Frankie, just a couple of days a week, desk duty. I'll beg if I have too."

Frankie laughed. "Okay. Two days a week, but only on desk duty. I hope you realise, that I won't get any work out of Adam while you're in. Does he know about this?"

Abi heard his key in the door. "No, but I think he's about to." Adam became instantly alert when he spotted Frankie. "Problem Captain?"

Frankie noticed how Adam's back went tense. "Relax, Abi's arranging to try and work again. You think she's up to a couple of days of desk duty? Says she'll beg."

Adam glanced at Abi, saw the hope in her eyes and knew precisely how brilliant she could be at begging. She'd been doing it a lot recently. Every time they went to bed. "I think she's ready," Adam smiled back at her.

Abi screamed in delight and threw herself at Adam. She kissed him hard on the lips. "Thank you."

Frankie took a good look at Abi. She's thrilled, and he knew now she'd recovered. The guys at the station would be happy to have her back. "I'll leave you two to it. Adam, I'll send you a copy of your rota's. I'll put Abi down to start Monday and have you working the same shifts when she's in."

*****

Abi drove Adam crazy on Monday morning. Her excitement at being able to go back to work became contagious. Adam couldn't

216

help smiling. His fiancé back in uniform and ready to go. Frankie decided she would do a couple of weeks of desk duty and then if all went well, she could go back to full duties. Julian had agreed, but only part-time. He didn't want her to push herself too much. It fitted into Adam's plan. She would have completed her first week on full duty, the week of his surprise. Adam drove them in. This time she didn't hesitate and entered the station with full confidence.

Nat spotted her first. "Abi," she called and hugged her. "Welcome back."

Adam's lost Abi in all the hugs she got caught up in and noticed that Morris held back.

"Morris, are you alright?" Adam walked over to him.

Morris couldn't be happier to see Abi. He'd been keeping tabs on her himself, but he couldn't forget that he hadn't protected her. He'd let Michael abduct her. "Yeah."

Adam knew what bothered him. "She doesn't blame you, never will. You couldn't have stopped Michael anyway, he had the perfect plan. Morris don't blame yourself. Look at her, she's fine now. Anyway, she'll be back on the streets soon, you'll be able to make it up to her. Merely keep her supplied with coffee."

Morris laughed as he walked over to her. "Abi, welcome back," and pulled her into a great big hug.

Chapter Twenty-Five

The day of Adam's surprise arrived. Being back on full duty, Abi couldn't be much happier. His family had flown down yesterday and had kept themselves hidden. Abi didn't have a clue. All he would tell her was that he'd arranged a meal for them both. Wanted to celebrate her recovery.

He somehow persuaded her to wear that silver blue dress. Told her it set her eyes off lovely. He didn't lie, it did. He would put on his best suit and hoped he managed to get everything perfect. "Abi," he called. "Car's here." He couldn't wait to see her face.

She walked into the lounge, and his breath caught in his throat. She was so damned beautiful. He took her arm, and they headed downstairs. She gasped as she spotted the limousine. He'd pulled out everything for this evening. Abi would get a perfect night to remember. The driver opened the door, and Adam handed her a glass of champagne, once settled.

"To new beginnings."

"Happy endings," replied Abi.

When they entered the hotel, and to Abi's surprised, they walked past the restaurant and went into the garden. It's now her turn for her breath to catch in her throat. Anthony must have arranged a marque, lit up with bright lights and an orchestra. Everyone's there. Adam's parents, brothers, Crystal, Jack, Frankie, Louise, Michelle, Nat and even Steve. The setting couldn't be more perfect. Abi turned to Adam and kissed him on the mouth.

"Get a room," Anthony yelled, and everyone laughed, including Abi. "Thank you," she said.

Adam showed her to a chair, and the waiters began to serve them.

The meal was lovely, Abi couldn't be more delighted. "How did you arrange all of this?"

"He didn't," Anthony answered. He motioned to the waiter who handed out some champagne. When he raised his glass, Anthony looked at the couple. Amazed this evening had happened. Everything Abi has been through, and she's back at his brother's side. They made such a lovely couple, and he hoped the worst was over. "To Abi and Adam," he said.

Everyone raised their glass and smiled at the happy couple. "To the future."

*****

The evening went perfectly. Adam couldn't stop staring over at Abi, she was so happy and relaxed. Something he'd never thought he'd see again. She excused herself to go to the restroom and Nat followed her.

"Abi, you are happy, aren't you?"

Abi smiled and nodded, but Nat noticed her quick glance at her ring finger. "Abi?"

Abi sighed. "He took my engagement ring, Nat. Made me watch as he smashed it with a hammer. Told me he'd take away all my happiness, that the ring was just the start."

Anger passed over Nat's face. The bastard. "He hasn't though, as he. You fought him and won again."

"Yes, but he's still out there. What if he's still watching, waiting for another chance? What if he tries again. Nat, I can't survive a third time." She let a tear fall.

"Abi, Adam's hired a bodyguard, who follows you everywhere when Adam's not with you. We're going to do our damned hardest, to make sure Michael doesn't get anywhere near you, ever again."

"I know about the bodyguard, spotted him ages ago."

Nat could only laugh. "Abi, you are way too observant."

Abi's eyes shone with tears that were ready to fall. "Not when it comes to Michael." She whispered. "He always manages to grab me. I know he'll try again. Nat, am I doing the right thing? Marrying Adam? Potentially putting him through it a second time?"

219

"Abi, you've been through a lot recently, it's taken its toll on you. Hell, on all of us, but you especially. Oh Abi, let it out." She pulled Abi close and held her while the tears fell. A few minutes later Abi pulled away.

"I'm sorry Nat. I guess I'm more worried than I thought."

Nat knew Abi would worry until they'd found Michael and preferable put a bullet through him. "Abi, we'll stop him. No matter what he tries. Is everything okay with Adam and you?" Nat became concerned that there may be more to it.

"Oh god, yes. Things couldn't be better. I love him, I really do, and he certainly loves me back."

Nat noticed Abi's blush. "Really don't want to hear the details," Nat said and they both laughed.

Abi sighed and stared back at her finger and made a decision. "Nat, I want my ring back. I want to feel engaged again. I know Adam's not going anywhere. God knows I've tried my hardest to push him away. But I want to feel like I'm truly his and I just can't get there. After everything, I need to feel like I'm engaged again." She glanced at her finger once more.

Nat had seen her glance at that finger several times during the evening. She needed to speak to Adam.

They went back out. Abi re-joined the family while Nat walked over to Adam. He'd separated himself slightly from everyone.

"Adam, exactly what is your plan for tonight?"

He pulled out a ring and showed Nat. It's a white eternity ring, with small diamonds running around the band. He'd had the inside engraved with, 'mine for eternity'.

"Lovely," Nat said sarcastically and knew it would not be enough.

"She not ready for an engagement ring yet."

Nat whacked him hard on the shoulder. "Adam Leroy, sometimes you are a damned idiot. For a cop your observation skills are crap."

"Nat, that hurt," he says as he rotates his shoulder to ease the pain.

"It was supposed to. Adam, haven't you noticed her looking at her finger. She's told me Michael made her watch while he smashed her ring. She's still feeling insecure, and worried he'll try again."

"I've hired a bodyguard, he's with her when I can't be."

"Yep, she spotted him ages ago."

Adam laughed. "Yeah, she could always spot a tail."

Nat looked at him. "Adam seriously. If you don't put an engagement ring on her finger tonight, I'll shoot you myself. Better still, I'll push her in Anthony's direction. After all, he's the one setting all this up."

Adam watched Nat walk away, then studied Abi. She smiled, but he could tell she'd been crying. Slowly she glanced at her finger, and he saw the look of sorrow on her face. Damn it, Nat was right. He called Steve over to him.

"Change of plan. Steve, I need you to get the perfect picture, and Abi a brand-new beginning." He pulled out another ring. He'd had an identical engagement ring commissioned. Steve nodded, Adam didn't need to explain. How many women could get two perfect proposals, from the same man? "Let me know when."

It didn't take long. Adam noticed Abi stood by the edge of the lake. The full moon shone down and lit up her hair. Now, he thought. He nodded at Steve and walked softly behind her.

Jack notice. Finally, he thought. He'd seen Abi look at her finger, the insecurity in her eyes. He'd been ready to speak to Adam himself but saw Nat hit him in the shoulder. Knew she had the exact same talk. They all watched as Steve moved into position and nodded back at Adam.

Adam's calmer this time, as he knelt on one knee, just behind Abi. He opened the ring box. "Abi," he called softly.

She turned, the look on her face perfect.

"Abigail Lawton, will you make me the happiest man alive and agree to marry me, again?" Abi didn't even hesitate. "Yes. Oh Adam, yes."

He placed the ring on her finger and kissed her fiercely. They didn't hear the cheers and applause. They only had eyes for each other.

Epilogue

Michael's angry, extremely angry. He'd had the perfect plan, thought it through and executed it with precision. Her abduction and torture went well. Jack distraught knowing Abi was back in his tender loving care and Michael knew he'd seen the rape. He smiled as he remembered how much pain he'd caused. It was so perfect. Moving her to New York, forcing her to allow him to continue raping her, brilliant. Oh, he'd already known pregnancy wasn't a possibility. Knew how his previous injuries would prevent that, but the torture of sex with her unprotected was too much to give up. She'd always wonder if he'd give her anything. Her escape was the perfect excuse to be rougher than ever before. Those injuries would have hurt, but he'd had so much fun.

Forcing her to stab herself had been a master plan, but the brothers had found her in time. He'd thought he'd still win, especially when she'd refused to see Adam. Oh Adam, how he'd witnessed the rape too. He'll have to send him the video of that one day, maybe send Abi one too. No, he'd do Abi again in person. Make sure Adam knew it too.

He'd been so sure that Abi would never let a man love her again. Her scars would make sex way too painful, but even then, the bitch had proved him wrong. The hypnosis was a masterstroke. As they got back together, she'd try to kill herself. But they outmaneuvered him on that too. He looked down at a photo. The one he got it last night. Adam on one knee and Abi looking rather delightful. He had been within reaching distance of her. Saw her head towards the restroom and hid in a cubicle. His plan to rape and stab her through the heart. Leave her for them to find. It would have been a fitting end to the evening, but no, that detective had followed her in. He'd heard every word and yes Abi, I am still watching, still waiting.

He picked up his hunting knife and stabbed the photo, right in Adam's face. They seemed so happy. He'll let them have their happiness, but only until the time was right. He'll wait and then he'll permanently erase Adam Leroy. The bitch won't be happy then and Jack? Well, he'll have to watch her fall apart all over again.

To be continued……

Thank you for reading this book.
If you have enjoyed it, please leave a review on Amazon/Goodreads and let your friends know. It will be appreciated.

Keep up to date on my facebook page
www.facebook.com/jmralley/

Look out for further books in the series.

Book Two Persecuting Adam

J M Ralley lives in the West Midlands, England and this is her debut novel.
When not writing she's busy with her day job, or spending time with her pets, reading or outdoors.

Printed in Poland
by Amazon Fulfillment
Poland Sp. z o.o., Wrocław